A HANDBOOK FOR SURVIVAL—

NO MATTER WHAT

- How to *make* a getaway airplane
- Hone your "crisis skills"
- Fleeing the firestorm: escape tactics for city-dwellers
- How to build a homemade fallout meter
- Civil defense, American style
- "Microfarming"—survival in five acres

And much, much more.

"[Ing writes] in the Hemingway tradition of personal, physical encounters with man and nature."

—*Analog*

DEAN ING

THE CHERNOBYL SYNDROME

To Ginny Heinlein, whom we all owe a lot.

THE CHERNOBYL SYNDROME

A Baen Books Original

Baen Publishing Enterprises
260 Fifth Avenue
New York, N.Y. 10001

First printing, May 1988

ISBN: 0-671-65345-8

Cover design by Carol Russo

Printed in the United States of America

Distributed by
SIMON & SCHUSTER
1230 Avenue of the Americas
New York, N.Y. 10020

CONTENTS

1. PREFACE by Nancy Tappan 1

2. THE CHERNOBYL SYNDROME 4

3. SELF-RELIANCE IN EVERYDAY LIFE 15
   - A. The Great Escape As A Hobby 17
   - B. Crisis Relocation 24
   - C. A Sensible Bias On Business As Usual 31
   - D. High Tech and Self-Reliance 38
   - E. A Lifetime Lesson Schools *Can't* Teach 43
   - F. Microfarming 47
   - G. Quickie Projects 55
   - H. Models Of Self-Reliance 60

4. NUCLEAR CALAMITY 69
   - A. Gimme Shelter! 71
   - B. Living Under Pressure 83
   - C. Power And Potties To The People 103
   - D. Stocking Your Tenacity Chest 119
   - E. A Homemade Fallout Meter, the KFM 137
   - F. Finding Truly Responsible Physicians 219
   - G. Is Nuclear Winter Exaggerated? 225

5. NON-NUCLEAR CALAMITY 229
   - A. Snowshoe Summer 231
   - B. The Woodpacker: Backpacker's Woodstove 245
   - C. Safetynet: Pestproof Headgear 257
   - D. The Backpacker's Saw Quandary 262
   - E. Biker's "Second Stage" Kit 269
   - F. Keeping Those Wheels Unstuck 272
   - G. The 12-Volt Solution 277
   - H. Making An Alternative Engine Oil 286
   - I. Teeth In Your Pocket 290
   - J. Chimney Fires 292

6. ING'S THINGS 295
A. Self-Reliance Scrapbooks 297
B. Know Thy Neighbor 298
C. Getting Organized 299
D. Weatherproofing Your Papers 300
E. Chimney Sweeping 301
F. Spring Outings 302
G. Safe Bicycling 303
H. Shining Those Survival Wheels 304
I. Towing in Safety 305
J. The Carton and the Candle 306
K. The Solar Trickle-Charge 307
L. Solder 307
M. High-Tech Pottery 308
N. Survival Shrubbery 310
O. Rose-Hip Tea 311
P. Toolkit in A Tube 312
Q. An Emergency Sole for Shoes 313
R. Weatherproofing Adhesives 313
S. Toy Kits for Self-Reliance 315
T. Trade Goods I. 316
U. Trade Goods II. 317

7. BOOK REVIEWS 319
A. The How-To Book For Woodcutters 321
B. Urban Alert! 322
C. High Frontier 324
D. How To Make Nuclear Weapons Obsolete 325
E. We Can Prevent WW III 327
F. Down-Home Ways 328
G. Nuclear War Survival Skills 329

PREFACE

Nancy Tappan

By compiling this book, Dean Ing has done me a favor, for it makes survivalism respectable. After all, he's offering self-reliance, an esteemed American virtue that's fallen from favor in the twentieth century. His credentials are impeccable. You cannot dismiss an Air Force veteran, an aerospace engineer who left that profession to get a Ph.D. in communication theory, taught, then quit academics to write award-winning science fiction, as a kook who doesn't know what he's talking about.

I first heard about Dean from novelist Jerry Pournelle, who called me after my husband's death to offer suggestions when he heard I was continuing to publish Mel's newsletter dealing with long-term survival. "There's a fellow in Ashland you really ought to know. He's a survivalist, and he's one hell of a writer. Name is Ing," said Jerry.

At that point in early 1981 I was sick of the word "survivalist," which had become a media catch-all for members of far-right extremist groups and nuts in general. In the popular imagination, a survivalist was a camou-clad gent carrying a semi-automatic rifle, living in an underground shelter waiting for the bomb to drop. This image contained much truth. The self-defense aspect of survivalism and its focus on the possibility of large-scale catastrophe—be it nuclear exchange, natural disaster, or economic collapse—attracted the mentally unbalanced. These people paid scant attention to the common-sense underpinnings of survival, and used the notion of impending doom to escape from personal problems and to buy quantities of expensive gear—"big boy toys."

I was besieged by so-called experts on the subject who had articles for the newsletter on everything from cyanide-tipped blowguns to algae as the perfect survival food. When I would meet these people face to face, and they saw that I lived in an everyday ranch-style house without machinegun turrets on the roof, they were crestfallen. I did not live up to their image of a survivalist. To me, they seemed a bit loony, which explains why I was apprehensive as I picked up the phone to call Dean Ing.

I was pleasantly surprised. Wonder of wonders, he turned out to be sane; he even had a sense of humor and talked about survival in a witty way. He had suggestions for articles describing steps the average householder could take to prepare for nuclear catastrophe. But he wanted to do more than write about nuclear survival. To my delight, he was full of ideas people could implement to become more self-reliant in all phases of their lives, which is the essence of survivalism.

As we talked, his message came through: there is an alternative to certain death from nuclear war, or caving in to Soviet demands because annihilation awaits us if we don't. Ordinary people, without millions of dollars, can take simple measures to protect themselves from disaster, non-nuclear as well as nuclear.

Dean's suggestions for articles were good, but still I had to read them. Knowing something of his engineering background, I envisioned pages of sleep-inducing technical jargon. Again, I was pleasantly surprised. His copy was *fun* to read and easy to understand.

I asked Dean to contribute to *Survival Tomorrow* on a regular basis. And contribute he has. Most of his newsletter pieces appear in this collection, where they can reach the general audience they deserve. He presents a valid case for every stand he takes, backing up his statements with facts, not ideology. And his projects work because he has built and tested them himself.

Forget your preconceptions about survivalism and nuclear war when you read this book. Depending on your political persuasion, you may find Dean Ing opinionated, at times flip and cocky. But I guarantee you'll keep turning pages until you reach the end. He may not change your mind about disarmament, but I bet you put together a pump and air filter and start doing "Ing's Things."

You are in for a treat reading *The Chernobyl Syndrome*, because Dean Ing is one of a handful of writers who can write about complex technical subjects in an entertaining style that explains the material so the layman can grasp it. His is a rare gift. Enjoy the book—and heed the message.

Nancy Tappan
Editor, *Survival Tomorrow*
Rogue River, Oregon

THE CHERNOBYL SYNDROME

"No need for any war here
save the good one of survival . . ."
—Ray Bradbury

In June 1986, an Associated Press team was preparing a feature story on that rare and elusive creature, the survivalist. The AP's Lisa Ryckman knew that public interest in survivalism had peaked twice before, first around 1960 and again some twenty years later, only to subside for various reasons.

Ryckman, savvy in the ways of the American public, guessed that survivalism in some guise might soon be peaking, or at least bubbling to the surface, a third time. Why? The answer, in a word: Chernobyl. Pieced together from Soviet and Western sources, the Chernobyl story makes quite a saga.

Prior to April 1986, few Westerners had ever heard of Chernobyl, a town roughly 80 miles north of the great Soviet city of Kiev—and eleven miles from four massive nuclear power reactors. But at 1:23 AM on Saturday, April 26, Chernobyl was suddenly and explosively on its way to a dreadful notoriety. During a planned shutdown of Number 4 reactor, its managers committed a string of errors which included the bypassing of safety procedures. These half-dozen mistakes, in the words of Dr. Conrad Chester of Oak

Ridge National Laboratory, amounted to a "prescription for a steam explosion." The explosion ripped into the night, heavily damaging the reactor and killing two workers instantly. Worse still, this reactor was the kind that used graphite as the fission moderator, and unlike U.S. designs it lacked some fail-safe features.

Graphite blocks, stacked around zirconium-clad nuclear fuel rods, are water-cooled. Maintaining a flow of coolant is so critical that its loss rates a special nightmare-term among nuclear engineers: LOCA (Loss Of Coolant Accident). If coolant flow fails, all the fuel rods and all that graphite just get hotter and hotter until, eventually, the graphite can reach its own ignition temperature. The cladding of zirconium, in these circumstances, may have suddenly released great amounts of hydrogen gas into the wreckage, producing a second—perhaps even more devastating—explosion and fire.

Graphite is a form of carbon, and it burns, and inside that hellish conflagration near Chernobyl was a tremendous concentration of fissioning nuclear fuel on its way to the final nightmare of the nuclear power industry: meltdown. If the great mass of a nuclear core melts, it could burn its way down into the earth until it strikes water, causing a subterranean explosion something like a small volcano.

That should have been the worst, but it wasn't. The worst was that the Soviets, perhaps trying to shave on costs, had not erected a sufficiently strong containment vessel—usually a pressure-tight concrete dome over the reactor. A containment vessel is designed to prevent clouds of radioactive matter from escaping, in the event of an accident. Its containment breached, the savaged Chernobyl reactor began spewing vast quantities of deadly radiation into the night sky.

And in Chernobyl, the good people slept on. The

smaller town of Pripyat was only three miles from the inferno, but even at dawn they too remained unaware of the implications of that smoke on their near horizon. The USSR has total control of its news media, and while Soviet officials scrambled to address the problem, they continued to hope that they could keep the lid on news of this nuclear accident. Meanwhile, and throughout the day, the Chernobyl reactor core continued to burn.

General Nikolai Antoshchkin of the Soviet Air Force got urgent orders Saturday evening to proceed to Pripyat with military helicopters. He arrived the following evening, according to the Soviet military newspaper *Krasnaya Zvezda*, but not to evacuate the citizens of Pripyat and Chernobyl. Antoshchkin's job was to supervise the dumping of sand, borates and lead pellets over the burning Chernobyl graphite using helicopters—a hair-raising feat, which Soviet pilots accomplished around the clock, initially without much effect. Weaving back and forth over the world's first full-scale nuclear meltdown, Antoshchkin's men earned their hazard pay while dumping bags of sand into its maw.

Meanwhile, some 36 hours after the accident, a convoy of buses had arrived to evacuate Pripyat's thousands. The media silence was still complete, the Chernobyl meltdown was proceeding to eat its way down through the reactor's thick concrete floor, and desperate Soviet officials conceived a plan for tunneling down below the molten nuclear witch's brew while those chopper pilots bravely slalomed overhead. And borne on gentle winds, the deadly cloud of radioactivity continued to drift toward Poland and Sweden.

By Monday, Scandinavians were measuring high levels of windborne radioactivity. The Poles were getting a dose, too. A few media people began to sense that something was terribly wrong in the

Ukraine, but for 64 hours after that first disastrous explosion the Soviets refused to acknowledge any nuclear accident whatever.

On Monday night, finally, *Tass* news agency confirmed what the West already knew: a nuclear accident of appalling dimensions. Western newsmen in Moscow began frantically searching for details. A Manchester *Guardian* correspondent wrote of newsmen evaporating into Moscow's back streets in search of unmonitored telephones, trying to shake their police shadows because Soviet citizens know better than to tell tales on their government while Big Brother is listening.

The rumors ran from dead accurate to pitifully far off the mark, and some of the most erroneous rumors got reported as fact. The United Press reported 2,000 immediate dead from radiation, though evidently the number was only 24. (A few more succumbed later.) Chairman Gorbachev furiously denounced Western media for their "malicious mountains of lies," and gradually Soviet officials began to release more details on the Chernobyl disaster, perhaps because the truth was not as bad as those rumors. Had there been *any* containment vessel? First reports said no. Later reports proved there had been a containment vessel, but the vessel had failed.

Meanwhile, monitors watched the cloud of radiation dwindle. When the prevailing winds shifted they blew the radioactive cloud back into the Soviet Union, now considerably less lethal but dropping moderate doses on a wide swath of Soviet republics. Eventually, with careful monitoring by the U.S., the tail end of fallout passed over the United States. By this time the radioactivity in those windborne particles had decayed so much that no obvious harm was done here. But by mid-May, raw milk and rainwater in the U.S. showed clear evidence of contamination by very tiny amounts of radioactive iodine and cesium.

To repeat: it was such a tiny amount as to be virtually harmless, three weeks and many thousands of miles from its origin. But it wasn't all that harmless in Pripyat, or in Chernobyl, or a lot of other territory immediately downwind for a few days. The Soviets evacuated a reported 92,000 people in their first effort, and another 20,000 later, not counting 250,000 children who got summer vacations early so they could take vacations far from Kiev.

That was the Chernobyl disaster. It was far worse than it might have been, not only because of the failure of containment, but because a vast close-mouthed bureaucracy allowed hundreds of thousands of its own citizens to live under a radioactive cloud *for days* before telling them of the problem. Robert Gale, an American marrow-transplant specialist who flew to Moscow to help save radiation victims, estimated that a hundred thousand Soviet citizens may suffer health problems because of the Chernobyl meltdown. How many lives shortened? No one knows.

As the Soviets slowly released more information, we began to assemble a kind of cautionary tale. The Soviets had thought Western safety procedures costly and unnecessary. As of now they evidently plan no stronger containment vessels around their 27 other reactors of the Chernobyl design. The *New York Times* reports that all radiation deaths at Chernobyl were workers so innocent of radiation monitoring that they did not know they were absorbing lethal doses of radiation. One bright note: the beleaguered Soviets seeded clouds to prevent heavy rainfall from reaching the Chernobyl site, thereby avoiding water-borne spread of radiation. This was a brilliant tactic which the West must bear in mind.

It has become a popular dictum, among many Americans, that a major nuclear fallout event is something so horrendous that we simply can't do anything about it. Therefore, they claim, we may as well shrug off any personal efforts at self-help in such an event. But Chernobyl proved that, for a given person anywhere on earth, awareness and training might make the difference between long life and lingering death.

Perhaps the greatest irony of the Chernobyl disaster is that the Soviets spend vastly more on Civil Defense than we do. Many of those lives need not have been shortened, because *Soviet citizens are trained to take proper measures to escape such disasters.* If a (Libyan?) nuclear weapon had exploded near Chernobyl, Soviet authorities would have announced the disaster so that citizens could seek shelter. For days, they did not announce it.

It was *their* nuke, an embarrassment they hoped to hide.

At least one victim innocently bicycled into a fiercely radioactive area. A reputable source which I cannot identify said that, two weeks after the meltdown, radiation was a ferocious 180 rads per hour in one spot, eighteen miles downwind from the reactor. An unprotected citizen would receive a lethal dose after two or three hours on that spot. A Soviet citizen is likely to have the training and determination to save his skin; but without awareness of his predicament, his prognosis is poor.

If a similar accident should happen in this country, our free media would quickly alert us—yet too many Americans seem to lack the training and determination. No wonder: our Federal Emergency Management Agency (FEMA) recently noted that our country spends about 55 cents a year, per U.S. citizen, on Civil Defense. This is a small fraction of the funds that, for example, the Soviets and the Swiss spend.

The infuriating truth, according to the *Washington Post*, is that the current FEMA plans for response to a nuclear attack include emergency centers for federal and state officials, while the general public would be encouraged to rely on "self-help." Translation: the American taxpayer's survival must be based on self-reliance. If we cannot heed this clarion call, our only option may be hearing the blast of Gabriel.

The nuclear nightmare, with its spectres of fallout and the possibility of "nuclear winter," is not our only goad toward self-reliance. Mount St. Helens has erupted twice in this decade, and could asphyxiate thousands next time. We are told by experts, as reported in the prestigious *Science* magazine, to expect a horrendous quake in California by the end of this century. Some pundits, perhaps with less justification, fear that economic collapse may put us in the position of self-help or no help at all.

Meanwhile, as the AP's Ryckman found, our own media have helped discredit self-help activities in several ways. First, news stories described heavily-armed paramilitary groups as typical "survivalists," though the typical survivalist was anything but offense-minded. "Survivalism," then, has become a pejorative word and those who promote sensible personal survival tend to call it "self-reliance." God knows, and FEMA tells us, we must not expect to rely on the government in widespread disaster!

Second, our media give much space to well-intentioned groups such as the Physicians for Social Responsibility. The PSR's pacifist bias includes the dogma that it is unethical for a physician to assist anyone who plans to survive nuclear war. Another physician group with exactly the *opposite* view, the Doctors for Disaster Preparedness, does not maintain a hefty public relations staff, so the DDP does not get as much press coverage (Ryckman and colleagues tried to remedy that to some extent). Without wide coverage of both views, Americans tend to think our physicians are uniformly opposed to nuclear survival.

To its resounding credit, the PSR announced on

May 6 after the Chernobyl disaster that we must obtain international, cooperative management of future disasters involving nuclear technology. To the PSR, this probably does not seem a philosophical turnabout; it's one thing to promote survival of a nuclear accident, and quite another to promote survival of a nuclear weapon.

This philosophical distinction need not loom very large to the U.S. public. It is crucially important to us, however, that the PSR is now offering to assist us in surviving nuclear disasters, whether or not our government helps shoulder that responsibility. The main body of U.S. physicians, factions aside, may at last be girding itself to help. The editorial of the August 1986 *Journal of the American Medical Association* focused on Chernobyl. A few salient quotes may be in order: ". . . it is disheartening to note that the medical and health care communities have not been very much involved since Three-Mile Island in emergency planning and public education for radiation accidents." And again: "These [nuclear accident] procedures are principally the responsibility of physicians, who must be intimately involved in each stage of emergency planning . . ."

The authors of the JAMA editorial were very careful to focus on the survival of nuclear accident, not nuclear war. The general public can be excused for contemplating both.

But even if the factions of our medical and health communities join to help us help ourselves, they will probably have a problem doing it through our mass media—and here the public itself shares media's lapse. We choose to use our media much more for entertainment than we do for work-oriented information. Media theorist William Stephenson detailed this trend years ago, and as we find more leisure time, we use more of it for instant gratification. Few of us are instantly gratified by news articles that urge us to work—even toward our own survival. A newspaper, or a TV station, is not likely to give much space to messages the public hates to hear.

A few media people do buck the trend in the public's own interest, which explains the scatter of self-reliance articles, and Ryckman's research. Natural disasters may always be with us; and advances of technology continue to add dangers which we must understand to overcome. Well, FEMA has warned us that in widespread calamity we must rely on ourselves. If we are to maintain self-reliance in the face of major calamities, both nuclear and non-nuclear, we must have three things: training, awareness of possible calamities, and determination.

That unfortunate Chernobyl cyclist probably lacked only awareness of his predicament, which in this country the media would provide. The Americans who risked silicosis while breathing non-nuclear fallout from Mount St. Helens probably lacked only the training to build temporary air pumps and filters—and this book will provide that training, along with many another project in self-reliance. And to bolster your determination, we hope to show in the following pages that self-reliance projects can be a lot of fun, while improving your confidence, whether you sit in a basement shelter or stand alone in deep Sierra snow.

A syndrome is a set of symptoms that characterize a disease. The symptoms affecting the human species are the lack of training for calamity, the lack of awareness even when we are squarely in peril, and a lack of determination to pull through, perhaps from a sense of futility. Any one of the symptoms *might* be fatal to us. Together, these symptoms characterize what could be a disease fatal to us as a species. I am indebted to Dr. Jane Orient for endorsing the concept of a Chernobyl syndrome, in her October 1986 keynote speech at the annual seminar of the DDP and the American Civil Defense Association. As reflected in its publications, the DDP's concerns go beyond strictly nuclear calamity in the attempt to lessen the horrors of any disaster.

For the same reason, the following articles do not focus entirely on nuclear dangers; they also cover a variety of sticky situations, from a flue fire to a backpacker's near-fatal mistakes. Their common thread is self-reliance, and they can help us treat those deadly symptoms I call the Chernobyl Syndrome.

Self-Reliance in Everyday Life

The Great Escape As A Hobby

Recently, I was privileged to be a member of a Life Management panel on the subject of self-reliance. Kevin Steele, Jerry Pournelle, Bruce Clayton and I listened to comments from the audience and sadly, inevitably, Topic #1 was How To Escape The City In A Major Exodus. Sadly, because we had no nifty answers that would serve the general audience. Inevitably, because a show of hands told us most of the audience lived in the Los Angeles area. Of course there wasn't time to confer with every member of that big audience, to discuss **answers that might serve each individual**. But there's time here and now. I propose that we look into various methods of escape that might uniquely suit some hobby of yours.

So what's this "hobby" stuff? Thanks for asking. In over thirty years of study, I've noted that very few of us can truly approach self-reliance as a vocation—a living. Most of us have to spend fifty job-connected hours a week; and to that we add family time, sleep, entertainment, and so on. This leaves very little for self-reliance studies—unless we develop a hobbyist's attitude about it. I used to become downhearted at times, worrying about things I needed to buy, or make, or learn. Not any more! I began tying hobbies (model building, backpacking, American Indian studies, race car development) together and found that I was learning more, while worrying less.

The best way to approach self-reliance in everyday life seems to be slightly less serious, more easygoing: the hobbyist's approach. You can indulge it longer without tiring of it, so you tend to learn more. You also don't worry your friends so much; I mean, of course, those improvident right-hearted, wrong-headed friends who think your personal pilot-light has gone out because you intend to affect your own destiny. When you approach self-reliance as a hobby, somehow it worries the dimwits less—**while teaching you more.**

Let's take the 'great escape' as this month's example. One of my friends ran the Boston Marathon. He's serious about it; come hail, sleet or sludgewater, that guy churns out the miles in all seasons. By now, he knows most of the runnable byways out of his city, and he knows how long it takes. He also pays attention to such things as prevailing winds, the location of people he knows near his routes, and places that might afford some cover from this or that. Here is a man who, wearing street clothes with a small pack, could make it from where he works to the backside of a mountain outside of town in roughly an hour! Yes, it would take longer if he lived in a really huge city; and some of us simply cannot become long-distance runners (my doctor would have me committed!), but for a dedicated few, running is a way to escape the Great Gulp, given any kind of luck.

Bicycling is another hobby that offers potential escape from city-wide disaster. I've written about the bike as a "second-stage" vehicle, one you carry atop your car. When you run out of fuel or road, you abandon your "first-stage" car and continue on the bike—hopefully, with a lightweight survival kit you've carefully assembled. But have you seen the new lightweight off-road bikes? If you haven't, drop in on the nearest bike shop and get your mind bent. There are several brands competing (and driving prices down) now: Stumpjumper, Univega, and Ritchey, to name a few. They must be tried to be believed. Huge brakes, whopping thick frame tubes, and knobby tires over two inches wide that'll navigate many a mountain trail, so help me! Thanks to chrome-moly tubing, they weigh in at only about 30 pounds. The 15-speed types are reputed to be more reliable than the 12- or 18-speed versions, and prices start at roughly $225. This compares well with prices of the better brands of classic ten-speed, and they're actually both lighter and sturdier than my old Schwinn. Be forewarned: the bikes will look "funny" to you at first. I suppose the first Jeep looked funny alongside a ritzy convertible, too—but it did jobs no stylish vehicle could do. If you're considering a new bike, by all means pay close attention to these new high-tech all-terrain bicycles that will literally jump obstacles with you.

Before we take leave of the bike hobby, let's pause to study the bike trailer. With a 20-pound two-wheel bike trailer you can carry a baby **under a windowed convertible top** plus a hundred pounds of gear. A trailer with child seat and top may cost upwards of $250, but lordy, think of all a biker could carry! Unless you have fiendishly steep terrain to cover, you could haul that trailer many miles in a couple of hours, carrying your toddler and fifty kilos of other stuff besides. For the ultimate in two-stage vehicles, consider a small rugged van with bikes and a bike trailer inside. Remember, this isn't a solution for everybody, but it might be one that dovetails with your hobby—or with a hobby your physician has suggested.

The motorcyclist has different options. For one

thing, a light scrambler bike (motorcyclists call their mounts 'bikes' too) can be lifted over fences or other barriers, while giving you a top speed that challenges most cars. Motorcycles are bloody dangerous because they combine speed with vulnerability. Please don't think you can buy a scrambler bike and keep it "handy" without you, yourself, getting "handy" with it. But you can cover a lot of ground in short order, if you're good with a scrambler. Or perhaps you have a Harley "hawg" or Kawasaki's equivalent. Again, you can gobble the miles fast with them, but they're just too heavy for most off-road travel. Presuming that your hobby involves a motorcycle, you need to study your 'escape' system to determine what it can do, and what it can't do; and then decide whether you need to tie your escape to a different hobby.

Without citing names, I'll say there's a couple very dear to me who live in Disasteropolis, the city that's doing its best to prove why cities make you vulnerable. There are times when they wish to aitch I'd quit telling them what they know already. But they live very near an urban airport—and they are currently investigating a new hobby called ultralights. The "ultralight" is a one- or two-passenger aircraft that combines the techniques of light aircraft and hang gliders, and many of them can be carried to the airstrip atop a car. The whole thing weighs perhaps 200 pounds. Its engine may put out 30 horses, and it'll take an hour, sometimes much more, to assemble; but given almost any treeless paved area a few hundred feet long, it can be your ticket from the jaws of the Great Gulp.

An ultralight doesn't need much speed or space to take off, and it costs about as much as a subcompact car. It may average 50 miles an hour in flight, but at this writing you still don't need a pilot's license to fly most of them. Check the hobby out; many owners of conventional private aircraft simply **hate** the little buggers for several reasons, partly because early ultralight hobbyists tended to graunch themselves and give flying a bad name—and partly because ultralights are an implied criticism of the wasteful ways of many big, fast, gas-guzzling, expensive aircraft that can't land on a dirt road because the old-timers come sizzling in at maybe 60 miles an hour, while the ultralights can do it at much slower speeds. Various versions of autogyro, such as the Bensen Gyrocopter, have some of the same short-field advantages, but I haven't seen one that can be quickly assembled from car-top stowage.

Naturally you should be bitterly realistic when considering this kind of escape. You won't go schlepping around the city all the time with your ultralight on the chevy, so consider the half-hour (sometimes considerably more) it'd take to stow it on your car; the time it takes to get to the nearest **reliable** takeoff strip; and the time it takes to assemble it. If all that time amounts to only two hours, you're lucky and adroit too. BUT: once you crank up the Cuyuna (or whatever little engine you have), you can forget about traffic jams and roadblocks. You can hedgehop a hundred feet over rooftops and be fifty miles away by the end of the third hour, with enough fuel for another fifty miles or so. Only a few models will accommodate passengers so far, but that'll change. This is a very, very good hobby-escape method for a very few people. But how d'you know whether you're one of those few until you've given it some thought? You may be nearer a good takeoff area for an ultralight than you think.

Are there waterways available? Then consider a hobby that involves a car-top boat, or one you can stow in your van. Good old Jacques Cousteau has shown us the value of a tough, inflatable boat of the Zodiac variety—but you won't make truly fast time without a hellacious big outboard engine. Those suckers are heavy, and they aren't cheap; but some such combination may be the best solution to your escape problem.

Many of us have seen the awesome performance of the high-performance off-road car, of which the Baja Bug—the off-road VW—is the best reasonably-priced example. You can't lift it over a fence or a roadblock, and it isn't silent (though it could be durn near inaudible if owners cared for silence). You don't have to become a competitive off-road racer to get good everyday use out of such a critter, but if you honestly expect to turn to it in your hour of escape, by all means do seek experienced off-road hobbyists. They can teach you many cute tricks that can extract you and three other people from otherwise hopeless snags.

I once wrote of a kid—fictional, but based on arguments by serious hobbyists—who used an up-to-date skateboard to speed him out of suburbs. Perhaps the best argument for the skateboard is that you can sling it over one shoulder with a strap, and it's so simple and sturdy it'll survive outrageous abuse with absolutely no damage. But will you fare that well? Those things are mayhem on almost anybody but a youngster. Maybe a skateboard could be a **third-stage** vehicle clamped on your bike! But don't even consider it unless you really do use a skateboard as a hobby. You could become what hobbyists term a "street pizza" with your first hard spill.

We've considered hobbies that take you on land, water, and in the air, and for most of us that covers just about all the general categories. But as a teenager, I engaged in one bizarre hobby in two cities that might qualify as another category. I refer to the usually silly practice of exploring storm sewers. There are many obvious drawbacks. Most sewers aren't navigable, but the big storm sewers are, if you know how to get into them. Is there one near you, that will take you somewhere you want to go? In every case in my personal experience, this means of escape would have offered no real advantage. But in fallout conditions, or when you're trying to get past a roadblock, this just might **possibly** be useful. Honestly, I can't recommend it, but there may be someone who lives in some circumstance that would make it work. I recall a mental institution where several inmates once used a storm sewer to wander out among the rest of us. I should also remind you that nuclear blasts often cause local heavy rains. A storm drain was intended to carry rain, remember; and it could be carrying lots of fallout too, so you could get drowned and irradiated at the same time. Great fun, hm?

Of course, whatever means you may choose to make your escape, you'll have only half your problem solved unless you've already planned where you're going. That can be a hobby too; more on that another time.

There is a real question of ethics in discussing some of these possible exits from the Great Gulp. Some may bc illegal under certain circumstances; some may be more dangerous than useful for you, personally. My personal ethic demands that I beg you to study the possible consequences of your choice, and to choose what you consider to be the hobby that best combines prudence with effectiveness. After all, it's ultimately you who will succeed or fail on the basis of your choice!

You might profit by brainstorming on all the hobbies or pastimes that dovetail with means for escaping your city—especially those pastimes I neglected to cover. That's a crucial part of self-reliance in everyday life; and it could convert a widespread disaster into your own Great Escape.

Crisis Relocation: Being Choosy, Getting Chosen

Previously we discussed a common problem, i.e., finding some way to escape a city in a major crisis; and we approached it as a low-profile hobby. We also promised to address the next problem, which is establishing a good haven. The same restrictions apply in all these problems: limited funds, limited leisure, low-profile. In fact, your efforts can be so low-key that neighbors and even some family members are wholly unaware of what you're doing! In short, you take a hobbyist's approach. Viewed this way, long-term survival isn't such a tiring effort and it doesn't get us tagged as fruitcakes by folks who don't understand.

Given that you intend to relocate in a crisis, your first logical step is to study whatever crisis relocation (evacuation) routes your officials have established. Crowds of other people would probably be evacuating too, and you'd have to expect armed officers funneling everyone along predetermined routes. In many locales, sheriff's emergency services departments are a good source of this vital information. Keep asking 'til you find out; it isn't a state secret, though you may have to persist because civil defense funding is so ridiculously tiny that such crucial information as this may not be known by every public servant who should know.

Armed with routes, you next take a detailed map of your locale and mark acceptable escape routes with a bright flow pen. No matter how much you *want* to take a certain freeway, you may find that officials have denied you access to it during a crisis. Can you change that ruling? Chances are against it unless you're a professional county planner (or can convince one); but if you're going to try, do it now. Surely you don't really intend to challenge a riot-gun-toting officer during a crisis? The prudent thing is to change what you can, while you can, and accept the rest. Your primary goal is to get somewhere with minimum fuss.

Now, take a second map that covers a region two hundred miles in all directions from you. Cudgel your mind for all the people you know who live in spots you'd like to use as havens within that distance. Mark those spots on the big map. If some of those potential havens are questionable, mark them with a question mark and settle the questions later.

Next, using a different color flow pen, mark any likely spots that might be sources of crisis. Examples: an active volcano (folks in Portland aren't laughing), a military base or major power plant (potential nuclear targets), or perhaps a city which may be barfing mobs of people toward you along designated evacuation routes. At this point you are mapping several scenarios—and it's entirely possible that each of your escape routes leads you straight into the jaws of some other potential Great Gulp. If that's the case, you're smart to get several maps and mark up one for each scenario: eruption, nuclear war, flood, and so on. It's highly unlikely that they'd all happen at once, and evacuation from a nuclear target might very profitably take you past the volcano, or vice-versa.

Obviously there's some path between you and the

source of each problem—a corridor bringing the problem to you. It may consist of prevailing winds (check your TV weatherman or some flight charter outfit for information on seasonal prevailing winds in your area), or it could be a canyon between a dam and your little valley, or a freeway carrying tens of thousands of frightened people. A little research will educate you, whereupon you mark your findings on the map. These are corridors you don't want to cross if you can avoid it. If prevailing winds are your problem, the corridor may be an awfully wide one. Try to find a route that takes you out of it in the shortest time.

By now you have some revealing maps. Chances are good that you see some areas that would probably be havens for you, no matter which disaster occurred. There's also a sizeable chance that you'll wish you lived in a "handier," more escapable part of your locale. Well, the average family moves every few years anyhow; we know couples who make a hobby of visiting open houses and model homes just to see what improvements can be made in their lifestyles. If you happen across a place that situates you in a safer area without entailing a change of job or friends, the house-shopping hobby may have paid off in the best coin of all.

Now, how about those friends within two hundred miles? We suggest roughly this distance because a single tank of gas, perhaps not entirely full when the alarm comes, may get you near enough to walk or bike the rest of the way. We once did some consulting for a man who'd already rigged his own haven in a near-perfect spot . . . except that the spot was many hundreds of miles from where he lived. He wasn't in shape to hike it and there were some formidable geographical barriers in between. This was a highly intelligent man who, like all of us, was capable of forgetting a crucial datum. In a crisis, your travel capability may come down to a matter of shoe leather.

Some of your hoped-for havens will be much more inviting than others. You'd be wise to make a listing of those sites and their advantages—and disadvantages. You'll be wiser still if you *don't* make a big point of "grading" these sites in front of, say, your kids—whose innocent tonguewagging might embarrass you later. Personal relationships with site owners will be a big factor. So can religious biases and views of the site owners on the topic of survival. Nobody but you can juggle your own variables properly, but somehow you'll wind up with a list that gives you a rough notion of which potential havens give you the best chance of safety and acceptance, if and when worst comes to worst.

Now comes time for diplomacy, especially if your clear first choice is occupied by acquaintances who may not yet be close friends. They could be touchy if you simply announced that you intend to cultivate them more because they offer a haven. Your choice may entail some ethical tradeoffs in the degree to which you share *all* your motives with others.

Once you've made a tentative choice, there's the not-so-little matter of getting chosen. To take an average case, let's say your choice involves close friends of your best friends—people you know and like, but you've never stayed overnight with them or vice-versa. Remedy that by finding some other *genuine* reason for such a visit to their home a hundred miles from you. Do they have summer stock theater nearby? Fishing? Some special sports event? Maybe you're an amateur photographer; if there weren't something highly appealing about their region (and worth a day of shutter-snapping), you wouldn't have chosen it! Perhaps you simply, honestly do wish you could live there, which is reason enough to make a weekend reconnaissance trip.

Make the visit and do what you said you'd do, meanwhile making mental notes. Do you really get along all that well with your hosts? Do some of you share hobbies or sports that could further cement friendship? So much the better. On the other hand, you may find that you're not well-matched for even a week of riding out some crisis. In either event, be the best guests you can, and invite them to descend on your home in return.

It's worth stressing that any such carefully developed relationship must truly be in everyone's best interest. (Many a sad marriage has reflected someone's failure to see the truth of this in advance.) Aside from the ethical question, your haven will be a poor one if it's crammed with people who don't get along. You must be toughminded enough on yourself to admit, if necessary, that your first choice wasn't a good one. There are almost certainly other choices available to you.

But if the visit works out, on a subsequent visit you should mention the idea of staying with them in case of need. By that time you'll know how you could pull your weight in such an event. Would they appreciate a whopping store of canned goods which they could use anytime? Does your family include someone trained in first aid or shelter construction? Would they like a free two hundred gallon storage tank for water?

If you're very lucky, you could find that your host has been considering ways to convert a game room or a basement into a shelter of come-what-may; and you should be willing to donate as much time and money as you can to make these plans a reality. Of course it isn't your place! Be an ideal assistant. And every time you visit, get more familiar with alternative routes with a view toward avoiding congested areas. Which routes would be best in rotten weather, and/or if you were afoot or on bikes?

Does this "ideal assistant" routine seem a lot to ask of you? Well, look at it this way: your host doesn't need you nearly as much as you need him. If you could afford simply to buy or lease a second home there, you would've already done it. The owner of that haven is offering you a lot. Compared to other options (or more likely, *no* options), the price is right. Make sure you pay your way. You want your host to be glad you joined forces, even if you never have to use the place for crisis relocation.

It's also important that you maintain the "hobby" outlook as you go about the gradual process of making someone else's home receptive to your small onslaught. When you visit, take your friends out to dinner or whatever entertainment they enjoy there—and if the cost bothers you, think of it privately as an investment. Take time to enjoy the visit. Meet their friends, too; become mutual friends because you do not want to remain a stranger. Since you chose the locale as a haven, chances are it's a smallish town or near one. The better-liked you are in that town, the better. If a crisis ever does come to stay awhile, you'll want to be someone who's already become accepted by the people around you, and that includes the entire host community if you can manage it. Simply put, you want to get chosen and stay chosen.

A few paragraphs back, we included the possibility that you really would prefer to live there. Well, especially in a smaller town, your chances of finding work there are infinitely better if you've already become known over a period of time. The opportunity may even arise for you to change careers there to good advantage—with the added advantage that you could pack up and leave your vulnerable site in favor of one you know, by now, to be much better. And moving to another locale isn't much of a hardship if you already have good friends there.

Getting back to the most likely scenario, however, you'll invest some time and money getting accepted as an occasional visitor. That may not be enough to make your presence a strong plus during a crisis, unless you also have needed skills and the desire to share them. These must be skills people need in a crisis.

As if you didn't have a good idea already, we'll recite a few crisis skills: nutrition, paramedical skill, construction, civil defense of the nuts-and-bolts type, mechanic, nurse (!), engineer, food storage specialist, electrician, farmer/gardener. If you haven't lived in a small town, you might be absolutely amazed how many village dwellers need help in those skills. And if your family includes a trained nurse, you can depend on a lot of acceptance. Why not include physician and dentist? Because if there's one of those in your household, you could almost certainly move to a haven site anytime you really wanted to, with very high assurance of a good income and high status. And some physicians I know have said they wouldn't evacuate at the very time when their patients would need them most.

Which brings up a final point. If your household includes someone who's beginning to consider career choices, you might stress the advantages of lifestyle in a small town. These days, small towns need computer repairmen, programmers, medics, teachers, and even TV anchor-critters just as the big cities do.

In a way, deciding on a career is a question of choosing to help the people by whom you'd most want to be chosen, if times get really bad. And if you're already glued to a career that doesn't favor those choices, there's always the hobbyist approach. . . .

A Sensible Bias On Business As Usual

In previous articles we pointed out that most of us simply can't afford to dwell on self-reliance constantly, and that the topic can be tiring on those around us anyhow. But we **can** adopt a special bias on everyday activities, making it low-profile for the most part without putting too much strain on business as usual. To take a few examples, there's nothing very unusual about buying presents, or attending garage sales, or driving a well-known route. Or is there?

Gifts

As long as you're going to buy presents during a holiday season anyway, you could hardly go wrong by asking, in each case, what potential value a given present might have. Your cousin may not give a good rap about self-reliance today, but a 12-volt plug-in spotlight for his car might save his personal bacon some rainy night—and give him a new outlook.

Then there are books, which aren't very expensive. Books of modest price can be manuals for surviving a variety of Great Gulps. For that cousin who doesn't want to be bothered you might select from a few fiction paperbacks that sugarcoat the message with entertainment.

And then there are the kids. Probably more than half the presents we buy are for minors, and all too often we give them things that are more harm than good. An example? Video games that keep the kid cemented to a chair for hours without teaching anything more important than the vagaries of a "joystick" when he's trying to zap the monster. There are educational games of course, including video games; but if the game seems to be one hundred per cent entertainment and zero per cent education, maybe that game is part of the kid's problem.

Before we leave the video game example, let's take hard note of a growing problem with our kids: their increasing demand for instant gratification. Now, as it happens, the writer has been asked to help design some video games, and to permit the use of some fictional plots by other game designers. Sure, there's money in it. There's also an insidious fact that keeps our interest at a pretty low ebb. Here it is: video game designers know by experience that kids—at least those who play video games a lot—are so impatient, so childishly demanding, of gratification **right now** that the game must be designed to let the play begin almost instantly. The video display could be very much more exciting, more realistic, than it is—if kids were willing to wait a half-minute or so for the highly complex display to be "loaded" into the circuitry. That means there could be more subtle colors, with full three-dimensional pictures that would change in a lifelike way, and more. There could be, that is, if kids were willing to defer their trivial little gratifications for the duration of a few breaths. They aren't willing. They demand something fast, not something good. How does the designer react? Why, the customer is always right, and the kid is the customer! The designer, in a sense, thus lets the monkeys run the zoo. If this trend expands, soon we will have fewer experts because, to get good at something, we have to work like blazes for a long time before we begin to enjoy the fruits of our labors. In short, the fewer kids who understand how to defer their enjoyment awhile, the fewer will be competent experts in the future. Meanwhile, video games will soon be giving the kids all those improved displays after all. It will cost more. It will improve computer graphics, too; but it will not say much for the training of our youth.

What kind of presents **will** train the kids? Probably, the kind that promises to give the youngster what she wants, if she's willing to invest a little time. (Translation: Defer gratification a little and promise a lot!) Does she plink at the piano? If she's of grade-school age, get her a small electronic organ kit! With an outlay of less than twenty bucks and an evening of adult help assembling the thing, she can make nine-volt music that isn't terribly loud while learning something about manual dexterity. Does he want to be a policeman or fireman? For less than twenty dollars, get him a quickly-assembled kit that tunes into VHF emergency frequencies. Does your teen terror ask lots of unanswerables about solar power? Again, for not much money, get him a kit that lets him tap solar power for radios, burglar alarms and so on. There are kits that teach computer science, electric power, gearing, auto mechanics, aeronautics, weaving and gardening.

We knew that all this "build-it-now, enjoy-it-later" stuff was working the first time we watched a nine-year-old girl's model rocket climb a thousand feet and return like a helicopter. The kid had small razorblade cuts on her fingers, but she'd built the thing with only advice and no adult fingers. She was ecstatic. In later years she studied the violin and architecture, both of which require a lot of deferred gratification. Nobody will ever be able to convince us that the early educational kits played less than a large part in this youngster's development.

So much for presents. How about, Lord help us, Hallowe'en? What's the value in buying a child a costume? Not much, unless the child had to work for the money. Instead, you might invest a bit of time helping (no, not doing it while the kid watches!) while the child sews, or paints, or tapes some outlandish creation together. If you have anything to do with judging costumes, surely you can give special prizes for those that reveal the most painstaking work by the children.

In all of the suggestions above, the same theme is stressed: there's long-term value in guiding our kids toward doing things for themselves. We've noticed another advantage, too: a child who assembles the hardware of his enjoyments will become an adult who takes better care of his things. And, not incidentally, he'll be one who knows how to repair things.

Garage Sales

Let's move on to another common pastime beloved by the All-American penny-pincher: garage sales. Many of us never learn certain skills because the equipment costs so much. But if you've ever seen a serviceable pair of snowshoes for ten dollars, or a fruit-drying unit for next to nothing, you've had the chance to expand your skills for peanuts. Don't lose sight of the fact that, after using the equipment, you can sell it in your own garage sale—maybe for more than you paid! So, if you have to justify it to yourself or your spouse, the resale potential means you can claim you're, um, ah, only renting it.

There's one trick (aside from checking the newspapers for such sales and getting there early) that can be of immeasurable help at garage sales: putting one and one together. To illustrate, we offer the example of a recent Saturday morning. Two garage sales offered little, though one had an expensive wheeled golf caddy for a mere $5. Time was short, and college football on TV waits for no man without a Betamax, so we went to a third sale for a quick once-over. That third site only had a few items; but one of those items was a whopping big carbon dioxide fire extinguisher for ten bucks. It was nearly empty, but a quick puff proved it still held pressure. Hmm; too bad it was so infernally big! When filled, it would douse a volcano, but was too heavy for anyone but a fee-fie-foe-fum type to carry. We'd long wished for one of those big wheeled extinguishers that anyone can lug to the location of a fire, but those were, and still are, priced like solid gold. We sighed and started home empty-handed.

Fire extinguisher rigged with caddy frame.

Are you already thinking what we realized on the way home? The extinguisher would easily fit in the caddy frame meant to carry a heavy golf bag. Quick U-turn; a fast stop to slap a tenner into the hands of the extinguisher man; then a prayerful trip back to the caddy folks, in hopes that no one else had bought the thing. When we got it all home, we found that twenty minutes of rigging made the big extinguisher fit into the caddy. A week later we had the extinguisher refilled. It sits in a corner now, fully transportable by any ten-year-old, looking almost new and costing roughly thirty dollars instead of three hundred—which is what such wheeled extinguishers usually cost. And we only missed the kickoff by a few minutes . . .

We found that friends had similar stories where tawdry treasures at different garage sales went together to yield prizes they could never have afforded otherwise. A cableless car winch at Sale One, and a coil of cable, cheap, at Sale Two; a beat-up but serviceable camera tripod at Sale Three, and a spotting scope without a mount at Sale Four. That's two hundred bucks worth of car winch for twenty, and fifty bucks worth of scope with tripod for ten. So the tripod looks a little funny; it sure beats squinting.

Alternate Routes

Nothing could be more "business as usual," for many of us, than driving a familiar route every day or every week—to and from work, or to a favorite relative. Well: is that route ever flooded, or plugged with traffic? There's no compelling reason why we can't start out five minutes early and explore alternate routes. Figure out for yourself whether there's any likely scenario that would make it necessary for you to get from point A to point B—and would also make it impossible. We know one common route which "everybody" takes between two towns, but which is clogged every winter during the periods of fog. One recent winter the fog squatted on the highway, thick as soup, for twenty-three successive mornings. It happens that there are two other routes that are much more free of fog. They wind along at higher elevations and, in good weather, take ten or fifteen minutes longer to make the trip. But on foggy mornings they take less time, and are lots safer. A few motorists always ducked off the highway at first opportunity, and one day we followed. Now we frequently seek out alternative routes, mindful of all the mornings when we took unnecessary risks because we hadn't explored those alternatives. An especially steep and icy stretch might be avoided; congestion during a relocation crisis might be another avoidable crunch.

We've termed these activities "pastimes" because we can pleasantly occupy ourselves with this low-profile hobby while pursuing other common activities. But there are lots of other hobbies that have special application to self-reliance. We'll take those up another time.

High Tech and Self-Reliance

When considering self-reliance, often as not we bump into the "high-tech" dilemma. One extreme opinion is that high tech is a trap to be avoided. The other extreme opinion holds that only high tech will provide self-reliance in style. Thirty years of study have convinced me that the best option lies midway between those extremes.

IMPORTANT FOOTNOTE: When it comes to keeping *our country* intact, high tech is absolutely essential, exclamation point. We may not keep it intact even with high tech; we will surely go down the tubes fast without it. The moment we begin to dull our nation's cutting-edge technology, the Soviets start leaning on us harder because they know they can afford to. We must never forget that "Star Wars" hardware means, literally, Civil Defense—defending our citizens. The Sovs are developing it anyhow, but we have an edge today. That edge cuts deeply into Soviet plans for dominion. Soviet high tech rarely gets to Russian consumers. Ours comes to the home; and that can be good if we know how to use it on a personal level.

Many people disagree on what "high tech" means. If it simply means some new technology, there's no real dilemma. If it means something very complicated to maintain, then maybe we *do* have a problem. Perhaps a few examples are in order.

The all-terrain bicycles are a new wrinkle, no more complicated than older types and a whole lot sturdier. As long as you're going to depend on any bike, sooner or later you must consider repairs. If the parts and repair techniques are just as easy, and the high-tech hardware is more dependable, then high tech is the way to go. Another example? I've been designing and testing survival hardware for many years, including a two-pound backpacker's woodstove that any tinkerer can build. The only high-tech part was developing certain shapes, baffles and flues, to triple the stove's efficiency. My own "Woodpacker" stove has kept me cozy in knee-deep snow and Sierra storms, and needs to be stoked only once every half-hour. Its design is clearly high-tech—but its construction is low-tech. In the same category is the "safety net," stiff mosquito netting sewn into a yard-wide sack so you can wear it, backpack and all, even while fishing.

High tech? Yes, in the sense that these things weren't previously available and had to be perfected (thin mosquito net won't qualify as a "safety net"; it won't stand away from your skin). But these gadgets can be made and repaired by low-tech means. They were new in concept, but could've been built and maintained with simple tools, generations ago.

Then there's the other kind of high tech, like solid-state electronics and the new H&K caseless ammunition. No matter how cheap it might be to buy, most of us have only the vaguest idea how to build or repair it. If a solar-powered hand calculator quits on you, chances are you'll have to toss it—but you might invest in a few cheap foil-wrapped spares. Just don't discard your old slide-rule, and make sure your kids learn how to use it. As for the new ammo: could it be manufactured locally? It takes a factory with special tooling and rare know-how to make caseless ammo. Many small-town chemistry teachers could manufacture guncotton, smokeless powder, even primers from basic chemicals, and handloading is an old art; but when you've fired your last caseless cartridge, that high-tech rifle is NO-tech!

Maybe for our purposes, high tech is anything that requires support which is beyond the means of the average small town. Has your car's fuel injection pump gone belly-up? If there's no mechanic near you with the parts and knowledge to repair it, this is the kind of high tech you *must not* depend on in a survival situation. Even mag wheels can be a problem if you have no special equipment to remount a new tire without gouging that tender cheesy magnesium. If you're now storing vital information on computer disks, you'd be smart to keep printed copies of it all, for that Great Gulp when permanent failure of power, or a computer chip, makes those disks useless.

None of these warnings should make you sell your fuel-injected car, or your home computer. They should make you think about low-tech backup systems for anything that requires sophisticated support beyond what's local and dependable. By "local," I mean within walking distance. And thereby hangs a tale . . .

Once, when I lived in a city, I knew a bachelor who was nuts about high tech. He didn't own a lot of things, but what he owned was nifty: foreign sportscar, solid state stereo, Cuisinart, gadgety camera and other mouth-watering boytoys. He used to joke that he ". . . couldn't survive beyond the city" because only a big city could provide the services to maintain his toys. He took pride in trading for new hardware that was so high-tech, few others had it and fewer still knew where it could be maintained. No problem, he said, so long as he kept a current list of all the wizards at adjusting Weber carburetors and troubleshooting electronics. He was a user, not a fixer.

This guy was carefully adjusting his life so that he needed the city's high-tech services, and his lifestyle could not survive without them. He assumed that he could always drive across the city to find somebody who could fix his problems. In other words, he lived a high-tech existence with the full intent of becoming utterly dependent on it. It seemed to me a little like an addiction, and it made me more than a little sick. The more I thought about that, the less I liked depending on distant folks to maintain equipment I depended on, but didn't understand.

I thought about it so much that now I live in a small town. As soon as I learned to fix my inexpensive home computer, I bought another one like it for a spare—but I have whopping big file cabinets and a manual typewriter with spare ribbons, too. I have a transistor radio, but I also have a 1933 GE brute with spare tubes, though its fifty-two-year-old original tubes still work and they were so over-designed they'll probably survive a nuclear weapon pulse.

I admit that I enjoy high tech; it's convenient—but when it gets too gimmicky for local repair, I try to make sure there's a more primitive backup system handy. High tech is a metaphor of the city: we can use it, but we must not depend on it.

And at this point, some readers will be objecting that they *must* have fuel, and spare parts, and technology that requires special expertise—including medicines. Take heart; so long as small towns are in business, we can enjoy many medium-tech conveniences and necessities. Almost any small clinic could manufacture penicillin, given the need. Many small shops can rebuild electric motors and generators. We can manufacture fuel alcohol from wood and grain; lubricant from castor beans; passable (barely!) bike tires from a length of water hose stuffed with bits of rubber and wired onto rims; and we can even melt and recast aluminum scrap for machining at any small machine shop. What we must not do on a personal level, is allow ourselves to become absolutely dependent on technology that can't be matched locally.

Meanwhile, don't curse the nation's pursuit of high-tech knowledge. It gave us penicillin (which could've existed centuries ago if we'd known what to do). It taught us heat transfer so some gadgeteer could develop an *efficient* woodstove anybody can build. And at present, with space-age experiments, it promises you and me the first real hope of defending most of our civilians against nuclear war. After all, isn't that the first duty of a government—to defend its citizens?

The Lifetime Lesson Schools *Can't* Teach

This article deals with a method for teaching children, on an everyday basis, how to plan for their many tomorrows. That's the very heart of self-reliance. Those children are more likely than most to grow up with keen judgment, and with a careful eye on problems that lie ahead.

After many years, I'm ready to report on a home project we first saw in a neighbor's home twenty-five years ago. It probably could not be duplicated in schools. It teaches grade-school children how to:

- Make long-range plans.
- Buy wisely.
- Take care of their belongings.
- Avoid waste.

And they *enjoy* the process! This may sound like a big promise, and it is. It is based on the upbringing of less than a dozen people—*all* of whom demonstrate that the idea works if the parents are steadfast. It also relieves parents from constant attention to the day-to-day expenses of kids. You can keep an eye on their progress if you like; but you won't be constantly nagged about it. This project began as a children's budget fifty years ago by parents of our neighbor, who became a brilliant closet survivalist if ever there was one. She raised her kids with the same love and the same budget scheme, and they ended up with the same virtues, ready to teach them to their own kids. We watched, and then did the same with *our* kids.

Well, our kids have flown the nest now; and though they are very different from each other, they are alike in one respect: they're willingly surviving hard times much better than most. We think they are thriving so well because we stuck with the budget project until, when our kids were roughly ten years old, it began to get progressively more pleasant. No wonder: by that time, the kids were taking much of the load—and liking it. I have never seen it fail, though sometimes it creates unexpected side effects. More on that presently; let me give you the budget schedule.

When your child enters the first grade, have a family meeting with milk and cookies while you explain: he's growing up, and you're ready to let him earn a salary AND make some decisions on his own. The salary you name will be higher than he expected—because, you explain, from now on, he will be allowed to choose all his own school supplies—*and his socks*. You may give advice, but the real choices will be his. The salary also must cover school meals, with a bit extra for whatever he wants; comics, gum, toys. Of course, it's important that you learn in advance what those costs will be. Chances are, they'll be higher than you thought. You'd hand over the money in any case; this way, you pay the child a weekly salary and let him begin, year by year, to plan more of his expenses.

In return for this salary, you have reasonable chores for him to do. No chores? No salary—or at least, so little salary that there's no money for the comics and toys. When they see that you remain firm, the kids do the chores.

In second grade, his salary is increased to cover purchase of all his underwear too. In third grade, add shirts. In fourth, the biggie: shoes. For some reason, kids always seem to buy one pair of fancy footwear that falls apart fast. And they want you to bail them out, of course. If you do, it must be a short-term loan *with interest*. They won't like it.

Right. They aren't *supposed* to like it, but that's the way the world works. They are supposed to learn from a dumb purchase, and to start understanding interest rates at a tender age. Mean ol' mom and mean ol' dad are teaching them things no school can teach, and few kids learn before they're twenty-five. Ours did. Yours can.

By the eighth grade, your kids are getting a sizeable salary every week—the envy of their friends. They are doing very sizeable chores for it, and by this time they are buying ALL of their clothes, supplies, and entertainment. You are spending no more money than you would anyway, and you don't have to spend hours on those purchases because the kids are doing it, perhaps as well as you could. Once in high school, they'll be running higher expenses. Maybe you can increase their salaries, or maybe they'll just have to find part-time work in addition to home chores. Extra payment for honor grades is no sin, if you can afford it.

The drawbacks? There aren't many. You have to do the original budgeting very carefully at first, and you must act as though ice water runs in your veins when your kids beg you to bail them out of dumb purchases which you probably advised them not to make. But whatever you told them, you didn't force them. That's important.

You may find, within a week after the last kid has left home, that he was doing more of the chores than you realized. Now you'll have to rake the leaves and prepare the gardens and feed the animals yourself.

Tough luck, parents; but think of how much help you got, all those years, for the "salary" you would have paid out as allowances!

We found one laughable drawback, of a sort. One girl discovered that if she dressed from Goodwill, she could buy more records with her salary. The result was that the local punker crowd applauded her weird-fitting garb and, for two years, she "went punk" in her dress style. No, she didn't do drugs or liquor—but boy, did she dress funny! She began to sink back into sane clothing as soon as she tried to get a job wearing clothespinned skirts and torn stockings. It took a lot of patience by her parents, but that young woman turned out very nicely, working her way through college and planning for her tomorrows.

Another side effect, less funny: the kids *do* mature sooner. They understand budgeting, they tend to get jobs sooner, and they grow independent sooner than most. This doesn't have to be a problem, if you realize that your child is wise beyond her years because you trained her to make her own choices, and to plan for hard times.

We've come to think of this as the "Salaried Child Project," and it does not produce slavish followers! They grow up as independent folks who train their kids the same way. The process isn't as troublesome as budgeting for your kids, so everybody gains. And in a very real way, the process trains them for self-reliance tomorrow.

Microfarming

Trying to cover the idea of microfarming in a few pages is a bit like biting off a big hunk of beef jerky: the more you chew on it, the bigger it gets. For some, a ten-acre spread producing familiar crops on a small scale is microfarming. For others—and I'm one of them—growing dwarf crops indoors or in corners of the back yard is *really* microfarming. If you have only those tiny backyard spaces, you may care more about pygmy corn than about micropigs. With five or ten acres, you might raise standard high-yield crops but not standard farm animals. Whichever situation you're in, the next few pages may expand your self-reliance options.

In a passage from a Max Shulman novel, dimwits tried to run a co-op farm with one cow and one sheep. They milked the cow all day long, and sheared the sheep constantly. The sheep, as I recall, finally surrendered itself to a meat packer. Well, Shulman was trying for laughs, and he got them. But there's nothing funny about needing beef *and* milk, when you've only got one cow and limited farmland. Some folks solve that problem by keeping a few goats, but goats and sheep aren't just everybody's pleasure. For one thing, they ruin pasturage by pulling grass up by the roots. Wouldn't it be nice if we could raise little bitty milk cows instead?

Well, we can; and the pint-sized critters have been around for a long time. The same is true for poultry, and now it's possible to grow incredibly tiny, full-grown pigs. A lot of food crops can be grown in miniature as well, including corn, grains, and fruits. This isn't to say that all these products can compete in today's commercial market. Maybe that's why we don't hear enough about them. It's high time we gave them some serious thought, if we want more self-reliance on less land.

Let's begin with that standard food producer, the cow. An ordinary milk cow often weighs over half a ton and requires an acre or more of pasture. Dexter cows, first imported here from Ireland in 1905 as "Kerry cattle," may weigh under 700 pounds when fully mature (a "big" bull might reach 900) but a Dexter steer has reached slaughter weight at only 450 pounds. Either all red or all black, they are gentle, with short horns and thick glossy coats. They don't damage fencing or sheds much, and they're easier to bully when you must, because they're only four feet tall at the shoulder. They don't need much pasture area or coddling because Dexters were bred from hardy stock for tiny Irish farms and less-than-ideal weather.

A 450-pound Dexter steer provides over 200 pounds of beef. No, the Dexter breed doesn't gain weight as fast as larger cattle; the hide, bone, and other non-edible parts are also slightly greater in proportion to the meat you get. But those drawbacks may become minor when you have a limited acreage and want a herd—even a very small herd—of cattle. You can't butcher half a beef. Unless, of course, it's a whole animal half the size of the usual critter. The American Dexter Cattle Association was formed to further the breed. From all reports, Dexters are inexpensive enough to be a practical buy today.

Maybe we need not take too much time describing bantam—often called "banty"—breeds of poultry. Sure, the eggs are smaller (a hen may be dumb, but she's not *that* dumb). A roasted bantam rooster won't feed a family of four, either, but it doesn't require much feed or room. (Incidentally, if you want plenty of eggs, don't crowd your hens.) On the plus side, you know bantam breeds such as the Rock Cornish Game Hen are fairly economical because you can buy the little birds, ready for roasting, at most markets.

On the minus side, bantam poultry aren't known for efficient egg production. And chickens of standard size, laying a nice big egg apiece every other day, don't take up all that much room. It's a tiny farm, indeed, that hasn't room for a dozen Leghorns and Rhode Island Reds. You can feed a dozen bantams or standard chickens mostly from table scraps, and let 'em scratch for the rest. The point to remember is that, while bantam poultry are a well-known option, they may not always be a smart one even for the smallest farms. You might consider a hutch for Homer pigeons, which might not bother the neighbors as much. Pigeons pair off quietly and produce a dozen squabs a year. Just don't expect pigeon eggs to make cost-effective omelets. Like the bantams, pigeons either fit a very special niche in your food plans, or no niche at all.

Now for a real mind-boggler: the micropig. A common farm pig will eat five pounds of feed a day, and weighs 600 to 800 pounds fully grown. A micropig eats maybe *one* pound of feed a day, and may weigh 60 pounds fully grown! *Science News*, in June 1986, reported that Colorado State University now has a colony of 100 micropigs and that in Wilmington,

Massachusetts, the Charles River Breeding Labs will sell micropigs.

Micropigs are virtually hairless; they're also clean and easy to handle. Several of them can be kept in a single four-foot by twelve-foot pen. Because they eat just about anything we do, we can feed them our leftovers. Micropigs were bred from a Mexican strain called the Yucatan Miniature, or "minipig." (In Quintana Roo, on the wild underside of the Yucatan, I noticed that the Maya word for pig was *k'eh-k'enh*. When pronounced the way the Maya do, the word sounds comically like a minipig's grunt.)

It's been ten years since swine researcher Linda Palepinto began breeding Mexican minipigs down to micropigs in Colorado, and Palepinto thinks she can create 40-pound pigs eventually, without breeding abnormal finicky beasts. The micropig already sounds like a paragon of farm virtue just as it is. There's got to be a catch, right?

The catch is that micropigs are still rare, and they're sold to medical researchers who would much rather deal with a 60-pound pig than its 600-pound cousin. Because the pigs will flourish on the same diets as humans, and have similar skins, stomachs, and teeth, they're in demand by universities and pharmaceutical labs. It may be years before the micropig colonies are expanded to the point where you can buy a pregnant sow for a reasonable price. Keep your eyes open for them, though. In the near future, you may be able to raise 50-pound pigs on your postage-stamp farm.

We can probably pass over some other miniature farm animals with a nod. Yes, tiny horses have been bred down to the size of a collie, but they have little value as farm animals. If oxen have pulled plows for thousands of years, we could employ a pair of Dexter cattle instead of balky Shetlands or smaller horses.

Even farm cats can be miniatures; I've seen Abyssinian cats that were no bigger than a Chihuahua dog. I also wonder how they'd stack up against a big feisty Norway rat. . . .

The fact is, it might just be possible to stock a working ten-acre farm with a weirdly appealing array of live miniatures. Three or four Dexter cattle; a few "banties" among your Plymouth Rock chickens; a microboar and a few sows that, altogether, wouldn't weigh as much as one half-grown Poland China hog; and a Chihuahua to chase your Abyssinian cat which is, at least, big enough to eat the mice that eat your miniature crops.

If you have several acres for crops, you'll probably realize a higher yield with common crop varieties. The smaller your crops area, the more you may appreciate plants that fit that available space. Miniature corn, of course, is older than the huge hybrid stuff that I have seen towering nine feet in the air. Some pygmy corn grows no more than shoulder-high, producing ears in proportion. The grain yield per stalk is low, but I grow a score of stalks in a plot scarcely bigger than a card table. And each little ear is as succulent as its bigger cousins. You could grow a stand of pygmy corn in a bathtub. Save the fattest ear for next year's seed!

As for flour, you can harvest ten or fifteen pounds of buckwheat grain from a plot that's ten feet on a side. You can grow it in cool climates too (but not in very hot ones), a bushy little plant that's more like a weed than a grass. It will attract bees when it blossoms. Just be sure to harvest your buckwheat before first frost and don't be put off by the fact that it's still flowering even though the seed—the grain you harvest—is already set. Could you harvest buckwheat bushes more than once? I don't know, but it might be interesting to try. The plants are still flowering when early seeds are ready. A friend reports that, when she lived on a Navajo reservation, she would beat up on her buckwheat to harvest the seed, then turn it under so it would come up again. It evidently fixed nitrogen in the soil as well as alfalfa does.

Some dwarf varieties of common garden vegetables can be grown in window boxes or pots. Both head and leaf lettuce, of the normal varieties, can be harvested while very young and tender. You can sow a small plot heavily, eat the plants you pull to thin the plot, and let the others grow full-size. The same is true for carrots, and baby carrots are a great delicacy.

A single cherry tomato plant in a pot can provide hundreds of small tomatoes for months, and can be raised indoors until warm weather comes. That way, you'll begin to harvest tomatoes a month or so early. Many varieties of tomato stay small. Some will climb a trellis to make use of a foot-wide strip of soil next to a fence.

Park Seed offers a potato for home gardens, the "Spud Bud," that sounds too good to be true. It's supposedly disease-free, with a yield 20% higher for a given space than other potatoes. If there's a catch, it's this: the potatoes are no bigger than ping-pong balls. But what do we care, if we harvest enough of them?

And then there are the dwarf fruit trees, in wondrous variety. Some are hardy specimens you can plant as a small orchard in an area no bigger than a one-car garage. Apple, peach and pear are common and inexpensive, many with full-sized fruit that are a snap to harvest because the tree seldom grows higher than you can reach. The "fruit salad tree," basically a plum tree with graftings of other fruit, is usually of normal size. It saves space by producing almonds, several kinds of plum, and something like an apricot on the same tree. The ones I've seen were not really dwarfs. In contrast, many citrus trees are dwarfs. Like their bigger cousins, they won't survive a hard frost.

Some dwarf citrus, in fact, are no bigger than bonsai. These can be grown indoors and will bear both fruit and fragrant blossoms all year long. The favorite in our home was an Otaheite, actually a type of lemon *that was bearing when it was a foot high.* Thriving in a 12-inch pot, it bore orange thin-skinned fruit as tart as limes, the size of a half-dollar, for years. I killed it by leaving it outdoors one October evening in a very mild cold snap. The Calamondin orange is not so tart, and will prosper indoors as well. Dwarf lime trees will do the same. All these citrus dwarfs produce fruit with great gobs of vitamin C, in laughably small spaces.

There's an asexual dwarf fig that will bear fruit indoors in a 12-inch pot without pollination. It may grow up to five feet high in that pot. Finally, the dwarf Cavendish banana tree will produce edible "hands" of bananas half the size of the common types. Just remember that commercial banana palms are big devils, so your "dwarf" will need a whopper of a pot two feet high and two feet across. The dwarf banana may not be worth its trouble indoors because it needs lots of sun and humidity. But in a protected corner of an atrium, a cluster of banana trees might reward you handsomely for the small space they need.

From the examples above, you can see that however you define microfarming, you can broaden your options with miniatures. A few acres of microfarm could make you virtually self-reliant today. Several firms are already developing crops that will probably be the first practical food crops for a moon colony, and they could add to your backyard microfarm options tomorrow. Given a larger spread with three acres of pasture, three more for grain, and an acre or so for garden, home and sheds, a microfarm could grow as broad a variety of foods as big farms grow today.

Quickie Projects

By now you know our theme: a low-key approach to self-reliance in our "normal" activities. It keeps us learning and preparing for the worst without wearing ourselves out or earning wary glances from friends and neighbors. This might be called a hobbyist's approach, and we would not be doing justice to our families if we failed to give them a shot at that hobby. Perhaps the best way to get them interested is to get their help on quickie projects; some of them take less than an hour.

This is especially true of our kids, who are likely to have a short attention span. If they're gonna work at something, they want results *now*. Probably the very best thing we can do for our impatient kids is to teach them patience: first with quickie projects that produce a reward in a half-hour or so, then in an hour, then a half-day, and so on. Unless your family members are already primed and pleased to begin such brief projects, you might do a new one every few weeks. Make haste slowly! There are quickies you can do in every season. We'll mention a double-handful below, listing them by the likely season and giving the amount of time they usually take.

Spring

One quickie project for early spring is the planting of seeds in window boxes. You can tape plastic or foil on a sunny windowsill to avoid water damage, then use egg cartons for planters. Avoid planting such items as corn in such shallow soil, but lettuce and other crops can be started this way very nicely. Experiment! Label each experiment, and urge the kids to do the same. You're teaching them some very important things, including soil science, and it might take an hour before your egg-carton planters are basking in the sunlight.

A bit later in the spring, one of the fastest projects of all is foraging for dandelions, as well as chicory and a few other hardy edible weeds. You can pick a popcorn-bag full of tender spring leaves in fifteen minutes, and have them washed and boiling in another ten. Boil ten minutes or so, drain, and season with vinegar or lemon juice. In less than an hour, you have a green veggie that tastes as good as spinach and has more Vitamin A than carrots. If you wanted to use the fresh greens in salad instead, you'd be done in less than half an hour.

What? Your kids don't like spinach anyhow? Then bribe the little infidels. If you would spend a half-dollar on spinach at the grocery, tell them you'll pay the same for a small brown bag stuffed with young dandelion leaves. After all, the main point of the exercise isn't to give them "spinach" now, but to get them familiar and confident with tricks that could save their bacon later.

Spring, or any other time, is fine for melting a few ounces of beeswax and using it to waterproof wooden kitchen matches. Get the wax just above melting temperature, and supervise the operation. A quick dip of the match so that its head and most of its shank are well-coated, then wait until the wax firms up and set the match aside. You can use metal clips to hold the ends of a dozen matches at a time if you want to make a production run of it. This is a half-hour project too, and will provide enough matches for your summer pack trips.

In later spring, set out those plants you've been watering on the windowsill. It could take the kids an hour. (Let's not talk about how long it takes to prepare the garden soil.)

Summer

By now those pesky dandelion roots in your yard should be ready for digging out, washing, drying to brittleness, and grinding up for dandelion coffee. You can still use the greens but be sure to strip the center spine from each leaf unless you want a bitter crop. Processing the root may take a couple of hours.

You can spend a summer hour foraging outside on your own, making sure you know which plants are really edible, then take the kids on a summer forage and teach them. Some fruits and berries are ripe now. So is most grain, which brings up another quickie.

You might ask the farmer first, but a hand-gathered bag of ripe wheat or rye or even millet can be threshed at home in a half-hour, letting the breeze separate the chaff while you catch the grain on newspaper. A hand grinder or even a blender can make it the basis for a boiled cereal. Or you can use it as coarse flour and bake bread. Ever see a kid who didn't drool over fresh-baked bread? Me, neither . . .

You can gather berry, mint, and other leaves to make teas of various kinds. Try dried orange rind shavings as an added spice. Leaves can be boiled fresh, or dried and kept in lidded jars. From plucking to sipping, you might spend a half-hour.

In late summer you might want to slice, pit, and dry various local fruits. They'll often keep through the winter, especially if you keep them dry in small packages. A couple of pounds of fruit—just for the experience—can be processed in an hour. Sun-drying may take days, but what do you care?

Fall

Fruit leather is a kind of candy made with leftover fruit, and it'll keep many months. Some recipes include methods you can complete in an hour or two.

Your kids can gather a pint of bug-free acorns in twenty minutes during the fall, and you can shell and split them in another thirty. Boiling the split nuts, changing the water every five minutes for about forty minutes, you will leach out nearly all the tannin that makes acorns so bitter. The nuts are dried (sometimes in an oven at lowest heat) until hard, then ground up for flour. Try mixing pancake flour with it, half-and-half, then making pancakes. Yep, the entire process may take a morning, but our acorn flour keeps for years and it might be the most important food discovery your kids will ever learn. Entire tribes of Indians lived mainly on acorns that weren't as well prepared as this.

Winter

During a season when almost all your greens are brown, it's fun to grow alfalfa sprouts. It takes longer to describe the process than to do it; and we won't describe it here, but it takes maybe two minutes, once a day, for a week. It also takes some water and a jar. No soil, no sun, no sweat. Unbelievable; the end product is a batch of sprouts ready for eating. It could've been done during any season, but we saved the magic for dreary times.

Winter is when you burn the most wood, and clean out the most white ash. Why not drip water through that ash to collect and concentrate the lye? (Don't use aluminum containers!) And why not collect some clear meat drippings? Those are the only materials you need to make soap. You might spend two or three hours (over several days' time) before you have a few bars of solidified soap created from those humble origins. But you will have demonstrated chemical processing at the kitchen-sink level, and our kids tend to use soap with pride, if they helped make the stuff.

The foregoing examples are only a few that might interest children enough that bribery would be unnecessary. But we really should do whatever is necessary—even if we harbor a bit of irritation on that score—to sweeten the effort our kids put into such brief projects. They (like some of us adults) might not fully appreciate what they're learning, today. Let's hope they will never have to *fully* appreciate these tips; but if they ever come face to face with absolute need, they will have some extremely valuable knowledge—thanks to quickie projects.

Models of Self-Reliance

It's almost impossible to dwell on self-reliance every minute—and in fact, you shouldn't try. Take it from one who did, a long time ago: it can isolate us more than is good for us. That kind of single-mindedness puts a strain on family, friends, and business. And a reputation for being somewhat flaky, on *any* topic, works against your best interests in the long run. Instead, we can put a self-reliance bias on our everyday activities; high potential, low profile. One of the most useful of those activities is studying construction projects by building models of them.

You don't have to be a radio-control freak, or boast a basement full of model trains, to cobble up a model. Those projects can be as simple as a small cardboard model of a basement shelter against Mount St. Helens ash fallout, or as complex as a full-scale wooden mockup of a high-tech windmill with moving parts. The aerospace industry has built full-scale mockups in plywood and cardboard for many years—for example, to make sure a mechanic can do maintenance inside some big gizmo before they build the real thing in titanium. It saves them a lot of money and grief because it's quick and cheap. It can do the same for you.

A favorite example: some years ago, my wife needed a big splash shield for her potter's wheel. I figured on making one from aluminum, but first I scrounged a big corrugated cardboard shipping carton. My wife knew what she wanted, but was no great shakes at sketching her needs. Instead, she cut out some cardboard panels and taped them all together, full-scale. Sure, it looked scruffy, but she had a mockup of her splash shield taped to her potter's wheel in an hour.

I grabbed a flow pen and a slitter—the kind of knife they use at the supermarket to slit cardboard boxes open, with a replaceable razor blade—and made a neater, final-version mockup of the splash shield from more cardboard. I taped it with heavy kraft paper tape and tried it for size. Since I had built mockups of race car cockpits this way, that part of the job went pretty rapidly. Gee, it looked so good I wished that I could use the mockup instead of expensive aluminum. And suddenly I realized that I could!

It took another hour to spread newspaper on a sheet of plywood to catch the mess I was about to make; cut the cheap "¾ ounce" fiberglass matt more or less to fit, with plain scissors; and mix up some boat resin with catalyst in an empty milk carton. Then I painted the polyester resin onto each cardboard face of the shield, laid the right piece of precut matt on it, and used a cheap paintbrush to paint more resin onto the fuzzy matt.

After the stuff cured for an hour, I trimmed the rough edges and finished it (wearing glasses, rubber gloves and a paper mask) with a rotary sanding head on my hand drill. It fitted nicely on my wife's potter's wheel and it required only a morning's work. It was waterproof, far stiffer than aluminum, fairly sturdy, and took a coat of paint. That was ten years ago, and the durn thing is still in use. I've used the same technique to waterproof other "mockups" since, including a shelter air filter and pump. Conclusion: Sometimes your mockup becomes the real thing!

On the other hand, mockups of property and buildings can be a thousand times smaller than the real thing. Not long ago, our family latched onto a few acres of sloping mountain property. We have a map of the place showing the elevation contours, so we decided to make a small scale model of the slopes where the three-dome complex would be built.

One of our teen-agers is pretty quick with her hands, so we turned her loose on the model of the upper slope. She was too lazy (translation: too smart) to make a relief map of the entire acreage. "Come on, Dad," she said; "why waste time and cardboard and glue?" I didn't argue; she obviously had her own picture of how it should be done, which was a powerful aid to *getting* it done—and anyhow, she was right.

She used cardboard for several reasons. It was free; it's earth-colored, and takes mastic cement well;

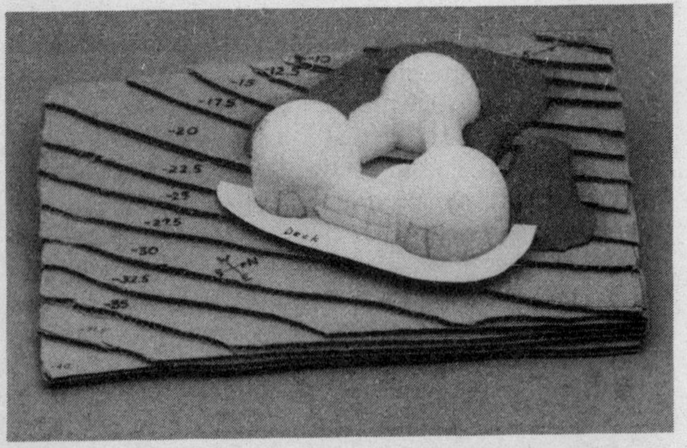

Scale model of elevation contours with dome complex.

it's ¼″ thick, which is just the right thickness; and it's easy to cut with a razor blade or even heavy scissors. (It's the right thickness in this case, because we wanted a model that was scaled down so that one inch on the model equalled ten feet in the real world. A ¼″ drop on the model equals a two-and-a-half-foot drop on the property.) That gave us a fairly realistic idea of the slope on our land, even though our model achieves its slope in stair-step fashion. Well, if it's good enough for architects, it's good enough for us. . . .

Our teen modeler's result is the "landscape" in Figure 1. She just followed the contours of our map (for the small area she was interested in), placed dollops of sticky mastic cement to glue each contour piece to the one below it, and kept going until she got "down" to the elevations below our homesite. It's good enough for our purpose, and it gives a realistic idea of the slope of the property. If the confounded kid didn't spend so much time on her jobs and studies and bicycling and soccer and young men, we'd hire her to do a map of the whole seven acres.

This girl does not list model-building as one of her hobbies, you understand; it's just a bunch of little things she learned while building Hallowe'en costumes (a robot from "Star Wars" movies, for example) and making furniture for a very weird bedroom, and reading maps while backpacking.

We built models to study another interesting problem when locating the site for a forty-foot windmill tower. The prevailing winds are hard to figure on our property, unless you can erect forty-foot towers with slender plastic streamers. (Sure, a recording anemometer would be great! Got any old ones lying around?) "Or," my bright cousin said, "one tower that you can erect and remove quickly." And when he said "You," he meant me—with my bad back. So we designed a plywood base that could be anchored with tent poles, and telescoping tubes that pivoted about four feet up on the base. Once you get a forty-foot pole up, it's easy to keep it there with guy wires; but it takes a real King Kong to raise such a pole from the horizontal, unless . . .

Unless you counterweight it below the pivot, with heavy weights on the short end of the pole. We decided to pour several disks of concrete which I could lift one at a time, then slide them onto the butt of the pole. It looked good on paper, but it all had to fit into the cargo door of a VW bus, too. We hate doing things twice, so we built a small model of the tower first. Model shops carry plywood sheets as thin as 1/16″, 1/32″, and even 1/64″. They also have aluminum and brass tubing of several sizes. The model shown in Figure 2 was our second try; the first one didn't quite fit through the opening we cut from cardboard to represent the cargo hatch of the VW bus. Can you imagine the frustration we would've had if we'd built the first version and then had to rebuild it? That model was worth its weight in liniment!

But the most useful model of this project was the one we made to check out the patterns of sunlight and shadow. This is an extended family scheme, with

Scale model of portable forty-foot tower.

three domes and earth ramps for insulation. If we put a small pool between the domes, or high windows to shed direct afternoon sunlight into a room, we want to *know* the sun shines where we want it, before we locate the domes and windows.

The best way to check it all out while a half-dozen critical adults can see it, was to build a very small scale-model of the whole blooming layout. This is what you see in Figure 1; about an acre of the property as interpreted by a teenager, to which I added the domes and insulation ramps of sod. We built the domes from styrofoam; and the earthwork ramps from modeling clay. It took a half-day to build. Knowing the seasonal patterns made by the sun, we used a flashlight to find where the shadows would fall at various times of the day, and various seasons of the year. And you guessed it: we can't get direct sunlight everywhere we want it. At least we know what to expect, and we didn't pay an architect to find out.

If you don't have an experienced modeler around when making your first models of important projects, you may want some new cusswords for your traitor fingers. Well, try muttering "Klutz!"; everybody's a klutz at first. The old-fashioned single-edged razor blade is still alive and well at the drugstore. So is fast-drying model cement and the slower, but stronger, carpenter's white glue. Most discount stores have styrofoam in sheets, blocks, spheres and other shapes. The stuff is very easy to cut or rasp, but test your glue before smearing it on a final piece of styrofoam because most model cements will simply melt a great hole in the foam. The aliphatic glue used by woodworkers doesn't melt styrofoam; it works fine. So does epoxy.

A hint on making things from common oil-based modeling clay: it only seems too hard until you have "worked" it for a few moments. Start with a gob no bigger than a golf ball, and knead the stuff until it is soft. Pull off pea-sized softened hunks and smear them onto the surface you want to coat, then add more pea-sized hunks until you have roughly the right shape. Then you can smooth it into a single mass with your thumbs. Later, if need be, you can cut sharp indentations in it with a knife or even a hardwood tool.

Hobby shops often carry special materials for model train enthusiasts—maybe a more complete assortment than you ever imagined. Those tiny little barns you've seen, built of teeny-weeny hardwood two-by-sixes and one-by-twelves? All that lumber can be bought at the hobby shop, already milled to size; and you can literally build the frame of your dream house as a table-top model before you tackle the real thing. You can also buy tiny I-beams, plastic pipe, and so on.

More tips, if you're building a small scale-model: make yourself a ruler that is to the right scale, and use it often. Also, don't try to make it too large or too small. You don't want it too large because you'll probably want to keep it awhile. And if you're like us, you'll wind up with a roomful of important models one day. You don't want it too small because it takes longer to do fine details of a dinky pocket-sized model, and little mistakes are more glaring on a tiny model. So don't risk the frustration of a really tiny model unless you're a skilled modeler or a surgeon.

If you've decided to make a cardboard layout of your proposed basement shelter, choose a scale that's big enough for you to handle without tweezers—say, an inch to the foot, which is 1:12. Take a straight, sturdy strip of cured wood about two feet long and mark it, in inches, as though they were feet. Then make smaller marks midway between the "foot" marks (which are the "six-inch" marks, of course). After that, it's easy to eyeball smaller marks to get tiny scale "inches," which are actually one-twelfth of an inch apart. If you use a regular ruler, you're likely to forget while converting some number (even the experts do) and foul up the job. If you spend fifteen minutes making the scale ruler, you make fewer mistakes. And the ruler will still be handy the next time you want to build a model of the same scale.

Of course the best tip of all is to talk with modelers. They are usually surprised and delighted to find anybody even faintly interested in the craft, and every last one of 'em has a trick or two that he discovered on his own. Examples? Small aluminum sheets, so thin you can cut them with scissors, are often discarded by print shops. You may have to clean the ink from them with acetone, but whattheheck. A hot coathanger, bent into a complex curve, can cut that shape through a thick sheet of styrofoam. Shortened pins can be pushed into balsa with their heads protruding to imitate nailheads or bolts, if you need to. Of course, we slapdash types just apply a dot with a flow pen and call it a nailhead.

You may also be surprised to see how much realism you get by coloring the model like the real thing. Plaster of Paris, cast with small gravel from a tropical fish tank and tinted gray with water color, can look astonishingly like real concrete—and it doesn't take long to add these touches.

Finally, when you have a pretty good-looking model of your project, try cutting a hole through a piece of cardboard and looking at your model through it *while masking off the surroundings.* With no telltale "house-sized" coffee cups or furniture in view, sometimes you get a really uncanny vision of the real, full-scale project as it will look one day. You may decide the thing is uglier than you figured it would be. More likely, you'll find the model is a guide and a motivator, pushing you gently toward completion of the real thing. It showed you how to build the project while avoiding pitfalls and waste; it gave you a chance to try several versions of the project fast; it's a three-dimensional map guiding you through the big project; and just looking at it, bribes you to keep working. If that isn't a model of self-reliance, I don't know what is.

Nuclear Calamity

Gimme Shelter!

A generation ago, Herman Kahn urged us to think about the unthinkable: nuclear war. He then proceeded to scare the hell out of us with his own scenarios on megadeath and civil defense (CD). Soon afterward we were deluged with plans, arguments for and against fallout shelters, and an open letter to the public by then-President John Kennedy. The President, New York Governor Nelson Rockefeller, Kahn, and many others were strongly in favor of public shelter programs in view of the awesome destructive power of nuclear weapons.

A loyal opposition quickly emerged, notably from a phalanx of educators in the Boston area and in the pages of the Bulletin of the Atomic Scientists. Freeman Dyson's argument was succinct: nuclear nations should *not* build shelters on a large scale because, while a lack of effective shelters may mean death for a warring nation, effective shelters may mean death for the entire human race. Dyson reasoned that effectively sheltered antagonists would go on pounding away at each other until not only the duelists, but the whole world, was fatally contaminated. Better that the warring nations die alone, he concluded, than to drag all mankind down with them. More recently, in *Weapons and Hope* (1984), Dyson said he couldn't imagine any scenario that would kill us all.

Dyson did not deal with the obvious, e.g., what happens when one duelist is protected and the other is not. We must deal with it now. Relatively speaking, the USSR is effectively protected. The United States is not.

Now that we have your full attention, let us remind you that Dyson warned us against shelters *on a large scale*. If a few thousands or millions of us choose to survive on a small scale, it shouldn't affect first-order terms of the megadeath equation very much.

No one can know today whether our lives would be worth living after a nuclear war, and we won't dwell on the moral questions of the individual's responsibility to oneself and to others. For the ultimate amorality, the survivor who envies the dead can join them any time he chooses. But you ought to have the option of nuclear survival, and that option starts with information. We can't expect to be as effective as the USSR has been in training tens of millions of Soviet citizens as a survival cadre, but we can help a few to train themselves. Much of the information is basic. For many of us, particularly urbanites, it begins *before* we step into a fallout shelter. This article is a beginning. Subsequent articles will show how, with a little foresight, you might reverse the odds against yourself once a shelter is reached.

In the 1950s we knew that the 20 KT (equivalent to twenty thousand tons of TNT) Hiroshima blast was almost insignificantly small compared to 20 MT—*Mega*ton—and larger weapons then in development. Was the public interested? Not much, until Kahn popularized the mathematics of annihilation and helped provoke the great shelter debate of the sixties. Suddenly in 1961 we were more than interested; we were fascinated, and then inundated by a tsunami of articles, pamphlets and books. Like the European tulip craze of the 17th century and our Muckraker Era after 1900, the topic blazed into focus. It didn't stay long; anyone can see by checking the Reader's Guide to Periodicals that by 1963 the topic was plummeting from public view. By 1979 it had fallen almost out of sight.

For several reasons, the U.S. public largely abandoned civil defense matters until very recently; and now the rules have changed! Government agencies spent most of a billion dollars locating and stocking potential fallout shelters in urban areas. With all those signs telling us where to go, we'd be okay when we got there; right?

Wrong. Language sets its own tripwires, and in our focal effort to find fallout shelters, we concentrated altogether too much on only one danger, i.e., fallout. Quick, now: how many victims in Hiroshima and Nagasaki succumbed to fallout? Evidently none. The bombs were detonated high in the air for maximum effect against the two cities. An air burst does its damage as a one-two-three-four punch. First comes the thermal radiation, moving out from the fireball core at light speed and lasting something under one minute. Next comes the blast wave, a hammerblow of air moving a bit faster than Mach 1 that can reduce nearby concrete structures to powder, the range of blast destructiveness weakening with the cube root of the bomb's energy. This means that a 20 MT bomb's blast effect reaches only (!) ten times as far as that of a 20 KT bomb. Third comes the firestorm, a genuine meteorological event caused by the burning of everything ignitable within range—and that encompasses many square miles—of the initial heat effects. Last and most lingering comes the fallout, a rain of deadly radioactive ash from the mushroom cloud that moves downwind, as it did near Chernobyl in 1986.

The bigger the bomb, the more preponderantly it is an incendiary weapon. Victims of conventional Allied incendiary air raids in World War II were found suitably protected from blast effects in shelters—suffocated and cremated by the firestorms that ensued. Even without nukes the toll was 200,000 in Tokyo, 300,000 in Dresden. In New York City fallout shelters, the toll might be twenty times as high, because the first bomb targeted against a big city will almost certainly be an air burst with appalling incendiary effects. Suburbanites far downwind may live long enough to worry about fallout.

The ground burst is the one that punches a vast depression in the earth and sends thousands of tons of vaporized dirt into the air. We can expect ground bursts against deeply-buried military installations and other "hard" targets. The fallout from a ground burst may be lethal hundreds of miles downwind, because the vaporized dirt will condense and drift down as radioactive ash—thousands of tons of it.

Incidentally, because so much of the ground burst's energy goes into punching that hole in the ground, the blast and initial radiation effects of a ground burst will not be as widespread. Your chances a few miles from a ground burst can be better than the same distance from an air burst, if you're far enough upwind, or sheltered well enough, to avoid fallout from the ground burst. But that mushroom cloud will be miles across; and if I'm near it, gimme shelter!

But what *is* effective shelter? Not an ordinary urban basement. Probably not even a subway tunnel, unless the tunnel can be hermetically sealed against the firestorm. Imagine a gopher in his tunnel, with openings fifty feet apart—under a bonfire a hundred feet across. The fire will rage for hours, causing updrafts of hurricane force toward the center that suck air right out of the tunnels. It simply withdraws the little varmint's oxygen while the heat gradually builds up deep beneath the bonfire. Well, a big firestorm is a miles-wide bonfire, and our subway commuter is the gopher. The Soviets have given that a lot of thought. Unlike us, according to Leon Gouré, they've done something about it.

Gouré, a RAND Corporation man, emigrated from Moscow in infancy and revisited the USSR in 1960. He found huge blast doors set into the floors of Moscow subway tunnels—and we can take hermetic seals for granted. Moscow might burn, but a million or so Muscovites can keep on breathing. Gouré also learned that Soviet civil defense officials, the MPVO (for Mestnaia Protivovozdushnaia Oborona, so from now on we'll just give acronyms; trust us, okay?), can call on twenty or thirty million members of a paramilitary civilian cadre called DOSAAF. DOSAAF people correspond roughly to a national home guard, and they all get compulsory training as population leaders in evacuation and shelter exercises.

The Soviets, with total control over the architecture of apartment buildings as well as municipal structures, have very special building codes for urban basements. Many apartment building basements have specially reinforced, thick ceilings and walls with load-bearing partitions and airtight steel doors. In addition, ventilation tunnels filter incoming air and provide remote emergency escape passages. Gouré cited toilet facilities, stored food and water with other supplies, and implied that bottled air may be provided. Thus protected, Soviet apartment dwellers just might live through all but the fiercest firestorm.

It's possible for us to build better urban shelters than these, but we are not doing it. Our civil defense posture has regeared itself more toward evacuation than to digging in. More accurately, at the moment we're between gears, idling in neutral.

A Boeing study revealed to a Congressional committee that, with its low-key, continuing civil defense; its carefully dispersed industry; and its less centralized population, the USSR might recover from a war in two to four years while the U.S. might need twelve years for recovery. Two per cent of the Soviets might die. Sixty per cent of Americans might die. *Now* do you see why the Soviets marched into Afghanistan with such confidence?

Anecdote time: we know a scientist who fled the Soviet bloc some years ago. Her eyewitness report on Soviet civil defense is more recent than Gouré's, and perhaps more scarifying. She insists that the USSR and its satellite countries feel confident that their people would easily survive a nuclear war because of their massive compulsory CD programs. Now in the U.S., our scientist friend moved as far from local target areas as she could, and modified her basement into an acceptable fallout shelter. She's still dismayed that her American friends have no hermetically sealed public tunnels and that they consider her efforts, in a word, weird.

China has her tunnels, too. Less elaborate than Moscow subways, Peking's tunnels are only a few meters below the surface and probably would be employed as an escape route to the countryside. Dairen, a big shipping port, is a likely target and its deep tunnels are stocked for 80,000 evacuees. The tunnels crisscross like a bus network and might be marginally suitable if they are effective conduits beyond the firestorm area.

Canada has her National Shelter Plan, several years in arrears of our own and still geared to identifying mass fallout shelters for urbanites. Undeniably, Canada harbors fewer prime targets than we do in both major categories; the hardened military sites for which ground bursts are slated, and the soft population targets so vulnerable to air bursts. But Canada's cities are just as vulnerable as ours. She needs an urban public that's drilled as well in evacuation as in cellar-dwelling, just as we do.

From all evidence, both U.S. and USSR civil defense officials count on being alerted many hours or even days before Time Zero, apparently on the basis of judgments of political events and evidence that the other side is battening down its hatches. This is a gamble we take collectively; but you, *personally*, don't have to take all of that gamble.

So how do you reduce the gamble to your immediate family? Being painfully aware that you may find some of the answers very unpleasant, we'll start with some generalizations, and some specifics.

1. Talk to your local CD coordinator, who is making do with absurdly low federal and local funding. Local officials usually have expert guesses as to the nearest target area. What common carriers are earmarked for evacuation? What should you carry with you? Where will you go and what facilities will you find there? Ask for a copy of the 1977 booklet, *Protection in the Nuclear Age*, or borrow theirs and copy it. The booklet strongly reflects the shift in emphasis toward evacuation—or in CD jargon, "Crisis Relocation." Among other things the booklet describes home shelters of several kinds, a source of free shelter plans, and your best tactics in evacuating a target area.

2. If you live or work in a primary target area, for God's sake seek other stomping grounds. This is far and away the best item in improving your chances—and the toughest one to implement.

3. Do your homework on fallout, prevailing winds, and target areas upwind of you. The November 1976 *Scientific American* is a good departure point.

4. More homework. Make a low-key, consistent hobby of studying survival and technology. Oldies like *Fortunes in Formulas* and any decent encyclope-

dia set may be more helpful than books on woodcraft. If you wind up in the woods you either know your stuff already, or you're up the creek without a scintillator. Mel Tappan's column on survival was a fixture in *Guns & Ammo* magazine for several years from December 1976 until his death, and Tappan was no wild-eyed troglodyte. His argument in favor of living in a smallish town, rather than metropolis or mountaintop, is eloquent.

5. Fill a scruffy rucksack with raisins and jerked meat, transistor radio, masking tape and monofilament line, first-aid equipment including water purification tablets, a few rolls of dimes, leather gloves, vitamins, steel canteen, thermally reflective mylar blanket from any outfitter, good multipurpose clasp knife, and so on. You might have to change plans and relocate without notice. We spent an evening once at Poul Anderson's place with several writers including Frank Herbert of *Dune* fame, arguing the merits of a survival kit that was originally stored in my specially-stiffened Porsche coupe. Basically, our kit was intended to get a tinkerer across country. It didn't look worth stealing. That's a vital point: when you can't expect a policeman to help, keep a low profile.

The kit had some of the items mentioned above, plus small slide rule, pliers, drill bits, wire and needles, compass, fishhooks, wax-coated matches and candle stub (a plumber's candle is high in stearic acid and burns very slowly), thick baggies, pencils and pad, all wrapped in heavy aluminum foil so that it could be swung like a short club. Huge half-inch-wide rubber bands looped around the handle end. Never forget that a slingshot with big rubber bands is quiet and flashless, and ammunition for it is everywhere. Why the masking tape? Whether you stay put or evacuate, you may need to tape cracks around openings to make your quarters as airtight as possible. Freshen the kit annually.

* * *

Pamphlets suggest you may have two days' warning. Don't bet your life on it.

No booklet can possibly cover all the problems you're likely to find if you choose crisis relocation, i.e., evacuation after the alert sounds. But another brief list might help you.

1. Keep detailed county and state maps. Decide where you'll go and learn alternative routes; chances are, major arterials will soon be clogged. Consider strapping bikes onto your car as second-stage vehicles. Roads that become impassable by car might still be navigable on a bike.

2. When you already have a good idea which way you will probably go, polish up your friendships with acquaintances who live in that presumably safer region. Establish agreements that they'll accept you, and do your part ahead of time. For example: buy a 100-gallon water storage tank and let them have it on permanent loan; furnish them with a survival library; help them build their shelter; and/or *be* an encyclopedia of survival lore which they'd rather be with, than without.

3. Get in shape. Stay that way. Regular exercise, particularly jogging, hiking, and bicycling, gives you stamina for that extra mile or edge of alertness when you need it. Physical exhaustion has its corollary in emotional exhaustion, and a sense of futility is a heavier load than a full backpack. Besides, if you use a cycle regularly you'll keep your bike in good repair. How long since you patched a bike tire at the roadside?

4. Collect a first-stage kit and a second-stage kit in your garage or storage shed, and be ready to stow both in your car. First-stage kits include saw, pick, and shovel, plastic tarps, extra bedding and clothes, all the food you can quickly pack into rugged boxes, a spare fuel supply for your car (store it wisely in the

meantime), the contents of your medicine cabinet, tools, sanitation items, and any books you may think especially useful. Second-stage kits include the rucksack we described earlier, small ax or hatchet, sleeping bag, plastic tarp, maps, and medication or other essentials according to your special needs. If you must abandon your car later, you can grab your second-stage kit and keep going afoot or on a bike.

5. Move quickly without panic if the time comes to relocate. Drill your family in the details, and obey officials in face-to-face encounters. Law officers coping with the crisis may not be willing to put up with much argument when you're en route. Choose the clothes you'll wear beforehand, and dress for a hike.

6. Pretend you've gone halfway to your destination, abandoned your car, and are afoot in a sparsely populated area when you perceive that you're downwind of a mushroom cloud. You may have several hours before you must have shelter, but the time to seek it is right *now*! A homeowner may take you in, especially if you look like you'll be more help than hindrance. If not, don't risk getting shot. Keep going until you find some structure that will shelter you. The more dirt or concrete above and around you, the better; a dry culvert could be much better than a bungalow. Establish your location on the map, seal yourself in for what may be days, and attend to your radio for information on local conditions. If you're one of the few with a radiation counter, you'll know when to stay put and when to move on. Fallout is like lust; it isn't forever, but it colors your decisions.

7. If you're heeled—carrying weapons—cache them securely before you enter any public or communal shelter. You'll almost certainly be required to give them up anyhow, and you'd be dangerously unpopular if it were known that you didn't surrender them. And you probably wouldn't get them back once you surrendered them. For most of us, weapons are more

harmful temptation than useful tools. Of course, a tiny pocket canister of Mace is another matter. Ever notice how some defensive items look like cigarette lighters—especially if spray-painted silver or white?

It's probably not necessary to justify all the points we've listed, but you'll find a rationale behind any advice that's worth hearing. Our embedded biases aren't hard to pin down. We believe that mass evacuation from target areas is a more viable response than most shelters in those areas. We know that our present CD planning is underfunded for the goals it is planning. Translation: Your local officials probably won't be able to cope with the evacuation after they call for it.

We also believe that, the more actively you study the problems and consider prudent means to avoid bottlenecks in your own relocation, the more likely it is that you'll become a part of CD solutions.

And consider the rationales in the details, e.g., bicycling. It does more than improve your stamina and speed your relocation. It can be equipped with a tiny generator and light; it requires no stored fuel; it can be bodily carried or even hauled through water; it is almost noiseless in use; and ultimately it can be abandoned without great financial or emotional loss. It's part of that low profile we mentioned.

By now it should be obvious that, for many of us, crisis relocation will precede effective shelter. Once you've relocated to an area where shelter can be effective, you'll need to focus on such things as fallout shielding; air filtration and pumping; hygiene; and other basic life-support needs. In the next article we'll show you how to build simple air filtration and pump units with a minimum of effort and time.

In the meantime, do yourself a favor. Talk with your local CD people, and visit your library for the articles we've mentioned. After you've studied the problem a bit, you'll be prepared to make a better response to an alert than to stand on the courthouse lawn bawling, "Gimme shelter!"

Living Under Pressure

We began this series of articles to update and alert you on the problems of survival after an all-out nuclear exchange. Briefly summarized: in "Gimme Shelter" we explained that twenty-mile-wide, thermonuclear-kindled firestorms would render many U.S. urban areas utterly uninhabitable. The government—much too quietly, in my opinion—now favors mass evacuation from high-risk areas following an alert. The problems with this new and more sensible civil defense (CD) posture lie in educating us about it; in the likelihood of clogged routes during the evacuation; in improvising shelters in low-risk areas; and in doing anything on a large scale with damnably low CD budgets. We also referenced some publications and promised to give you some tips on making a shelter more effective, starting with air filtration and pump units that you can make on short notice. We're making good on that promise now. In a phrase, one key to clean air is living under pressure.

We assume that you have your free copy of the government's CD pamphlet of February 1977, *Protection in the Nuclear Age*, which admits the wisdom of "crisis relocation" and suggests that you find a shelter completely surrounded by two or three feet of masonry or dirt. But even if you have such shelter, you still aren't safe from fallout unless you can make the place airtight. In 1986, Mount St. Helens threatened another kind of fallout event (again!), and its ash could make air purification a "must."

If you've ever fretted through a dust storm, you know how air supports dust particles, and how a breeze sifts the finest ones past infinitesimal cracks around doors and windowframes. While a lot of fallout will be large visible ash, too much of the stuff will be invisibly small hunks of airborne grit, settling hundreds of miles downwind of a detonation. They are lethal dustmotes if you breathe enough of them during the first two or three weeks after a nuclear strike. That's why a shelter should be stocked with caulking material and tape; so that every crevice in the shelter can be sealed. In short, you must turn the shelter into a pressure vessel and bottle yourself up in it.

Which means that you could swelter in your body heat and asphyxiate in your own carbon dioxide waste if you stayed inside very long without a fresh air supply. We'll give figures later in this article; for the moment, the rationale's the thing.

If your supplies are adequate, you might stay in the shelter for weeks—but almost nobody will have a week's supply of bottled air. What you need is a means for pumping cool filtered air from the outside, and for exhausting the stale humid air from your shelter. Believe it or not, the solution isn't necessarily very complex once you've practiced doing it, even on a small scale model.

We infer from sources on Soviet CD that the first stage of their civilian shelter filters is through something called a "blast attenuator"—a wide vertical conduit pipe filled with big rocks and gravel. The pipe has a raincap on top, aboveground, and a removable grille covering one side of its bottom end. The grille is sturdy enough to hold the gravel and coarse enough to let air through. Notice that a conduit of twenty-four-inch diameter can be used as an emergency exit, once the grille is removed and the gravel drained out. The gravel lets air through while trapping large fallout particles and baffling concussion waves from any nearby explosions. The Soviets use finer filters for the air that is sucked down through the gravel by pumps. Incidentally, if you're building such a "blast attenuator" for a shelter, specify rounded quartz gravel. Hunks of damp limestone can eventually cement themselves together to become a rigid sponge that impedes airflow.

In extremis, you could build a medium-mesh filter by taping a towel over a square-foot-sized inlet into the shelter. You might find it clogged after a day or so. A finer-mesh filter can be made with corrugated cardboard, large juice cans, replaceable rolls of toilet paper, and tape.

Our demonstration rig was designed to provide air for two adults. It uses a standard household furnace filter element taped securely over the intake hole of the filter box—because we assume that you *won't* have a yards-long gravel-filled conduit. After you build your air filtration unit, you'll have to place it in some weatherproof spot just outside the sealed shelter. Thus, you can get to the unit quickly in case filter elements become clogged.

The standard furnace filter has a coarse fiberglass element. Particles that get past it will be small, but many would be visible to the naked eye. That calls for a second and finer element.

For its second element, our model uses the same stuff employed by a great many industrial air filters: nothing more than a piece of flannel. As it happens, we spent a dollar on a yard of cotton outing flannel, enough for a one-square-foot filter element with eight spares. That might be enough for two weeks, depending on how much fallout is in your area. We could've used a new diaper or a flannel shirt; it's the soft fuzzy nap of the flannel that traps so much dust. Flannel that's been washed until its fuzz has gone the way of all lint is, ah, washed up. Don't use it, or use two layers. Terrycloth could be used, but to less effect.

So far our scheme calls for a coarse fiberglass filter element taped over a shallow frame of some sort and, right behind it, one fuzzy flannel element. In a pinch, these elements would probably protect you from 95% of the fallout without finer filtration. But the particles that get past these two coarse elements might still zap you if fallout is heavy. What we really need is a still finer element, or a set of them in parallel, to take out particles of micron size. That's where toilet paper rolls come in.

For many years, some engine oil filters employed a roll of toilet paper as the filter element. The oil was forced under pressure to pass between the many circular layers of paper—and the central hole was, of course, plugged. Note well: the oil didn't pass from one *side* of the paper cylinder to the other; it passed from one circular *face* to the other. In the process, even very small solid particles in the oil were trapped in the paper. Only the smallest particles, reportedly on the order of a half-micron, could get through such a filter element.

The same kind of filtration works in extracting tiny fallout particles from air. However, we assume that your air pump (like ours) will be the sort that provides high volume but not much pressure. Since a paper roll restricts the airflow somewhat, it's necessary to use at least four of the rolls simultaneously, in parallel, to allow enough airflow for two adults. It's worth repeating: a four-roll filter is minimal. Use more if you have the materials.

In Figure 1 we see the filtration unit during assembly. The coarse filter elements with their shallow cardboard frame are ready for mounting, the fiberglass element hinged by masking tape and ready to swing down over the flannel element. The shallow frame will fit over the canisters holding the (fine) paper elements. Our small model uses only four paper roll elements, fitted into juice cans. The can with Fine Element #1 is already taped in place; Fine Element #2 is in place, ready for taping; Fine Element #3 is ready to be thrust into its hole; and the hole for Fine Element #4 hasn't yet been cut. Element #4 lies beside the filter box with the paper roll inside its canister. To prepare the hole for Element #4, first cut out the central hole; then cut the radiating slits; and finally fold the slit tabs of cardboard outward so that the hole allows passage of the juice can, in the same manner as Element #3. The white paint on the unit isn't just cosmetic; a gallon of quick-drying latex paint will seal the pores of lots of corrugated cardboard.

FIGURE 1

You'll probably find that a roll of toilet paper won't fit in a juice can until some paper has been unrolled. Strip off the necessary layers and stuff some of it into the can before you insert the roll. Stuff the rest of the paper tightly into the central hole of the tissue roll. Lastly, insert the roll into the can so that it's a snug, but not crush, fit. Of course there must be holes in the other end of the canister through which air can be drawn. In the demo model we've punched four triangular holes next to the closed end of each can, orienting the holes so that when the filter box lies in its normal position, air must rise up through the holes. This gives fallout particles one more chance to drop out. In Figure 1, the filter box stands up-ended so that you can see assembly details.

In Figure 2, the filter box lies in its normal operating position. The coarse elements and their cardboard frames have been taped in place on the filter

FIGURE 2

box. Hidden within the coarse filter frame are the four canisters with the fine-filter rolls, taped securely in place. Every seam on the unit has been double-taped, and you can see its size from the meter-sticks in the illustration. The small soup can inserted at one rear corner of the filter box has both its ends removed. It merely provides a connection to the air conduit tube leading from your filter unit to the pump in your shelter.

Our pump unit is a simple bellows pump, made from another cardboard box. Obviously, if you have a commercial pump that will suck air through a filter, you're way ahead. We're taking the position that, like almost everybody else, you failed to buy such equipment and must either make your own at the last minute or die trying.

Before starting on the pump body, make its conduit tube. If you don't have the equivalent of a three-inch-diameter cardboard tube, grab a thick section of old newspaper and roll it into a tube. Tape the long seam and tape the ends to prevent fraying, then slather latex paint over it. Make it no longer than necessary, remembering that the longer it is, the more resistance it has to airflow. Ideally your filtration unit will be only a step from your shelter, so you'll need only a few sections of newspaper conduit. Our demo model uses one section, just to show how simple it is.

Chances are, a newspaper conduit won't be sturdy enough on its own to withstand the partial vacuum created when the pump is working. So why didn't we use a heavy cardboard tube or, more efficient, smooth-walled metal stovepipe? Only because we assumed you won't *have* any. As it happens, there's a quick remedy for the "collapsing conduit" problem. You make a long cruciform stiffener of cardboard, or several short ones, and insert it into the conduit. The conduit might still buckle a bit, but it won't collapse.

If you can make conduit that's stiffer, without incurring a heavy time penalty, do it.

Now cut a round hole in your shelter wall near the floor and run the conduit through, taping around the hole, and tape the conduit to the filter unit outside (as we did in Figure 2). At this point you can retreat into your shelter and seal yourself in with tape. You're only half-finished, but you can breathe shelter air while you build the pump.

The pump unit is absurdly simple, really, even with its two flapper valves. In Figure 3 it's half-finished, the inked lines showing where you must fold and cut, including the flat piece that eventually becomes our admittedly gimmicky pump handle. For our bellows material, we used transparent flexible sheeting so that we could see through it to watch the

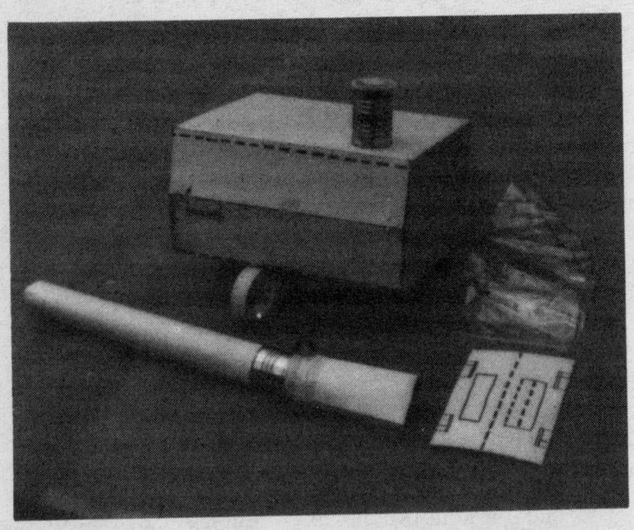

FIGURE 3

inlet valve operate; but plain translucent, or even black, polyethylene sheeting would do. You should choose four-mil-thick or thicker sheeting.

You can see that the pump begins as a rugged corrugated cardboard box, with seams taped to make it airtight. As the dotted lines show, one rectangular face and the adjoining triangular halves of two other faces must first be cut away. The removed cardboard can be used as a pattern to cut the flexible plastic bellows material. Or you can cut the flexible plastic free-hand, as we did. In Figure 3 the flexible stuff is folded double, lying between the box and the pattern for the pump handle.

Next make the pump handle. We like to play with cardboard, so we built a rigid cardboard handle that locked into the top of the pump with tabs, and we taped it around the tab slits to prevent air leakage. It probably would've been quicker to merely punch two holes in the box and to run a rope handle through the holes. Knots in the ends of the rope handle would keep it from pulling through, and tape around the holes would minimize air leaks. The point is, you can do it any of several ways—so long as you don't leave sizeable holes in the pump box which would dramatically lower the pump's efficiency.

Now for the moving parts: the two flapper valves. Here again, we deliberately made them of different materials only to demonstrate that you can use whatever's handy. In Figure 3, the valves aren't yet in place. The outlet valve is sitting atop the pump. The body of the inlet valve has been mated to a conduit tube via a soup can. We made the inlet valve from an empty macaroni carton; a sloppily-cut rectangle of cardboard slightly larger than the mouth of the carton; and a piece of masking tape as a hinge. Simply tape the cardboard rectangle—the flapper—at the top only, so that it hangs down over the mouth of the carton. Blow through the carton and the cardboard flapper swings out to let the air pass. Blow against the face of the flapper and it swings shut, preventing airflow. That's it; a one-way flapper valve. It isn't completely airtight, of course, but so long as it fits neatly over the mouth of the carton it's close enough. And it only takes a moment to make.

Cut a hole through the rear face of the pump box to accept the carton; shove the carton halfway through; and tape it in place. The valve works better if you mount the carton at a slight angle, protruding upward into the box. That way, gravity makes the flapper lie flat over the carton's mouth. In Figure 4 you can see the inlet valve flapper through the transparent bellows—about which, more later.

Make the outlet valve and install it the same way, except that the outlet valve flapper is mounted on the outside of the box. *Inlet flapper inside; outlet flapper outside.* In our model, we made the outlet valve from a soup can and a throwaway plastic lid. Even at the risk of boring you, I repeat: there was no special reason why the inlet and outlet valves were

FIGURE 4

different shapes and made from different materials, except to prove that there are lots of ways to do it. For you perfectionists: with rubber faces between flapper and valve body, and with very slight spring-loading to help them close, you could make better valves than we made. But it would take longer. Our model worked so well that the observer's typical first response was delighted laughter. The little bugger'll blow your hat off!

You're almost finished when you cut a long trapezoidal piece of flexible plastic sheeting (the same size and shape as the piece of cardboard you cut away along the dotted lines) and then tape the sheeting onto the box in place of the missing cardboard. When you finish double-taping and latex-painting the pump box (you don't have to paint the handle), grab the handle and raise the lid of the box. You should hear the pump draw a mighty breath, then a faint "clack" as the cardboard flapper of the inlet valve drops back into place inside the pump box. Now push down

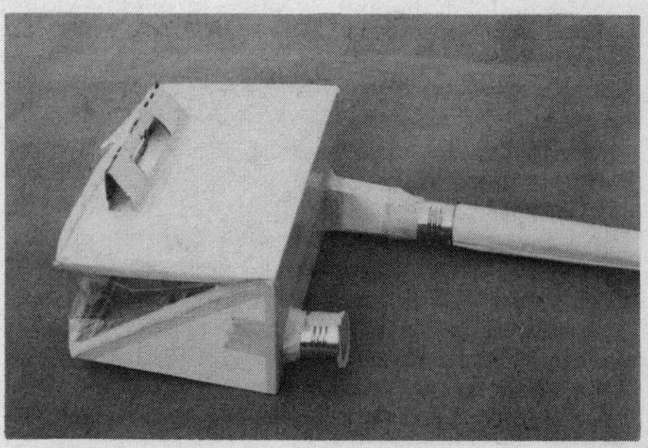

FIGURE 5

firmly on the handle. The pump should exhale with a whispery 'whoosh', followed by another 'clack' as the outlet flapper drops back into place. Check for air leaks; if air is expelled from anyplace besides the outlet valve, those leaks must be sealed. In Figure 5, the completed pump is in "inhale" position and the tape-hinged outlet flapper is visible.

Our small model displaces about two-thirds of a cubic foot of air with every inhale/exhale cycle. If you can start with a bigger box, naturally your pump will move more air—which is all to the good, as we'll explain later.

The last step before drawing clean air is simply to mate the conduit from the filter unit to the pump inlet; tape the joint; and start pumping. It may not keep absolutely all radioactive particles out of your shelter, but the little rig assembled for testing in Figure 6 should make your breathing air cleaner than outside air by several orders of magnitude—a thousand times as clean. For somebody who started three hours ago, you're doing pretty well! If two of you are building the units together it could be closer to two hours. Incidentally, in Figure 6 you can see

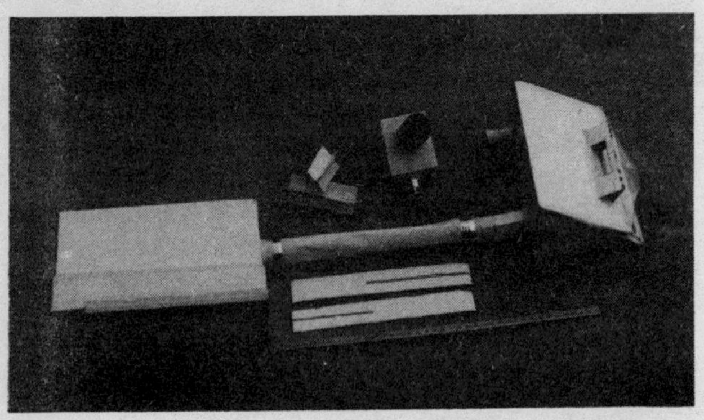

FIGURE 6

cruciform conduit stiffeners of various lengths—the longest one not yet assembled—and a stale air valve we haven't yet discussed because, when minutes count, it should be built last.

Though you now have a means to pump clean air into the shelter, you still need to consider how you'll get rid of the stale air you've already breathed. That stale air will normally be a bit warmer than it was when it entered the shelter but it'll be more moist, too, from water vapor given off by every animal in the shelter. The stale air will also be loaded with your exhaled carbon dioxide, which is slightly heavier than air. All in all, you can expect the moist, carbon dioxide-laden stale air to lie near the floor. There-

FIGURE 7

fore, the stale air exhaust valve inlet should be placed at floor level, and far away from the fresh air squirting into your shelter from the pump.

Before you ask how much more mickey-mouse gadgeteering we need for the system, a glance at Figure 7 will show you. The job of the stale air exhaust valve is to permit the escape of stale air when the shelter air pressure is raised by a very small fraction of a pound per square inch—in fact, by a fraction of an *ounce.* This little exhaust valve is the last part of our air supply system.

Our stale air exhaust valve consists of a small box for the valve body; a perforated soup can sticking up into the box from below as an inlet and flapper support; a piece of styrofoam taped atop the soup can as the valve flapper; and a cardboard tube leading from the side of the valve box, through a hole in the shelter wall, to the "outside." Note the penny glued atop the styrofoam flapper. Styrofoam is so light, it needed a tiny weight to ensure that the flapper would always close. The flapper will rise when shelter pressure is very slightly elevated above ambient, i.e., outside, air pressure. If a windstorm brews up outside and gusty winds try to blow in through the exit tubes, the flapper stays put. Little or no unfiltered, fallout-laden air gets in.

By studying Figure 7 you can see that, like the other parts of our system, the stale air exhaust valve can be made from whatever's handy, so long as it's airtight. We punched triangular holes around the bottom of the soup can for stale air to enter. We taped the can securely into the box, then did the same with the cardboard exit tube. We tape-hinged the styrofoam flapper atop the soup can, then taped the box shut so that any air passing out of the shelter must pass through the triangular vents at floor level,

FIGURE 8

up through the flapper, and then out of the shelter via the exit tube.

Finally, in Figure 8, we pushed the end of the exit tube through a hole in the shelter wall and taped it in place so that the valve stands on its inlet tube.

Unlike the valves in the pump, the stale air exhaust valve won't clatter much during operation. In fact, you might want to install a piece of plastic or glass as a window into the little box so that you can inspect it now and then while someone operates the pump. If it never opens at all, start looking for leaks in the shelter while the pump is in operation. A few wisps of cigarette smoke might help you trace a leak. Otherwise, don't smoke!

* * *

You now have all the necessary elements for a minimal air supply system for two adults in a small shelter. It's a far cry from an automated system. In fact, if alone in your shelter, you could still be in serious trouble if you fell asleep for many hours.

Engineering texts on ventilation systems call for two or more air changes per hour in a meeting room—more for lavatories, locker rooms or assembly halls. They also call for roughly a thousand cubic feet of air, per person, *per hour*. Frankly, this approaches the upper airflow limit of our small demo unit even if you kept it going all the time. Luckily, as the texts admit, these figures are greatly in excess of general practice.

How much in excess? Well, you probably needn't worry about CO_2 poisoning or sticky-wet humidity if you manage to get 400 cu. ft. of fresh air into the shelter per person, per hour. It's my personal suspicion that you could get by on a fraction of that when sleeping, or sitting quietly. But if you begin to feel headachy, dizzy, or drunk, get to work on the pump.

For a rough approximation of your pump's output, measure the outside dimensions of the pump when it is fully open, then find the volume inside. Next, bearing in mind that the pump doesn't entirely close down to half of its maximum volume, multiply the maximum by 0.4; in other words, take 40% of the pump's maximum volume. That's roughly how much air the pump gives you every time you open and close it fully.

Example:

Our pump box dimensions are 20″ × 14″ × 10″.
Maximum volume, then, is 2,800 cubic inches.
40% of 2,800 cu. in. = 1,120 cu. in.
And since 1 cu. ft. = 1.728 cu. in.,
each pump stroke yields 1,120/1,728 cu. ft. of air,
which is roughly ⅔ **cu. ft.** per stroke.

For those of you who think these calculations are too elementary: please knock it off, you guys. We want to make this clear enough for a smart sixth-grader.

Since we can operate our pump at about 20 strokes per minute without tearing it up, we find that our little demo unit will give us 14 cu. ft. of fresh air per minute, or 800 cu. ft. per hour. I think—but with so many variables of shelters, valve seals, and such I wouldn't swear to it—that you might get by with three adults in a shelter using this little rig half the time. To put it another way: each of you three would probably have to operate our little pump for four or more hours every day to assure a decent air supply. That implies a lot of work, which means heavy breathing, which means elevated humidity.

As we said before, the pump provides more than just oxygen; it also keeps the humidity and temperature down to bearable levels in the sealed shelter by forcing out the stale air.

What if you're alone? There's no one to pump while you sleep, so you should choose a shelter that contains a thousand cubic feet of air, or more. And bring an old windup alarm clock with you. Far better to be awakened by a clattering bell every two hours to pump for awhile, than never to wake at all.

No alarm clock? Lordy, what are we gonna do with you! Just remember that sand or water can be metered to trickle slowly into a container on a teeter-totter. When the teeter-totter shifts, it can knock something over noisily in approved Rube Goldberg fashion. Sure, this is all a lot of trouble. Why didn't you invest in good, commercially available equipment *before* the klaxon tooted?

No one is suggesting that the primitive life-support system illustrated here is any match for a commercial unit. To repeat: this article is for the ninety-five per cent of us who may know what we ought to do, but aren't doing it. It's easy to critique the system—and to make this one better.

The filter unit could be improved several ways: by being larger with more fine paper roll elements; by having a quickly resealable panel for fast replacement of paper rolls in case they become clogged; and by being more rugged than cardboard. Duct tape is stronger than the masking tape we used, but much more expensive. Buy some anyhow; tell yourself you're worth it.

The pump is the weakest link in our model; it should've been bigger. But even using the box we used, you could increase its capacity by altering the pattern for the bellows so the pump would open wider. We found that a single thickness of cardboard is almost too flimsy for the top face (the one with the handle) of the pump. A doubler sheet of cardboard, plywood, or even thin wooden slats taped across the flimsy top face would make it last longer.

You'll find that the pump's light weight can be a problem. It creates so much suction, the whole box wants to rise up when you lift the handle. If you don't want to wedge the pump in place on the floor, you could weigh it down. Just unseal the bellows, lay several bricks down on the pump's bottom face between the valves, then reseal the bellows. In that position the bricks won't reduce the pump's output, and they'll keep the pump from jumping around while you use it.

When we characterized this model as "minimal," we weren't kidding. With only four paper rolls in the filter unit, airflow is so restricted that you must exert some effort to lift the pump handle. You'll be dog-tired after using it awhile. You'll wish you'd built a filter box with more roll elements so you could pump more easily. Well, you still can! Just build another filter unit, go outside briefly, and connect the filter units by a short conduit.

You could elect to build a filter without the paper roll elements. It won't purify the air as much, but it's much quicker and it makes pumping much easier. Of course, the flannel element can be quite large.

We won't go into great detail on the subject of negative-pressure shelters because they aren't as secure. But you could opt for such a system, in which the shelter air pressure is very slightly *lower* than ambient. Essentially, you install a stovepipe from your shelter to the roof and install a simple, commercial wind-driven rotating ventilator atop the pipe. When the wind blows, the ventilator sucks air up and out of the shelter. If you taped a couple of layers of flannel over a window-sized opening into your shelter, the ventilator would do your pumping for you, drawing fresh air in past the flannel elements. The pressure differential in the shelter would be too low, however, for you to hope it could suck air in through paper roll elements.

Summarizing the low-pressure shelter scheme: it's attractive because it doesn't require you to pump by hand. On the other hand, it won't pull air through a really fine filter element—and besides, the low shelter pressure can draw unfiltered air in through crevices. Moreover, when the wind isn't blowing your air gets stale anyway.

Whatever system you use to provide fresh clean air in your shelter, what do you do if it proves less than adequate? Well, you trouble-shoot it to check for something clogging any part of the system. You breathe through a flannel (or something better) mask while the shelter is open to ambient air. You remind yourself that you're buying time during the hours when your system *is* working, because day by day the radioactivity of fallout particles should diminish.

In forays outside the shelter, you wear gloves and all-enveloping raingear, leaving it just outside the shelter when you seal yourself in again. You treat clogged elements as radioactive.

Now we're getting into hygiene. What do we do about hygiene in a shelter, including disposal of body waste? How about lights and other niceties? We'll get to those topics in subsequent articles; for the moment, it's enough to know you can live under pressure.

Power and Potties to the People

The average citizen would have fair-to-excellent survival chances after an all-out nuclear exchange—but only by having certain awarenesses, and acting on them. To summarize briefly: we have explained that the government now favors mass evacuation from high-risk areas following an alert, since firestorm is a more immediately lethal threat for city-dwellers than is fallout. But you will probably be on your own when evacuating and improvising shelter because no sufficiently powerful lobby group has fought to fund the machinery—software and hardware—of city evacuation. The Federal Emergency Management Agency (FEMA) admitted in July 1986 that we must rely only on self-help. We discussed the logistics in some detail and suggested that you relocate *now* from primary target zones.

We have showed how to build air filtration and pump devices from household materials in a few hours, so you can breathe relatively uncontaminated air once you find shelter beyond a firestorm-candidate area. Finally, we promised some tips in future articles on making your shelter more liveable; things like lights, hygiene, and so on.

Okay, it's time to power your shelter. Take heart: even though our premise is that you haven't amassed special equipment, we've tested enough commonplace equipment to prove it's rather easy to generate enough electricity to run lights, radios, even a cassette recorder—from at least one source we'll bet you never thought about.

A moment's thought will remind you that cars, motorcycles, boats, even many bicycles are equipped with subsystems that you could use in a shelter. It's a sorry automobile that doesn't have a complete electrical system with a hefty battery to store electricity; a generator to generate more electricity; many yards of wiring; several electric motors, some connected to fans that you might use for shelter air; and more light bulbs than you'll need. Of course we don't suggest that you run your car inside your shelter. We do suggest that you familiarize yourself with a car that you can park in your garage and then strip of some life-support items when the time comes. You can always replace the hardware quickly if you need it in the car again.

We won't go into detail on removing car parts because electrical systems differ a lot. Study your own, and ask any mechanic for details on cannibalizing it. We will mention a few things that could free you of frustration when you're trying to set up an emergency power system.

To start with, be advised that a good car battery can strike sparks if its "positive" terminal (also called the "hot" or "+" terminal) comes in contact with metal parts of the car. This does *not* mean the battery could shock you. Its twelve-volt jolt is much too low. You simply have to remove the cables from the battery terminals with care.

The average car battery has enough energy stored in it to operate a small light for a week or more without a generator. You can find tiny lamps with

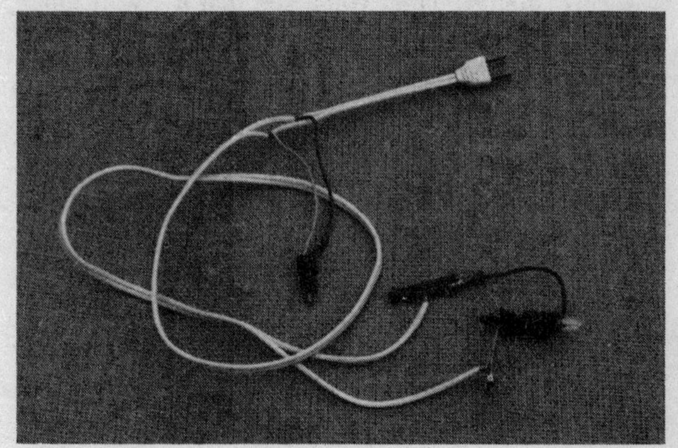

FIGURE 9

removable sockets in glove compartments, in instrument panels, on roof interiors, and next to license plates. Many of the interior lights are designed to be installed and removed instantly, socket and all. In Figure 9 we have wired a tiny transmission shift selector light, and a slightly larger light pried out of a glove compartment with its socket, to the remains of an extension cord. The wires lead to a 12-volt power source that could be a car battery. Or it could be something else—about which, more later.

Light bulbs in your brake and tail-lights, directional and backup lights, and so on require more power and provide more light. Finally you could remove a headlight, which sheds tremendous light on the subject but also gobbles up a battery's stored energy in a few hours.

Generally, the brighter the light, the more power it consumes. You may think you need a high-wattage bulb in your shelter until you plug off the last window with old books, and find out how dark it gets in a secure shelter. Then you'll see that a 6-watt glove compartment light makes the difference between merely shadowy, and downright scary. Remembering that

1 watt = 1 volt × 1 amp, so that
6 watts = 12 volts × 0.5 amps,

you can see that a "half-amp" rating for a bulb in a 12-volt system means it draws about 6 watts. When considering a 12-volt motor that has a wattage, but no amperage, on its ID plate, you can solve for the amperage. Select appliances that use little power, so the battery will last longer. If you must do a lot of reading, cuddle up near a small light and put a mirror or other reflector where it will help. If you have a fluorescent drop-light intended to plug into a 12-volt system, good. It's stingy with power and doesn't give off much heat. In the days when shoemakers and tailors worked by candlelight, they found a nifty way to concentrate what little light they had. They suspended a water-filled glass globe so that the globe created a lens effect, giving a powerfully concentrated beam of light from a candle onto a small working area. Try it with a wineglass; you'll probably find a long slender patch of light, intense enough for threading needles.

If you haven't already noticed; we make a worst-case assumption that you don't have welding equipment, special tools, or arcane talents with you. Probably you won't have rolls of insulated wire or tinkerer's alligator clips for making test connections. But you can use extension cords and, in lieu of alligator clips, hair-curl "clippies." That's what we used to cobble up some power and light devices for this article. You can slice through an extension cord and bare its wires with any sharp knife. Yes, it'd be better if you could clamp or solder your final connections; but if you tightly twist copper wires together and tape over the connection, it will usually work well. Millions of temporary electrical connections have been made by forcing a sturdy safety pin through insulated wires; this is often done when hooking up trailer lights to the wiring in cars.

We also assume that you can recognize the places where you must connect a wire to a light bulb or its socket. In the simplest use of your system, just bind one naked wire-end to a battery terminal and one naked end of your second wire to the other terminal. Then touch the other ends of those wires to the cannibalized lamp and you should have light. Since 12 volts won't shock you, you can even do it by hand.

Don't worry about the battery burning out the tiny lamp if the lamp was taken from a similar 12-volt system; the lamp will draw only the few watts it needs. You could probably have a string of tiny lamps going simultaneously (connected in parallel, not in series) with less use of power than if you used a brake light.

Electric motors usually use electricity faster than several small lamps; be advised. For God's sake don't use a battery to run a heating element, e.g., the little elements that plug into cigarette lighters to keep cups of coffee warm. A heating element really squanders electricity. You'd be better off using a candle for heat.

If you're up to it, you might remove the generator from your car and mount it against the rear wheel of a bicycle. Most modern car generators are called "alternators" because they generate AC, and they're quite efficient. But if you intend to build such stuff, remember that an alternator won't generate any juice at all unless a battery can supply at least a trickle of power to it to energize its field coils. You don't believe me? Disconnect your car battery and get your car going downhill at any speed you like, then try to start your car with the alternator alone. The nice thing about the old DC car generators was that they'd start your car even if your battery had been stolen! Talk to your friendly junkyard man; some old DC car generators are still around.

Now, about that bicycle that took you past the traffic jam . . . You must somehow jack the rear wheel clear of the floor so you can pedal in place, the rear wheel spinning the generator pulley that's snubbed against it. If you align the pulley against the rubber tire, the friction of tire against pulley will serve as a pulley belt. You may have to dismember a chair, or even rip into a wall somewhere, for sturdy wood to whittle and bind a frame for mounting your car generator to the bike. Here we're talking about fairly rugged rigs, and at this point many of you may be deciding to forget a generator. Hold it: if you have a bike, you may also have a quicker answer.

The fist-sized little DC generators built for bike lights are so cheap, every bike can and should have one. They mount on the bike frame, spring-loaded so they can ride against the tire as it spins, generating enough amperage to run a bike headlamp and tail lamp. If you can, get one that is rated at 12 volts or thereabouts. Because, so help me, it can also power an AM/FM radio or cassette player of the sort you can plug into a cigarette lighter. Our kids are the only ones on the block who have had tape decks on bikes! It was just a guess, but we guessed right: the cheap commercial adaptors sold to adapt a car's 12-volt system to 6- or 9-volt hardware, can also be wired to the little bike generator.

Figure 10 shows how handily a bike generator can be adapted to power an AM/FM-cassette recorder. The only trick is in wiring the generator to an adaptor that was intended to plug into a cigarette lighter, as shown in Figure 11. Our adaptor came with sev-

FIGURE 10

FIGURE 11

eral different plugs, to fit the different kinds of small appliances. For instance, one of the plugs fits a hand calculator. Our adaptor also has a tiny switch that lets you choose 6- or 9-volt output. Our cassette machine uses 6 volts; most hand calculators use 9 volts. Don't try to run both simultaneously.

In Figure 12, the bike's rear end is suspended with pieces of broomstick across the backs of two folding chairs. We bound one broomstick with cord and the other with strapping tape just to show that either will serve. Then we mounted *two* bike generators on the broomsticks so that they engage the bike tire on its tread. If mounted on the sidewall as is often done, the toothed generator pulley tends to chew the tire's sidewall up. We could've mounted three or even four of the little generators on that tire. The point is, the generators don't cost much and they don't load the tire down much either. You can actually recharge a great whopping car battery by trickle-charging it with a bike generator—more quickly using several bike generators wired in parallel.

FIGURE 12

One brief gimmick: ordinarily a bike generator is grounded against the bike's metal chassis. Of the two terminals protruding from the aft end of the generator in Figure 12, one accepts a wire leading to the weak little tail lamp while the other accepts a wire leading to the headlight. So neither of these terminals is a 'ground' terminal. By mounting our generators on nonconducting broomsticks, we made it necessary to supply a ground wire from the generator mount to a ground connection on the adaptor as shown in Figures 10 and 11.

If you buy bike generators for this broad-spectrum use, *don't* get the kind with both lamps built into the generator body. You'll want to run wires here and there in your shelter; to a battery, or to a bike headlight used as a reading lamp, or maybe to that cassette player so you can have Beethoven to keep you company.

A bike generator will light its little bulbs even if you haven't lugged a car battery into your shelter as a storage tank for electrical energy. But without a battery, you'll have to keep pedaling as long as you want light. The pedal effort is slight, and does not seem appreciably greater when two generators are mounted against the tire; but even with no generators, the effort will tire you and cause you to use a lot of air during a half-hour of steady pedaling. That's a good reason to have a car battery, and to install more than one tiny generator.

We tried some other ideas that didn't work well, so we didn't illustrate them. One idea was to tape bricks on the bike pedals, turning the bike upside down, so you could crank the pedals by hand and use the mass of the bricks to get a flywheel effect. If you could somehow fill a bike tire with lead weights it might be marginally effective, but the bricks added little inertia because they weren't very heavy and their moment arm was short. Sorry 'bout that.

FIGURE 13

On the other hand, we're still playing with some other ideas that sprang from the bike generator.

Example 1. Find a way to mount an adult's bike on the end of your roof, so that the front wheel minus handlebars can pivot easily. Now cut pieces of venetian blind slats and, with tape or wire, mount the slats like turbine blades among the front wheel spokes. If the slats have a modest angle of incidence (that is, angled like propeller blades), the wheel should spin in a decent breeze. With a homemade weathervane mounted through the handlebar socket—ours was a mop handle with a cardboard rudder tacked onto it—you can make the device turn itself into the wind, pivoting as it would with handlebars. Voila: a small windmill. If you use a big 26-inch wheel, it should barely run a bike generator in a good breeze. *Certainly* it's primitive, nowhere near as effective as some other systems; but it's a free power source. Oh: don't forget to mount the generator on the front wheel *fork* so that it pivots with the wheel, as we did in Figure 13.

Example 2. A wind-driven bike wheel can also let you convert a bike speedometer to a small power drill or other rotary-motion tool.

Example 3. A big-motha' windmill, with 4-meter epoxy-coated high-aspect ratio blades and a capstan drive made from a wheelchair (why didn't Oklahoma State U. toy with such handy little windmill drives in their development work?) is in development on a ranch near us. But it runs a chevy alternator which wouldn't be worth a cent if something happened to the huge truck battery below, because there'd be no initial jolt to energize the alternator field. Well, we're going to put a tiny little bike generator on the site just for emergency engagement to energize the big alternator. We're not saying it will be an optimal answer—only that it may be one very quick answer. We don't even have to mount the bike generator up high; it could be kept on the ground, out of the weather.

So much for those ongoing experiments. Now it's time to inject what we can call an in-text footnote because it isn't really a digression: candles and other combustion devices. Combustion uses up your oxygen; sometimes it stinks, too. Unless you have plenty of air, don't use up much of it with candles or kerosene lamps. If you use a kerosene lamp, trim the wick and keep it adjusted for minimum combustion without smoke. For years we've used a tiny kerosene lamp, a Japanese scale model of the big ones, to read while backpacking. It uses an ounce of fluid every three hours; neither it nor its fuel takes up much room in a pack; and it's a cheery companion when you're on a Sierra solo, with a wire gizmo made to let a coffee cup stay warm atop the little lamp. A quart of fluid can keep such a lamp burning for ninety hours but, unless you have air to spare, think twice about it.

Oh, yes; we played with the stubby little candles of the votive or "fondue warmer" type. When free-standing, they become a broad puddle of wax all too quickly. Placed in a container that keeps molten wax from running away, one of the little candles can burn for nine hours or more. Just remember, it's using a lot of oxygen and adding to the heat and carbon dioxide in a semi-closed life support system. Make sure your air supply is adequate.

We also made experiments with flashlights using two 'D'-size cells. Standard heavy-duty cells powered a bulb for 18 hours, while alkaline cells powered it for 30 hours. We burnt out several bulbs before we learned to accept the fact that the duty-cycle of most flashlight bulbs is brief. That is, you mustn't expect a common flashlight bulb to burn more than an hour in one session. Use it for awhile; let it cool awhile; then turn it on again when you must. Flashlight batteries will recover a bit after they've rested for a few hours. But if you depend on flashlight bulbs and batteries, keep spares for both.

A few people will be ahead of us with gasoline-powered electrical systems or windmills. Just remember that even the smallest gasoline engines use a lot of fuel and oxygen, put out a lot of noxious exhaust, and make a lot of noise. You'll almost certainly want to keep such bellowing little brutes outside your living quarters. A windmill is much quieter and uses no precious fuel.

Summarizing your power-and-light options, and presuming you don't have solar cells or a hydroelectric plant handy, a windmill seems a very good bet if you can make one. But for every shelter boasting such a power source there'll probably be hundreds making do with a bike-powered generator and perhaps a car battery. If you manage to haul two fully-charged car batteries into a shelter, you might have enough stored power to dispel the dark for the better part of two weeks without a generator of any kind. And many pundits are guessing that, if you can stay put that long, radiation from fallout will have greatly diminished.

In two weeks of continuous occupation, a shelter can get pretty ripe, considering body wastes and other odors. You must find or make a portable potty.

A sturdy bucket or even a cardboard box, with a garbage bag for a liner, makes an acceptable john. It is important that you sprinkle household bleach or hydrated lime into the bag after defecating into it. Not only the smell, but the danger of disease, will be lessened by disinfectants. If possible, train all shelter occupants to do their doo-dahs at roughly the same time. If you have no plastic bags, you may have to use brown paper bags or newspaper as a liner. In that case, you'll quickly learn to urinate into an old milk carton or other waterproof container to minimize the mess when emptying the john.

For: empty it, you must; and as soon as practicable after use, if you expect to live in an enclosed area for several days. If you have reason to suspect that even a moment outside shelter might be lethal, you'll have to store body wastes in a covered garbage can or the equivalent until the first possible chance to get rid of the waste. It should be dumped in a hole far from the shelter, then covered with dirt.

Figure 14 shows an emergency john made from a wastepaper basket, several layers of cardboard taped together with a hole cut through them, and a plastic bag taped into the hole. Okay, so it ain't the Waldorf; it only took ten minutes to build and it's fast, fast,

FIGURE 14

fast relief. Once the john has been used by all who will, some hardy soul must sprinkle a few ounces of lime into the bag, extract the bag, tape it shut and dispose of it.

Hygiene is more than simply a system for disposing of fecal material. It involves staying as clean as you can; using dilute bleach solution to clean messes with minimum waste of precious water; donning rain gear for any essential forays outside the shelter; shaking dust particles off of yourself before you get to the shelter opening; carefully shucking the rain gear before you enter the shelter itself; and more. Don't forget that your hair is a dandy dust-trap; wear a shower cap or other cover to keep from trapping fallout particles in your hair when you're outside. And as we've cautioned before, make a dust mask from flannel, or use something even better, to avoid breathing unfiltered outside air. All this is hygiene. It keeps you relatively free of contaminants you cannot afford.

Mental hygiene fits in here somewhere. Sensory deprivation studies suggest that we might get through the shelter ordeal much better if we do have light, some meaningful activity, and games of some sort to occupy us while the clock ticks away. If we don't have playing cards we can make them. The same is true of checkers, chess, dice, and many other games. Anyhow, the sooner we get used to manufacturing what we can't buy, the sooner we'll be back in charge of a high-tech existence.

Each shelter occupant might keep a journal, jotting down any ideas that might be fruitful for the future—including a log the radio provides on daily local and not-so-local survival conditions. In between reading favorite books, you could do worse than read some basic texts on gardening, electricity, food preservation, first aid, and appliance repair, to name only a few. Whatever you need to know that you don't know already; start learning it while you have enforced leisure.

If you've digested the information in the three articles so far, you have a good chance of emerging from a shelter two weeks after a major fallout event, without serious illness. A healthy adult *can*, if necessary, live for nearly a week without water, and over three weeks without food. If you've provided yourself with food and water, you might survive with no ill effects—except that you might have a mild case of claustrophobia. If personal experience is any guide, we expect that you'll also have a brand-new outlook on life. How sweet it is to be alive, when you look back on the nearness of death!

Even if you're still breathing through a homemade flannel mask, you're still breathing; planning; making ready for whatever comes next. We hope you've given some previous thought to the day when you emerge from shelter because, as Freeman Dyson has opined, a lot of people will probably outlast an all-out nuclear war. In the next article we'll suggest some things you should know—for example, that castor oil is easily extracted from castor beans and is a good engine oil. And we'll mention some things you should have all packed away for the post-shelter era.

Not in a hope chest. In a tenacity chest.

Stocking Your Tenacity Chest

Many Americans could survive an all-out nuclear exchange if we knew what to do, and if we did it. FEMA, in July 1986, admitted that we would be on our own, without much government help. We started this series of articles by describing a firestorm, a more lethal and immediate threat than fallout for city dwellers. You can be asphyxiated and roasted in a blastproof shelter—as three hundred thousand casualties proved in Dresden.

The U.S. Government has agreed about firestorm; has suggested that you relocate from target areas if war seems imminent. We suggested that you relocate *now*—or at least prepare for evacuation with a bike rack on your car for your "second stage" vehicle.

We showed you how to build air filtration and pump devices from household materials, so you can breathe clean air in a shelter beyond the firestorm area. Oak Ridge National Lab (PO Box X, Oak Ridge, TN 37830) has put a little tax money to excellent use in developing and testing other homebuilt rigs, including jury-rigged shelters and a high-volume air pump. Their pump will not pull through a fine filter as ours will, but without filter restrictions it pumps much more air than ours.

Our third article illustrated ways to rig toilets and lighting systems in a shelter. Briefly summarized: You build a small potty using thin plastic bags to catch solid waste, and sprinkle hydrated lime or Clorox into the bag before sealing it. Small lights, cannibalized from a car, can be run by auto batteries, or even by tiny 12-volt bike generators that will also power tape recorders and calculators. Wiring is safe and simple.

Finally, we promised to add some tidbits on post-fallout survival; call it cottage industry if you will. If you've read our previous articles, our texts and photographs will testify that we've spent a lot of time developing gadgets and trying advice collected from others. Amerinds, settlers, guerrillas, anthropologists—survivalists all—have taught us how to make fuels, treat illness, and scrounge food; well-informed Americans need not face a hand-to-mouth existence when first emerging from fallout shelters. So we promised to suggest some things to store in your "tenacity chest" for the post-fallout world. Much of that storage will be in the form of information.

We decided to break our information package down into five groups: shelter, food, health, energy, and utensils. There's a great deal of overlap here; you'll need to build utensils to make your own fuels and lubricants, for example.

Your most intimate shelter is clothing. It was Sylvan Hart, a modern mountain man with an engineering background, who said he was afraid of only one thing: a cold wind. He was talking about hypothermia, the situation when your body heat is drawn away faster than your body can replace it. When you read that someone died of "exposure," chances are he died of hypothermia.

You can insulate yourself from cold by wearing

several layers of clothing, but not if those clothes are wet. The air trapped between clothing layers provides good insulation. Water conducts heat and replaces the air, so your body heat is conducted from your skin through the damp clothes to the cold wind. Conclusion: stay dry in cold weather.

If you can't stay dry, try wearing leather. We find that thick elkhide trousers, though soaking wet in mountain snow, provide much more insulation than heavy jeans. But they dry more slowly, and we swear they weigh fifteen pounds wet!

You can dry your damp socks by putting them inside your shirt just above your belt. It takes awhile, but it's worth it for warm dry feet. Clothes should be vented so body moisture can escape. Rubberized or other entirely moistureproof fabrics tend to trap moisture inside to make you clammy. Outfitters can steer you to a nylon cloth, Goretex, so densely woven that it will shed rain while allowing water vapor to escape. For that matter, a weekend with a veteran backpacker can lead you to the items you need from an outfitter's shelves. Weatherproofing shoes (mink oil), keeping unlined leather gloves on during chores, and rigging a pack are three things that immediately come to mind.

Need oilcloth? The original stuff was, literally, cloth drenched with linseed oil and sun-dried. The sunlight polymerized the linseed oil to a flexible solid. You can start with plain cloth; just remember not to store it folded. The stuff tends to glue itself together into a useless lump.

We considered clothing as shelter because it's likely that you'll be more mobile—personally mobile; on foot—than you are today. But what if you're afoot and soaking and cold?

If more than an hour from known shelter, stop and get warm. It's nice to have a little hemispherical nylon-and-stiffener tent on your pack, preferably one of drab color. Next best might be a rectangle of ten-mil plastic for a tent, big enough that you can lie on it as well as under it. A down mummybag can be as small as a ten-pound bag of flour. People have also found refuge from that cold wet wind in hollow trees, abandoned cars, haystacks, bridge foundations—even warm compost heaps.

For more permanent shelter, architects are beginning to rediscover the virtues of dirt, citing the 'soddy' dugouts that insulated settlers from ferocious great-plains weather. Oddly, they don't often cite Wright's berm house of the 1930s, but they should. A berm is an earth ramp. If you build a wooden or stone house, you'll find yourself better protected and insulated with berms shoveled along the outside walls up to the windows or eaves. Since a berm will hold rain and ground water, you should place a water barrier (thin plastic sheet will do, but be careful not to tear it as you shovel dirt against it) between the wall and the dirt berm. A gravel-filled, stone-covered trench at the foot of the wall and under the berm will let ground-water percolate away—if your trench leads away downhill. If you build in a depression you're asking for flooding. We know, we know: there's lots more to it, but we're only touching the high spots.

A semi-permanent shelter requires amenities like verminproof storage, a firepit with smokehole, and a bough bed or lath-lashed sleeping platform. Study old National Geographics to see how the Ashanti or Blackfoot or Polynesians coped with special environments similar to yours.

We haven't the space here to dwell on ways to fortify shelters; your best protection is probably camouflage—including a grassy berm—and inconspicuous multiple exits also make sense.

Our second category is food, and we'll start with meat. Recently canned food should be okay, of course. Why waste space on the dressing-out of large animals? You probably won't see many. Among common domestic animals, swine and chickens seem to have superior powers to survive high radiation doses. Fish might be plentiful, and the radioactive particles they absorb seem to be concentrated in the organs we normally discard, so fish may be a staple. But remember not to eat shellfish unless you eat only the muscle tissue.

Extrapolating from the known hazards of irradiated fish organs, we suspect you should discard *all* animal organs. And we know the edible meats aren't all represented at Safeway. Frogs and snakes, for example, can be delicacies. Skin the snake and remove the head and organs, cut the flesh into manageable segments, then fry or roast the segments like chicken. Frog legs are skinned, then fried or roasted, the same way.

Insects? Many people have survived on such a diet—but not on insects recently subjected to high radiation. Some edible creepies such as grubs, termites, and nightcrawlers might be relatively safe because they don't live in the open—but all have organs which might concentrate irradiated particles, and the energy you spend collecting them might surpass the energy you get from digesting them. Several months after the last fallout, it might be safe to dine on those crawly critters. They have been praised as soup stock, but not by us!

Vegetables will probably compose 95% of your diet. We'll admit that corn, wheat, legumes, and other staples will be important, and go on to lesser-known foods. The lowly acorn is plentiful, easily-shelled, and (aren't we all?) bitter as hell when raw. You must leach out the tannin (a substance also boiled from oak bark for tanning hides) by boiling, say, a pint of shelled acorns in a quart of water, changing the water every five minutes, for about forty minutes. Then let the acorns sun-dry. They can be munched as is, or ground into flour for flatcakes or soup stock. When salted, they're so tasty we wonder why they aren't marketed.

We all know about fruit and nuts, but had you thought of crushing nutmeats and pressing them to get oil for cooking or lamps? If you can't rig a powerful hand press, boil and stir the crushed nutmeats and skim off the oil that floats to the top. Save the nut soup, dry it, and use the dried nutmeats for flour or nutcake.

Fruit "leather" is easy. Boil the fruit whole, drain it, saving the drained liquid to drink, and press the boiled fruit pulp through a sieve—perhaps a metal can with lots of nail-holes. The thickish paste can be sweetened with honey or with the boiled-down juice of fruits. Pour the paste onto a flat surface and dry it, protecting it from insects. When it's leathery, roll it into small tubes and store it as candy.

Cattails have a pulpy inner stem you can mash and eat raw, or better still, boil it first. Where the stem joins the root you'll find a lump that you can peel and eat like a potato.

Learn to identify the salsify weed, or "oyster root," which has a purple or yellow blossom and later a puffball like a huge dandelion. In Europe its root is a delicacy. Pull a double-handful of salsify roots, clean and boil them awhile. Big roots can be too fibrous for our taste, but we've seen guests take third helpings of the smaller roots with their faint delicious oysterish taste. The dandelion makes marvelous salad greens, or the leaves can be boiled like spinach. The cleaned, dried, ground-up root makes a tea-colored, coffeeish-flavored brew, and the Vitamin A in dandelions puts a carrot to shame.

Vitamin C is found in tomatoes and citrus, of course; but also in rose hips, the moderately bitter seed pods of the common rose. We pampered a tiny "decorative" citrus tree two feet high because it winters indoors in Oregon and yields sour fruit the size of ping-pong balls. The little zingers are loaded with Vitamin C and are fresh in January.

Incidentally, the leaves of mint, blackberry, and strawberry can also be brewed as tea. You might grow spices (sage, thyme, mint, oregano) as a barter crop. A pound of dry oregano might be worth a block of sea salt.

Winemaking is an art lauded in many books. Remember that you can make it from berries and fruit, too. It won't be sweet unless you add sugar. Brandy is made by distilling wine to obtain the ethyl alcohol and some of the original wine. If you have the right apparatus, including a sensitive chemical thermometer, you can wind up with almost pure ethyl. If your apparatus includes metals like lead you can wind up poisoned.

If you aren't a gardener, find a plot of bathtub size or larger and start now. A compost pile is a small art, and the pile can be quite small. The finer the particles of food scraps and decaying leaves you start with, the sooner it becomes good plant food—and if it starts to mildew, it's too damp. Some plants like marigolds and mint repel bugs, and you should learn which veggies you can grow best in your locale. Why only in your locale? Because you're not likely to travel very far from it. Long-distance travel may become hazardous for most of us.

We could go on for volumes, rehashing Euell Gibbons and Brad Angier on the subject of common edible plants—but what for, when others have done it so well? Choose a text or two; stalk the wild whatsit for fun—and for longevity.

For health problems: again, you should have advice and texts by experts. We can help a little by parroting them. Aspirin can reduce fever and aching of many kinds from flu to rheumatism. Ethyl or isopropyl ("rubbing") alcohols are among the best general disinfectants without side effects of iodine and merthiolate. Disinfectant should be daubed *around* an open wound, *not* directly into it. Unflavored vodka is about half ethyl alcohol and might serve as an emergency disinfectant. We suspect that germs aren't just wild about acetone, either—and soap and water are among the best cleansers of wounds, especially if you must scrub debris from them.

Bleeding helps to cleanse a puncture wound. A clean bandage, *not* airtight, should cover a break in the skin after disinfecting the surrounding skin.

Burns can be relieved first by cold compresses, followed by a gauze bandage smeared with clean petroleum jelly. The jelly helps prevent secondary infection while your body repairs the burn. We've read about mountain men covering a burn with tallow or bear grease—but if trying such a remedy with animal products, you'd better cook the stuff first to kill the bacteria it may harbor.

In the special case of a profusely bleeding surface wound, try to pull edges of the wound together and tape them that way. Don't use a tourniquet unless absolutely necessary; gangrene from tourniquets has caused as many deaths as has blood loss. You can lose a pint of blood without serious loss of mobility. To prevent shock after a burn or other injury, have the victim sip a quart of water containing a level teaspoon of salt and a half-teaspoon of bicarbonate of soda. No booze!

You can often relieve a cough by sucking hard candy, by inhaling over a bowl of steaming water, or by sipping hot drinks. Constipation can be countered by adding fruit, especially prunes, figs, or raisins, to your diet. If the fruit is dry, soak it in water awhile.

For many skin problems—poison oak, rash, fungus infections—calamine lotion will help. Athlete's foot is a fungus infection, by the way. The fungus thrives on soft, soggy skin, which explains why you must keep your feet and footgear dry—and brings us to an area of special concern: your feet.

When you can no longer buy fuel for your moped and the barter market or paramedic is two miles away, you will begin to give your feet the respect they always deserved. If you don't think corns or athlete's foot can have you walkin' on your knees, you've led a charmed life. A corn, often from improperly tight shoes, can cause excruciating pain. Commercial preparations can dissolve them, but you may be reduced to shaving one away with a razor blade. Don't imagine that you can get away with wearing a corn pad indefinitely, unless your shoe was designed for that pad—and it wasn't, was it? So treat the symptom (the corn), and correct its source (usually tight or run-down footgear).

Athlete's foot isn't as painful at first, but it can fill your boot with blood and yuchh, and may lead to serious systemic infection, and the itch can drive you right across the ceiling. Oh, yes; and if you scratch it with fingernails, you can spread the fungus to other parts of your infection-weakened bod. *Now* will you take athlete's foot seriously? Cotton or wool socks help absorb moisture from your foot, while synthetics don't. You could also put tiny lambswool pads between your toes if your feet sweat a lot. Always dry between your toes after a wetting before your socks go on; and a dusting of talc between toes and into shoes will help.

Choose ankle-protecting footgear for ruggedness and reasonably loose fit, and wear two pairs of socks if you need to. Keep shoes pliable and water-resistant. If you try to dry them next to a fire, you're risking serious deterioration of leather. Don't choose the sexy overlap-closure boots that hint of the downhill racer unless you live in snow. Those closures keep snow out, but water doesn't give a damn for any but the most perfect overlap; step into a creek up to the closure and it may mean instant sog in your boot. Instead, choose the accordian-fold closure, and inspect the lace 'D' rings to be sure they weren't anchored through the leather in such a way as to leave a path for water to trickle through to your sock. Your walking boots should let you step into water nearly up to the lace tie, without letting water in.

If you have a persistent skin sore, whether on your foot or from a hangnail, you might try a last-ditch remedy we've tested: man's best friend. We'd read of people with jungle rot letting a healthy dog treat the wound by licking it, but never tried it until 1978. An infected hangnail then defied our two-week treatment with antiseptic. Then our neighbor's canine medic, Bozo, took a sniff of the offending digit and did everything but write us a prescription. Whatthehell, we thought, and let him treat it twice a day. We can't swear that Bozo licked the swollen hangnail well in a week, but we *can* swear that we used no other medication during "saliva therapy," and it got well in a week. We were only trying what American guerrillas on Leyte had tried, and got the same excellent results. Hardly a controlled experiment; but it's an idea you might keep on file.

Energy technology, especially alternative sources of heat and fuel, is a fad right now. Pay attention to the simple alternatives. We've seen a cardboard box, with sloping clear glass front and foil-lined insulated inner walls, cook pastries by sunlight. It could just as easily dry fruit leather or cure meat strips into jerky, even in a light overcast.

Many stored fuels, including gasoline and diesel fuel, are perishable within a year. If you use old stored fuels you risk fouling the engine or carburetor by gums and shellacs. There are special stabilizer chemicals you can add to stored fuel, but you might just use alcohol. Rubbing alcohol is about half water and won't work. Methyl ("wood") and ethyl ("booze") alcohols are a bit tough to store because they readily evaporate, but they won't foul an engine. For a diesel, alcohol won't work well. For a gasoline engine, it works well *after you modify the carburetor.*

The optimum gasoline-to-air ratio is different from the optimum alcohol-to-air ratio, and there are two ways to easily modify that ratio in the carburetor. You can ream the carburetor's main jet with a drill bit so that its cross-sectional *area* is about half again—i.e., 150%—the size of the original hole through the jet. That way, the tiny hole can supply half again as much liquid fuel to provide roughly the same power as always—though your mileage will be poorer with alcohol. Or you can adjust the choke, a much easier process, by mechanically wiring or jamming the carburetor's "butterfly" air intake valve partly closed. This restricts the carburetor's air intake instead of increasing its alcohol intake—and of course your maximum power will be reduced somewhat. If you don't understand this paragraph, ask any mechanic to show you what we mean.

But where do you get alcohol? You can distill corn mash or wine for ethyl alcohol. You can (because we've done it) distill wood chips or kindling to get methyl alcohol, which is poison if taken internally. Remember that the charcoal left in the container after methyl alcohol distillation is a perfectly good fuel for stoking the next "charge" of the still. Don't use charcoal in a closed room; its carbon monoxide effluent can kill you.

When you begin to produce alcohol you'll shoot your thirsty Thunderbird in favor of a Honda or moped. Even a five-gallon yield is more than a tabletop operation; you'll need a big metal drum or its equivalent to contain the wood to be heated. An airtight lid on the drum is essential. The condenser of a still may be a coil of tubing, or may be simply a long water-cooled pipe which is much easier to clean out. Water, acids, wood tars and turpentine are all recoverable from heated wood, along with the alcohol and acetone that will collect in the condenser. Consider a second distillation to separate the alcohol from the acetone by careful control of temperature. Acetone can fuel an engine with alcohol, but is also a particularly good solvent. You can make quick-drying wood cement by dissolving shavings of many plastics in acetone. When the wood cement is thinned with more acetone it makes lacquer.

On a more modest level, study fire-kindling techniques. Lint and stored dandelion fluff will kindle from a strong spark, from flint-and-steel or some other device. Wooden matches can be waterproofed by a dip in barely-molten wax, especially beeswax.

A windmill or watermill can power generators taken from old cars, which in turn can power lots of things including pumps, blowers, radios, and lights. Yes, clever folks can extract energy from warm water springs and chicken flickin's, but your most available energy sources will probably be sunlight, wind, and wood.

Sad to say, you may have your pick of utensils in a post-fallout world. Sad, because you will be picking from the belongings of people who didn't pull through as you did. Stainless steel utensils will last longer than other metals, which is why they're favored by restaurant kitchens.

You may have to make your own utensils to process, e.g., soap. Start with a gallon container with nail-holes in the bottom, packed nearly full of white wood ash—*not* black charred ash. Trickle a gallon of water through the ash, catching it in another container, which may take a few days. Sprinkle the sodden ash around the rim of your garden plot to discourage snails and focus on the collected lye water. Filter the lye water if necessary, then boil it or let it evaporate down to a half-pint or so. It's concentrated lye when an egg or a scrap of potato floats in it (specific gravity over 1.2). Meanwhile you've rendered tallow from fat and filtered it clean. A half pint of lye and a pound of grease make a pound and a half of soap. When the tallow is melted, nearly too hot to touch, and lye is body temperature (feel the container), slowly pour the lye into the tallow, stirring for a half-hour. Then pour it into a shallow pan and let it cure a week. Sometimes it won't come out perfectly; unmixed tallow will set on top and lye will be on the bottom. But much or all of it will be firm soap. Don't use aluminum containers; the lye will eat aluminum.

How about glass containers for chemical work of this sort? Learn to cut and smartly rap gallon jugs with a glass cutter, so the top makes a funnel and the bottom, a wide-mouthed vat. Grind sharp glass edges with a stone for safety. There's also a grease-soaked, flaming twine-and-water-shock method, too. You'll break several jugs learning these tricks. Hacksaw blades are available today with carbide chips for sawing through glass.

How can you make twine? Soak long pulpy leaves of flax or yucca plants for a week in water, then strip and save the long leaf fibers from the leaf pulp. Fibers can be twisted or braided into twine, thence into rope. The Anasazi braided sandals that way.

Pottery? Find clay that can be squeezed and twisted without crumbling, make it into soup ("slip"), screen it to remove crud, then evaporate it to a plastic solid. Slap a piece repeatedly on a hard surface to remove air bubbles (it's called "wedging") before you hand-form it. Let hand-formed pieces sun-dry, then stack them loosely within a specially-built chimney. Build a fire gradually up to roar right through that chimney for an hour or so. Or stack the pieces on a heavy metal grid over an intense and long-lasting fire. You potters will sigh at the things we've left out; you others might watch a potter sometime. We've seen water pumps, tobacco pipes, and toilets built of clay, then fired and glazed for watertightness. You could build distillation heat-exchangers that way, making several parallel tubes instead of a coil, the way metal steam boilers are built.

For strong wood glue, boil and stir shavings of horn or hoof in water until you have a sticky gum. Use it while hot and wet, and give it a day to sun-dry. To save the rest, twirl it on a stick and let it dry, then immerse and boil your glue lollipop the next time you need it, as the Comanche did.

Weaving is too complex an art to detail here; study primitive methods like the simple bow loom as well as modern craft methods. Strips of rabbit fur can be interspersed with fibers when weaving a marvelously warm blanket. You can also knit or tie fiber into fishnet, bird trap, or a blanket grid for those fur strips.

If you have the electricity, the expertise, and the need, you can build a mile-long telegraph line as our guerrillas did. They unwound barbed wire and ran the separated strands from tree to tree, using pop bottles for insulators.

If you can't get lubricating oil for an engine, you might try fractionally distilling old oil to reclaim it. Or perhaps you can locate a few castor bushes. Castor beans, though poisonous, are easily crushed for castor oil. Process them as you would for nut oil, with one exception: don't breathe the vapor while boiling the mush. We found the vapor an all-too-efficient laxative. Don't worry that good castor oil will damage an engine; many a racing engine has thrived on it. It leaves a varnish on parts eventually, but it's an excellent lubricant.

For hunting small game, consider the sling and slingshot. Both are easy to make, they're quiet, and ammunition is plentiful. A longbow will drop a deer, but takes a good arm and carefully-crafted equipment. If pondering which gun to buy, avoid the calibres for which ammunition may be rare. The most commonly available rounds in the U.S. are the .22, .30-.30, .45 ACP, 12-gauge—and, at almost every drugstore, the BB. The .22 won't reliably and immediately drop game over thirty pounds, and needs at least an 8″ barrel for reasonable accuracy. For birds and rabbits, there are some excellent air pistols with rifled barrels that shoot either lead pellets or BBs interchangeably. An air rifle is more accurate but also pretty big to lug around. We're talking about real, pump-up air guns, not spring-loaded or CO_2 -powered guns. A pump pistol is relatively quiet with muzzle velocity up to 500 ft/sec, and will sting the bejeezus out of a mean mutt. Perhaps the best thing about a good air pistol is that you can quietly practice using it for pennies inside your house, using plywood or a dozen thicknesses of corrugated cardboard as backstop.

Jerzy Kosinski once described a simple fire-carrier made from a big juice can, for travelers without matches who need warmth while traveling. Punch ten spaced holes around the side of the can next to its bottom, and cut its top completely out. Add a long wire handle, borrow some fire, and keep a small bed of coals glowing as you hike along. For a fast fire, drop in a few hunks of wood and kindling and swing the can around in a circle; the forced draft does the rest. Kosinski claimed it was called a "comet" because of the trail of sparks it makes as it whirls around your head, and we found that the metal can is glowing in less than a minute. If it doesn't discourage an unarmed intruder, he must be desperate. As a small space heater and stove, the "comet" is a lifesaver. Our kids learned to make them at age six. Since then, we've developed sophisticated versions, testing new wrinkles by stoking a comet in a handy fireplace. It's a low-profile hobby, and it could save the hobbyist's life.

Perhaps you've noticed: we've begun to segue from the software of your tenacity chest to its hardware. Check on the shelf life of seeds and medicines you keep (even aspirin eventually decays with a vinegary odor), and next time you spot a sale on needles or injector blades, get a handful. A dime may have more purchasing power than a paper bill, so keep a roll of coins. Get a quarter-mile spool of strong monofilament nylon fishing line for lashings, sewing, traps, and so on.

Pick up a hand-cranked meat-grinder at a garage sale. We cut the clamp from one and made a small T-handle so the whole thing, spare grinder heads and all, fits into a bike's handlebar pouch as a mass the size of a grapefruit. It'll grind tough meat or hard corn, and when you have dental trouble it can make life bearable. It's also useful for processing nut and vegetable oils. Why did primitive plant gatherers seldom live past forty? For one thing, grit from their stone grinders wore their teeth down to the gumline by that age, in a chain reaction of events that impaired digestion and health. Get the bloody hand grinder! It's more crucial than you think.

There's one item we won't suggest that you buy, because you wouldn't; radiation monitors are expensive. But you can make one for next to nothing! Oak Ridge document ORNL-5040 is a little book that gives astonishingly complete instructions on building a calibrated foil electroscope that measures ionizing radiation—i.e., a fallout meter. Its calibration lets you know how much fallout is in your area, so you can judge your tactics better, and the little meter is built entirely of common household materials. We've rarely seen any sophisticated device as well-engineered to be built by rank beginners—and have never seen one as potentially crucial to human survival. Copies of the manual have been sent to libraries in Stanford Research Institute, National Technical Information Services, Illinois Institute of Technology, and defense documentation centers. Your congressbody can probably locate one which could be reproduced for you. Newspaper editors please copy; the document is in the public domain.

We've covered only some bare necessities to be packed into your tenacity chest, but we must stop somewhere. The one thing you must keep stored, above all, is your own tenacity. If you weren't interested in the history of technology before, you'd be wise to get interested now. Herbert Hoover and wife translated Agricola's mining/smelting treatise, *De Re Metallica*, into English. The conquistadores processed nitrates from horse manure to make gunpowder, and might have used bat guano from caves as well. Platinum jewelry can make catalyst grids for making industrial chemicals including acids. What do you care about thumb-pumped hairspray? Well, the spring-loaded ball check valve is visible inside, and can teach you how larger pumps can be built.

Presuming a post-fallout world, you'll find yourself becoming a generalist, much more self-sufficient—but you'll be smart to specialize as well, so you can trade special skills and products. Concrete begins with mortar from crushed, kiln-baked seashells. Repeated flooding and evaporation of sea water yields acres of edible salt. Sugar can be extracted from beets or cane. Smokeless powder begins with cotton steeped in a mixture of nitric and sulfuric acids for guncotton which is then washed, dried, dissolved in solvent such as acetone, and extruded to dry as flakes or tiny pellets. It has its dangerous moments, just as producing nitric acid from sulfuric acid and nitrates does. You'd best leave the production of primer explosives to chemists—though guncotton, in its dry fluffy form before solvent processing, can be detonated by a blasting cap or shotgun shell primer and might have brief popularity as a commercial explosive.

Commercial? Positively, yes. Even if governments fail and most citizens die, survivors will clear away the debris and eventually build a new commerce, a new government, a new society. If you've stored enough tenacity with your information and hardware, you may find that life can still be long and sweet and useful. And if you would be fondly remembered, you could hardly do more than demonstrate the pleasures of a life that's long, sweet, and useful.

A Homemade Fallout Meter, The KFM How to Make and Use it

FOLLOWING THESE INSTRUCTIONS MAY SAVE YOUR LIFE

The complete KFM instructions include patterns to be cut out and used to construct the fallout meter. At the end of the instructions are extra patterns on 4 unnumbered pages. The reader is urged to use these extra patterns to make KFM's in normal peacetime and to keep the complete instructions intact for use during a recognized crisis period.

If Xerox copies of the patterns are used, they should be checked against the originals in order to make sure that they are the same size as the originals. Some older copiers make copies with slightly enlarged dimensions. Even slightly enlarged copies of all the KFM patterns can be made satisfactory provided: (1) on the PAPER PATTERN TO WRAP AROUND KFM CAN, the distances between the 4 marks for the HOLES FOR STOP-THREAD are corrected; and (2) the dimensions of the FINISHED-LEAF PATTERN are corrected.

These instructions, including the heading on this page and the illustrative photos, can be photographed without additional screening and rapidly reproduced by a newspaper or printer. If you keep the KFM instructions intact, during a worsening crisis you will be able to use them to help your friends and thousands of your fellow citizens by making them available for reproduction.

1. The Need for Accurate and Dependable Fallout Meters

If a nuclear war ever strikes the United States, survivors of the blast and fire effects would need to have reliable means of knowing when the radiation in the environment around their shelters had dropped enough to let them venture safely outside. Civil defense teams could use broadcasts of surviving radio stations to give listeners a general idea of the fallout radiation in some broadcast areas. However, the fallout radiation can vary widely from point to point and the measurements are likely to be made too far from most shelters to make them accurate enough to use safely. Therefore, each shelter should have some dependable method of measuring the changing radiation dangers in its own area.

During a possible rapidly worsening nuclear crisis, or after a nuclear attack, most unprepared Americans could not buy or otherwise obtain a fallout meter—an instrument that would greatly improve their chances of surviving a nuclear war. The fact that the dangers from fallout radiation—best expressed in terms of the radiation dose rate, roentgens per hour (R/hr)—quite rapidly decrease during the first few days, and then decrease more and more slowly, makes it very important to have a fallout meter capable of accurately measuring the unseen, unfelt and changing fallout dangers. Occupants of a fallout shelter should be able to minimize the radiation doses they receive. In order to effectively minimize the radiation doses, a dependable measuring instrument is needed to determine the doses they receive while they are in the shelter and while they are outside for emergency tasks, such as going out to get badly needed water. Also, such an instrument would permit them to determine when it is safe to leave the shelter for good.

Untrained families, guided only by these written instructions and using only low cost materials and tools found in most homes, have been able to make a KFM by working 3 or 4 hours. By studying the operating sections of these instructions for about 1-½ hours, average untrained families have been able to successfully use this fallout meter to measure dose rates and to calculate radiation doses received, permissible times of exposure, etc.

The KFM (Kearny Fallout Meter) was developed at Oak Ridge National Laboratory. It is understandable, easily repairable, and as accurate as most civil defense fallout meters. In the United States in 1986 the least expensive commercially available dose-rate meter that is accurate and dependable and that measures high enough dose rates for wartime use is a British instrument that retails for $375. Comparable American instruments retail for over $1000.

Before a nuclear attack occurs is the best time to build, test and learn how to use a KFM. However, this instrument is so simple that it could be made even after fallout arrives **provided** that all the materials and tools needed (see lists given in Sections V, VI, and VII) and a copy of these instructions have been carried into the shelter.

II. Survival Work Priorities During a Crisis

Before building a KFM, persons expecting a nuclear attack within a few hours or days and already in the place where they intend to await attack should work with the following priorities: (1) build or improve a high-protection-factor shelter (if possible, a shelter covered with 2 or 3 feet of earth and separate from flammable buildings). At the same time, make and install a KAP (a homemade shelter-ventilating pump)—if instructions and materials are available. If not available, at least make a Directional Fan. Also store at least 15 gallons of water for each shelter occupant—if containers are available. (2) Assemble all materials for one or two KFMs. (3) Make and store the drying agent (by heating wallboard gypsum, as later described) for both the KFM and its dry-bucket. (4) Complete at least one KFM.

III. How to Use These Instructions to Best Advantage

1. Read ALOUD all of these instructions **through Section VII,** "Tools Needed," before doing anything else.
2. Next assemble all of the needed materials and tools.
3. Then read ALOUD ALL of each section following Section VII before beginning to make the part described in that section.

> A FAMILY THAT FAILS TO READ ALOUD ALL OF EACH SECTION DESCRIBING HOW TO MAKE A PART, BEFORE BEGINNING TO MAKE THAT PART, WILL MAKE AVOIDABLE MISTAKES AND WILL WASTE TIME.

4. Have different workers, or pairs of workers, make the parts they are best qualified to make. For example, a less skilled worker should start making the drying agent (as described in Section VIII) before other workers start making other parts. The most skilled worker should make and install the aluminum-foil leaves (Sections X and XI).
5. Give workers the sections of the instructions covering the parts they are to build—so they can follow the step-by-step instructions, checking off with a pencil each step as it is completed.
6. Discuss the problems that arise. The head of the family often can give better answers if he first discusses the different possible interpretations of some instructions with other family members, especially teenagers.
7. After completing one KFM and learning to use it, if time permits make a second KFM—that should be a better instrument.

IV. What a KFM Is and How It Works

A KFM is a simple electroscope-ionization chamber fallout meter with which fallout radiation can be measured accurately. To use a KFM, an electrostatic charge must first be placed on its **two** separate aluminum-foil leaves. These leaves are insulated by being suspended separately on clean, dry insulating threads.

To take accurate readings, the air inside the KFM must be kept very dry by means of drying agents such as dehydrated gypsum (easily made by heating gypsum wallboard, "sheetrock") or silica gel. (Do not use calcium chloride or other salt.) Pieces of

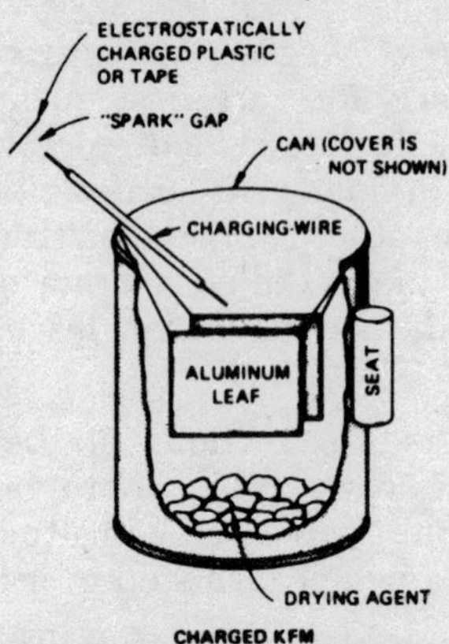

CHARGED KFM

drying agent are placed on the bottom of the ionization chamber (the housing can) of a KFM.

An electrostatic charge is transferred from a home-made electrostatic charging device to the two aluminum-foil leaves of a KFM by means of its charging-wire. The charging-wire extends out through the transparent plastic cover of the KFM.

When the two KFM leaves are charged electrostatically, their like charges (both positive or both negative) cause them to be forced apart. When fallout gamma radiation (that is similar to X rays but more energetic) strikes the air inside the ionization chamber of a KFM, it produces charged ions in this enclosed air. These charged ions cause part or all of the electrostatic charge on the aluminum-foil leaves to be discharged. As a result of losing charge, the two KFM leaves move closer together.

To read the separation of the **lower** edges of the two KFM leaves with one eye, look straight down on the leaves and the scale on the clear plastic cover. Keep the reading eye 12 inches above the SEAT. The KFM should be resting on a horizontal surface. To be sure the reading eye is always at this exact distance, place the lower end of a 12-inch ruler on

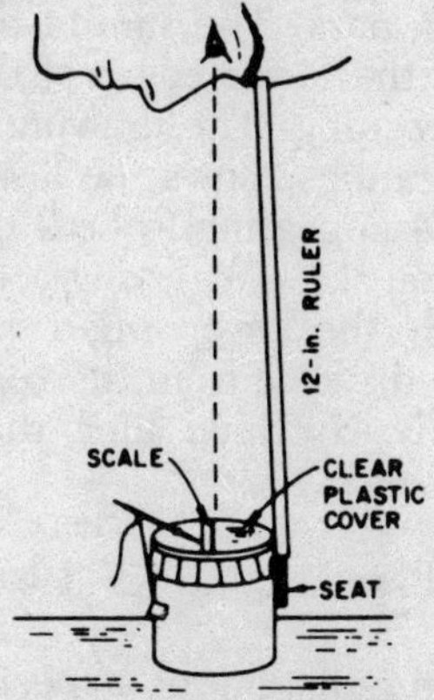

the SEAT, while the upper end of the ruler touches the eyebrow above the reading eye. It is best to hold the KFM can with one hand and the ruler with the other. Using a flashlight makes the reading more accurate.

If a KFM is made with the specified dimensions and of the specified materials, its accuracy is automatically and permanently established. Unlike most radiation measuring instruments, a KFM never needs to be calibrated or tested with a radiation source, if made and maintained as specified and used with the following table that is based on numerous calibrations made at Oak Ridge National Laboratory.

The millimeter scale is cut out and attached (see photo illustrations on the following page) to the clear plastic cover of the KFM so that its zero mark is directly above the two leaves in their discharged position when the KFM is resting on a horizontal surface. A reading of the separation of the leaves is taken by noting the number of millimeters that the **lower edge** of one leaf appears to be on, on one side of the zero mark on the scale, and almost at the same time noting the number of millimeters the **lower edge** of the other leaf appears to be on, on the other side of the zero mark. The **sum** of these two apparent positions of the lower edges of the two leaves is called a KFM reading. The drawing appearing after the photo illustrations shows the **lower** edges of the leaves of a KFM appearing to be 9 mm on the right of zero and 10 on the left, giving a KFM reading of 19 mm. (Usually the lower edges of the leaves are not at the same distance from the zero mark.)

As will be fully explained later, the radiation dose rate is determined by:

1. charging and reading the KFM before exposure;

2. exposing it to radiation for a specified time in the location where measurement of dose rate is needed—when outdoors, holding the KFM about 3 ft. above the ground;

3. reading the KFM after its exposure;

4. calculating, by subtraction, the **difference** between the reading taken before exposure and the reading taken after exposure;

5. using this table to find what the dose rate was during the exposure—as will be described later.

TABLE USED TO FIND DOSE RATES (R/HR FROM KFM READINGS

*DIFFERENCE BETWEEN THE READING BEFORE EXPOSURE AND THE READING AFTER EXPOSURE (8 PLY STANDARD FOIL LEAVES)

DIFF.* IN READINGS	TIME INTERVAL OF AN EXPOSURE 15 SEC. R/HR	1 MIN. R/HR	4 MIN. R/HR	16 MIN. R/HR	1 HR. R/HR
2 mm	6.2	1.6	0.4	0.1	0.03
4 mm	12.	3.1	0.8	0.2	0.06
6 mm	19.	4.6	1.2	0.3	0.08
8 mm	25.	6.2	1.6	0.4	0.10
10 mm	31.	7.7	2.0	0.5	0.13
12 mm	37.	9.2	2.3	0.6	0.15
14 mm	43.	11.	2.7	0.7	0.18

Instructions on how to use a KFM are given after those detailing how to make and charge this fallout meter.

To get a clearer idea of the construction and use of a KFM, look carefully at the following photos and read their captions.

A. An Uncharged KFM. The charging wire has been pulled to one side by its adjustment-thread. This photo was taken looking straight down at the upper edges of the two flat, 8-ply aluminum leaves. At this angle the leaves are barely visible, hanging vertically side by side directly under the zero mark, touching each other and with their ends even. Their suspension-threads insulate the leaves. These threads are almost parallel and touch (but do not cross) each other where they extend over the top of the rim of the can.

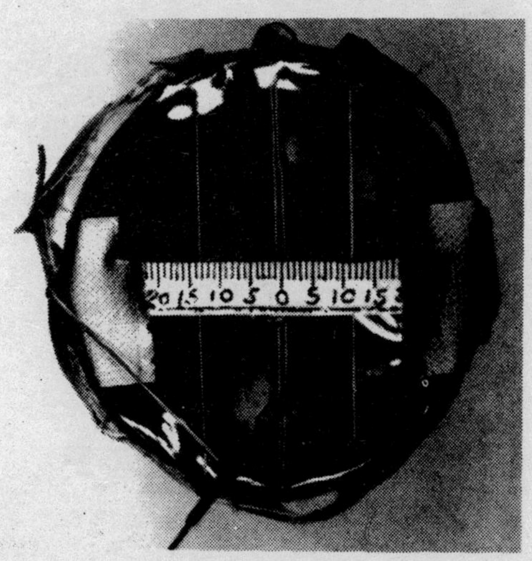

B. Charging a KFM by a Spark-Gap Discharge from a Tape That Has Been Electrostatically Charged by Being Unwound Quickly. Note that the charged tape is moved so that its surface is perpendicular to the charging-wire.

The high-voltage electrostatic charge on the unwound tape (that is an insulator) jumps the spark-gap between the tape and the upper end of the charging-wire, and then flows down the charging-wire to charge the insulated aluminum-foil leaves of the KFM. (Since the upper edges of the two leaves are ¾ inch below the scale and this is a photo taken at an angle, both leaves appear to be under the right side of the scale.)

C. A Charged KFM. Note the separation of the upper edges of its two leaves. The charging-wire has been raised to an almost horizontal position so that its lower end is too far above the aluminum leaves to permit electrical leakage from the leaves back up the charging-wire and into the outside air.

Also note the SEAT, a piece of pencil taped to the right side of the can, opposite the charging wire.

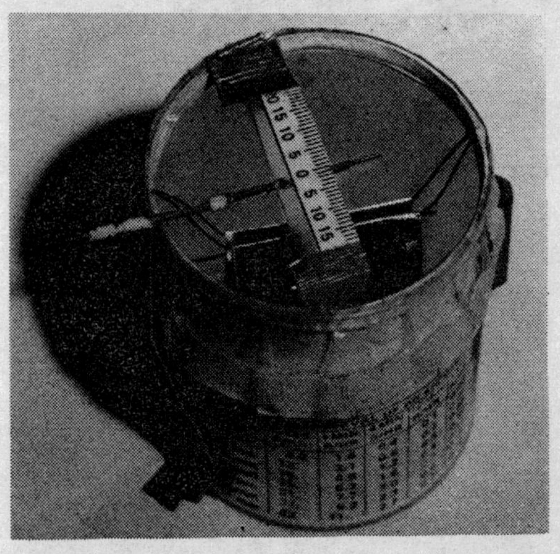

D. Reading a KFM. A 12-inch ruler rests on the SEAT and is held vertical, while the reader's eyebrow touches the upper end of the ruler. The lower edge of the right leaf is under 8 on the scale and the lower edge of the left leaf is under 6 on the scale, giving a KFM reading of 14.

For accurate radiation measurements, a KFM should be placed on an approximately horizontal surface, but the charges on its two leaves and their displacements do not have to be equal.

NOTE: In these photos, the paper scale is taped to the top of the transparent plastic-film cover. It is better to tape the scale to the under side of the cover, where it is less likely to be damaged.

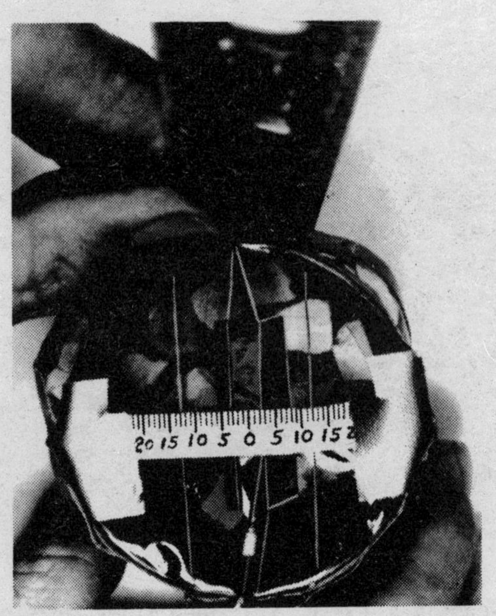

V. Materials Needed

A. For the KFM: (In the following list, when more than one alternative material is given, the **best** material is listed first.)

1. Any type metal can, approximately 2-9/16 inches in diameter inside and 2-7/8 inches high inside, washed clean with soap. (This is the size of a standard 8-ounce can. Since most soup cans, pop cans, and beer cans also are about 2-9/16 inches in diameter inside, the required size of can also can be made by cutting down the height of more widely available cans—as described in Section IX of these instructions.)

2. Standard aluminum foil—2 square feet. (In 1986, 2 square feet of widely sold U.S. brands of aluminum foil weighed between 8.0 and 8.5 grams. One gram equals 0.035 ounce.) (If only "Heavy Duty" or "Extra Heavy Duty" aluminum foil is available, make 5-ply leaves rather than 8-ply leaves of standard foil; the resultant fallout meter will be almost as accurate.)

3. Doorbell-wire, or other light insulated wire (preferably but not necessarily a single-strand wire) inside the insulation—6 inches.

4. Any type of clean lightweight thread that has not been anti-static treated will serve. In 1986 the best widely available excellent insulating thread is unwaxed dental floss: floss is not anti-static treated. Most unwaxed dental floss is too thick and stiff for properly suspending KFM leaves, but, since dental floss is not a twisted thread, you can make flexible strand-threads from it. Make each no more than one-quarter as thick as the floss, and about 12 inches long. First separate several strands at the end of the floss outside its dispenser. Then separate strands while pulling one way on the end of the strand-thread that you want and the other way on the unwanted strands. Use only

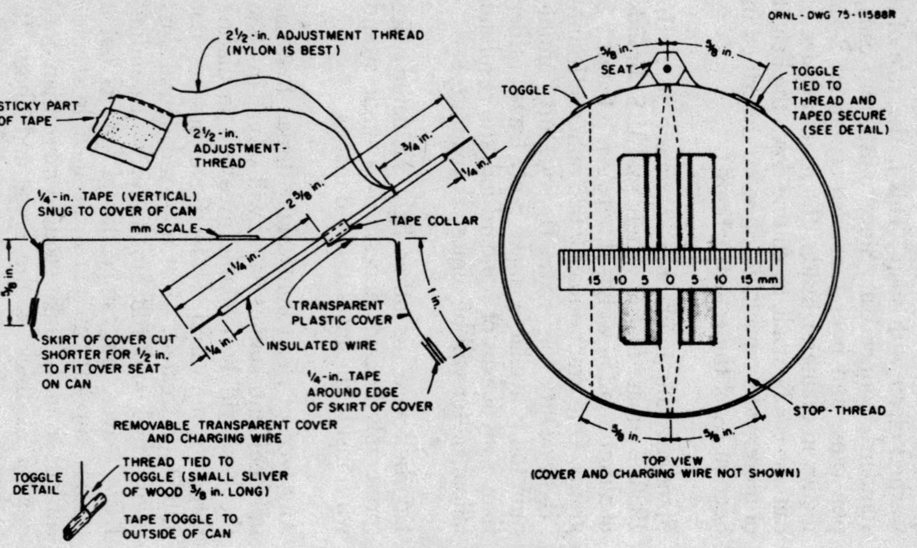

(This is not a Full Scale Drawing).

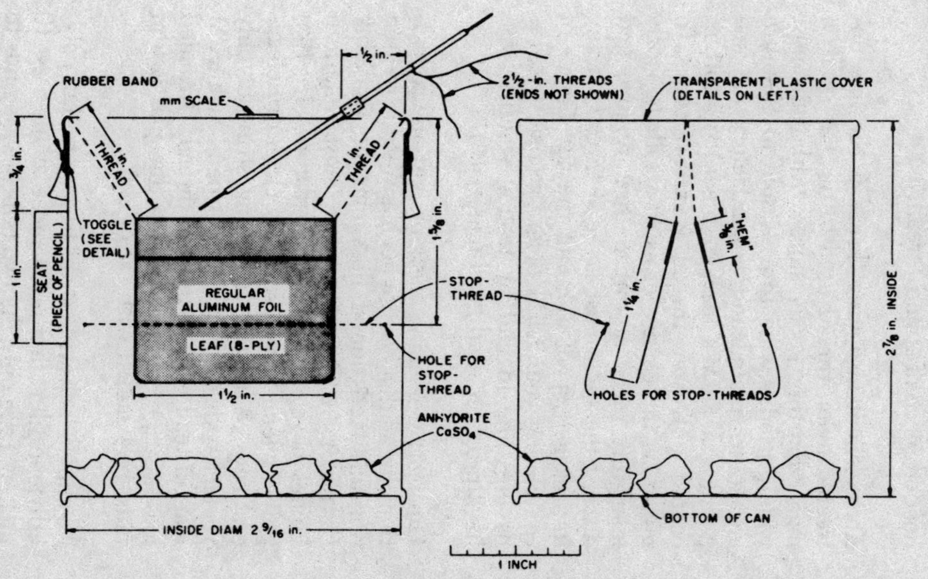

(This is not a Full Scale Drawing).

a clean needle to touch and separate the approximately 6-inch-long central part of the needed piece of strand-thread.

An excellent insulating thread is the fine untreated nylon thread used to tie flies, sold in many sporting goods stores. Although most widely used sewing threads sold in 1986 are anti-static treated and unsatisfactory for suspending a KFM's leaves, some 1986 cotton-coated polyester thread is satisfactory. To minimize the chance of using a soiled, poorly insulating piece of thread, first remove and discard the outermost layer of thread on any unpackaged spool. (One of the advantages of completing your KFM before a crisis arises is having time to find by testing whether you have properly used good materials.)

During a worsening crisis or post-attack, neither thread that has not been anti-static treated nor unwaxed dental floss may be available for making KFMs. However, most American homes have an excellent insulator, very thin polyethylene film—especially clean dry cleaners' bags. A narrow insulating strip cut only 1⁄16-inch wide can be used to suspend each KFM leaf, instead of an insulating thread. (Installed leaves suspended on strips of thin plastic film must be handled with care.)

To cut 1⁄16-inch-wide strips from very thin polyethylene film, first cut a piece about 6 × 10 inches. Tape only the two 6-inch-wide ends to a piece of paper (such as a brown grocery bag), so that the film is held flat and smooth on the paper. Make 10 marks, 1⁄16-inch apart, on each of the two tapes that are holding the film. Place a light so that its reflection on the film enables you to see the edge of the film that you are preparing to cut. Then use a very sharp, **clean** knife or **clean** razor blade, guided by the edge of a firmly held ruler, to cut 9 strips, of which you will select the best two. When cutting, hold the knife **almost horizontal,** with the **plane of its blade perpendicular** to the taped-down film. Throughout this procedure avoid touching the center parts of the strips.

5. A piece of clear plastic film—a 6 × 6 inch square. Clear vinyl (4 mils thick) used for stormproofing windows is best, but any reasonably stout and clear plastic will serve. The strong clear plastic used to wrap pieces of cheese, if washed with hot water and soap, is good. Do not use weak plastic or cellophane. Plastic film made from cellulose (such as Flex-O-Pane) and roasting bags are too permeable to water vapor.

6. Cloth duct tape ("silver tape"), or masking tape, or freezer tape, or Scotch-type tape—about 10 square inches. (A roll of Scotch Magic Transparent Tape, if available, should be saved for use in charging the KFM).

7. Band-Aid tape, or masking tape, or freezer tape, or Scotch transparent tape, or other thin and very flexible tapes—about 2 square inches.

8. Gypsum wallboard (sheetrock)—about ½ square foot, best about ½ inch thick. (To make the essential drying agent.)

9. Glue—not essential, but useful to replace Band-Aid and other thin tapes. "One hour" epoxy is best. Model airplane cement is satisfactory.

10. An ordinary wooden pencil and a small toothpick (or split a small sliver of wood).

11. Two strong rubber bands, or string.

12. Several small, transparent plastic bags, such as sandwich bags, to cover the KFM when it is exposed where fallout particles may get on it and contaminate it. Or pieces of thin, transparent plastic film, such as that from bread bags. Also small rubber bands, or string.

B. For the Charging Devices:

1. Most hard plastic rubbed on **dry** paper. This is the best method.

    a. Plexiglas and most other hard plastics, such as are used in draftsmen's triangles, common smooth plastic rulers, etc.—at least 6 inches long.

    b. **Dry** paper—Tough paper, such as clean, strong grocery-bag or typing paper. Tissue paper, newspaper, or facial tissue such as Kleenex, or toilet paper are satisfactory for charging, but not as durable.

2. Scotch Magic Transparent Tape (¾ inch width is best), or Scotch Transparent Tape, or P.V.C. (Polyvinyl chloride) insulating electrical tapes, or a few of the other common brands of Scotch-type tapes. (Some plastic tapes do not develop sufficiently high-voltage electrostatic charges when unrolled quickly.) This method cannot be used for charging a KFM inside a dry-bucket, needed for charging when the air is very humid.

C. For Determining Dose Rates and Recording Doses Received:

1. A watch with a second hand.

2. A flashlight or other light, for reading the KFM in a dark shelter or at night.

3. Pencil and paper—preferably a notebook.

D. For the Dry-Bucket: (A KFM must be charged inside a dry-bucket if the air is very humid, as it often is inside a crowded, long-occupied shelter lacking adequate forced ventilation.)

1. A large bucket, pot, or can, preferably with a top diameter of at least 11 inches.

2. Clear plastic (best is 4-mil-thick clear plastic used for storm windows). A square piece 5 inches wider on a side than the diameter of the bucket to be used.

3. Cloth duct tape, one inch wide and 8 feet long (or 4 ft., if 2 inches wide). Or 16 ft. of freezer tape one inch wide.

4. Two plastic bags 14 to 16 inches in circumference, such as ordinary plastic bread bags. The original length of these bags should be at least 5 inches greater than the height of the bucket.

5. About one square foot of wall board (sheetrock), to make anhydrite drying agent.

6. Two 1-quart Mason jars or other airtight containers, one in which to store anhydrite and another in which to keep dry the KFM charging devices.

7. Strong rubber bands—enough to make a loop around the bucket. Or string.

VI. Useful but not Essential Materials

(Which Could be Obtained Before a Crisis)

1. An airtight container (such as a large peanut butter jar) with a mouth at least 4 inches wide, in which to keep a KFM, along with some drying agent, when it is not being used. Keeping a KFM very dry greatly extends the time during which the drying agent **inside** the KFM remains effective.

2. Commercial anhydrite with a color indicator, such as the drying agent Drierite. This granular form of anhydrite remains light blue as long as it is effective as a drying agent; it turns pink when it becomes ineffective. Or use silica gel with color indicator, that is dark blue when effective and that turns light pink when it becomes ineffective. Heating in a hot oven or in a can over a fire reactivates them as drying agents and restores their blue color. Obtainable from laboratory supply sources. Use enough to cover the bottom of the KFM's can no more than ½ inch deep.

3. Four square feet of aluminum foil, to make a moisture-proof cover for the dry-bucket.

VII. Tools Needed

Small nail—sharpened
Stick, or a wooden tool handle
(best 2-2½ inch diameter and at least 12 inches long)
Hammer
Pliers
Scissors
Needle—quite a large sewing needle, but less than 2½ inches long
Knife with a small blade—sharp
Ruler (12 inches)
Desirable but not essential tools: a file and a fine-toothed hacksaw blade.

VIII. Make the Drying Agent

(The Easiest Part to Make, but Time Consuming)

1. For a KFM to measure radiation accurately, the air inside its ionization chamber must be kept **very dry.** An excellent drying agent (anhydrite) can be made by heating the gypsum in ordinary gypsum wallboard (sheetrock). Do NOT use calcium chloride.

2. Take a piece of gypsum wallboard approximately 12 inches by 6 inches, and preferably with its gypsum about ⅜ inches thick. Cut off the paper and glue, easiest done by first wetting the paper. [Since water vapor from normal air penetrates the plastic cover of a KFM and can dampen the anhydrite and make it ineffective in as short a time as two days, fresh batches of anhydrite must be made before the attack and kept ready inside the shelter for replacement. The useful life of the drying

agent inside a KFM can be greatly lengthened by keeping the KFM inside an airtight container (such as a peanut butter jar with a 4-inch-diameter mouth) with some drying agent, when the KFM is not being used.]

3. Break the white gypsum filling into small pieces and make the largest no more than ½ in. across. (The tops of pieces larger than this may be too close to the aluminum foil leaves.) If the gypsum is dry, using a pair of pliers makes breaking it easier. Make the largest **side** of the largest pieces no bigger than this.

4. Dry gypsum is **not** a drying agent. To drive the water out of the gypsum molecules and produce the drying agent (anhydrite), heat the gypsum in an oven at its **highest** temperature (which should be above 400 degrees F) for one hour. Heat the gypsum after placing the small pieces no more than two pieces deep in a pan. Or heat the pieces over a fire for 20 minutes or more in a pan or can heated to a dull red.

5. If sufficient aluminum foil and time are available, it is best to heat the gypsum and store the anhydrite as follows:

   a. So that the right amount of anhydrite can be taken quickly out of its storage jar, put enough pieces of gypsum in a can with the same diameter as the KFM, measuring out a batch of gypsum that almost covers the bottom of the can with a single layer.

b. Cut a piece of aluminum foil about 8 in. × 8 in. square, and fold up its edges to form a bowl-like container in which to heat one batch of gypsum pieces.

c. Measure out 10 or 12 such batches, and put each batch in its aluminum foil "bowl."

d. Heat all of these filled "bowls" of gypsum in hottest oven for one hour.

e. As soon as the aluminum foil is cool enough to touch, fold and crumple the edges of each aluminum foil "bowl" together, to make a rough aluminum-covered "ball" of each batch of anhydrite.

f. Promptly seal the batches in airtight jars or other airtight containers, and keep containers closed except when taking out an aluminum-covered "ball."

6. Since anhydrite absorbs water from the air very rapidly, quickly put it in a **dry** airtight container while it is still quite hot. A Mason jar is excellent.

7. To place anhydrite in a KFM, drop in the pieces one by one, being careful not to hit the leaves or the stop-threads. The pieces should almost cover the bottom of the can, with no piece on top of other pieces.

8. To remove anhydrite from a KFM, use a pair of scissors or tweezers as forceps, holding them in a vertical position and not touching the leaves.

IX. Make the Ionization Chamber of the KFM

(To Avoid Mistakes and Save Time, Read All of This Section ALOUD Before Beginning Work.)

1. Remove the paper label (if any) from an ordinary 8-ounce can from which the top has been smoothly cut. Wash the can with soap and water and dry it. (An 8-ounce can has an inside diameter of about 2-9/16 inches and an inside height of about 2-7/8 inches.)

2. Skip to step 3 if an 8-ounce can is available. If an 8-ounce can is not available, reduce the height of any other can having an inside diameter of about 2-9/16 inches (such as most soup cans, most pop cans, or most beer cans). To cut off the top part of a can, first measure and mark the line on which to cut. Then to keep from bending the can while cutting, wrap newspaper tightly around a stick or a round wooden tool handle, so that the wood is covered with 20 to 30 thicknesses of paper and the diameter (ideally) is only slightly less than the diameter of the can.

   One person should hold the can over the paper-covered stick while a second person cuts the can little by little along the marked cutting line. If leather gloves are available, wear them. To cut the can off smoothly, use a file, or use a hacksaw drawn backwards along the cutting line. Or cut the can with a sharp, short blade of a pocketknife by: (1) repeatedly stabbing downward vertically through the can into the paper, and (2) repeatedly making a cut about 1/4 inch long by moving the knife into a sloping position, while keeping its point still pressed into the paper covering the stick.

Next, smooth the cut edge, and cover it with small pieces of freezer tape or other flexible tape.

3. Cut out the PAPER PATTERN TO WRAP AROUND KFM CAN. (Cut one pattern out of Pattern Page A.) Glue (or tape) this pattern to the can, starting with one of the two short sides of the pattern. Secure this starting short side directly over the side seam of the can. Wrap the pattern snugly around the can, gluing or taping it securely as it is being wrapped. (If the pattern is too wide to fit flat between the rims of the can, trim a little off its lower edge.)

4. Sharpen a small nail, by filing or rubbing on concrete, for use as a punch to make the four holes needed to install the stop-threads in the ionization chamber (the can). (The stop-threads are insulators that stop the charged aluminum leaves from touching the can and being discharged.)

5. Have one person hold the can over a horizontal stick or a round wooden tool-handle, that ideally has a diameter about as large as the diameter of the can. Then a second person can use the sharpened nail and a hammer to punch four very small holes through the sides of the can at the points shown by the four crosses on the pattern. Make these holes just large enough to run a needle through them, and then move the needle in the holes so as to bend back the obstructing points of metal.

6. The stop-threads can be installed by using a needle to thread a single thread through all four holes. Use a **very clean** thread, preferably nylon, and do not touch the parts of this thread that will be inside the can and will serve as the insulating stop-threads. Soiled threads are poor insulators. (See illustrations.)

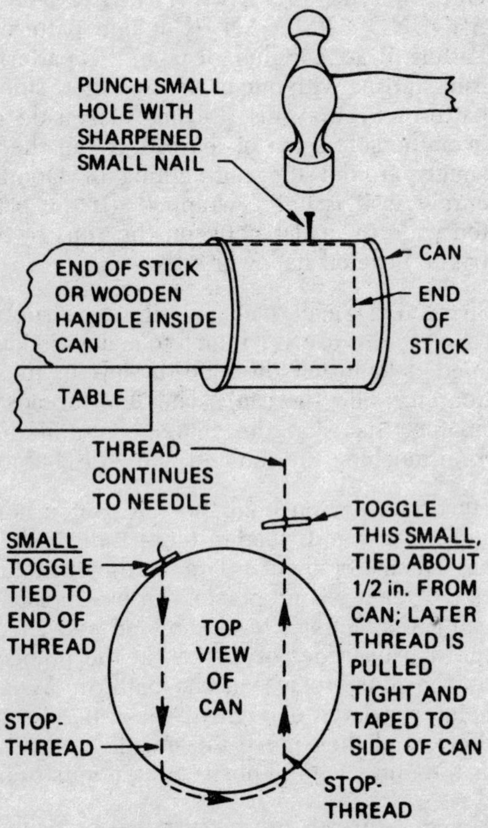

SINGLE THREAD THREADED THROUGH 4 HOLES
TO MAKE 2 STOP-THREADS

PATTERN (A)

The paper patterns on the next two pages are the exact size for a KFM. These patterns should be cut out and glued together so that their center lines align exactly. Each page has an overlap area to make this easier. Once glued together this pattern should be wrapped around a KFM can and glued or taped securely to it. *Caution:* Xerox copies of these patterns may be too large.

PATTERN A

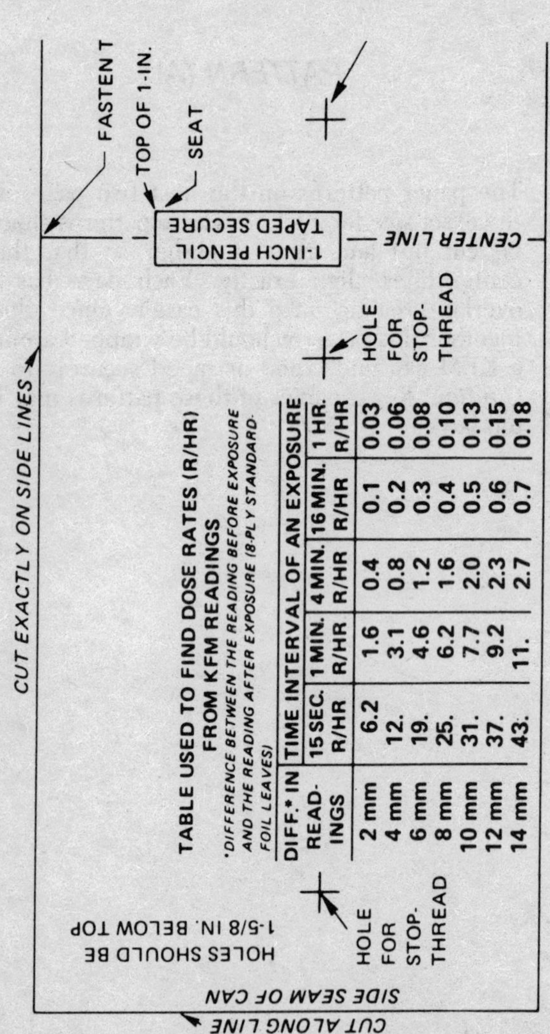

TABLE USED TO FIND DOSE RATES (R/HR) FROM KFM READINGS

*DIFFERENCE BETWEEN THE READING BEFORE EXPOSURE AND THE READING AFTER EXPOSURE (8-PLY STANDARD-FOIL LEAVES)

DIFF.* IN READINGS	TIME INTERVAL OF AN EXPOSURE				
	15 SEC. R/HR	1 MIN. R/HR	4 MIN. R/HR	16 MIN. R/HR	1 HR. R/HR
2 mm	6.2	1.6	0.4	0.1	0.03
4 mm	12.	3.1	0.8	0.2	0.06
6 mm	19.	4.6	1.2	0.3	0.08
8 mm	25.	6.2	1.6	0.4	0.10
10 mm	31.	7.7	2.0	0.5	0.13
12 mm	37.	9.2	2.3	0.6	0.15
14 mm	43.	11.	2.7	0.7	0.18

PATTERN A

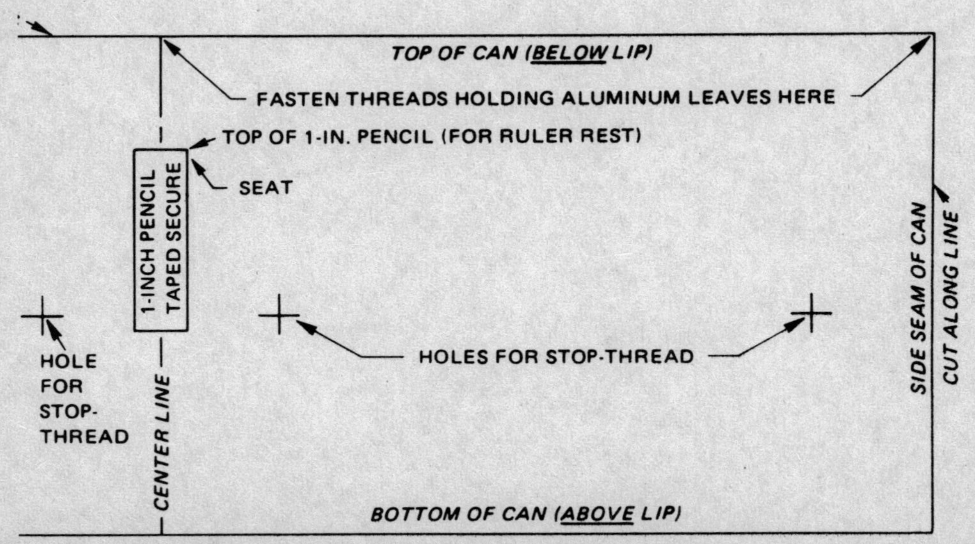

TOP OF CAN (BELOW LIP)
FASTEN THREADS HOLDING ALUMINUM LEAVES HERE
TOP OF 1-IN. PENCIL (FOR RULER REST)
SEAT
1-INCH PENCIL
TAPED SECURE
HOLES FOR STOP-THREAD
HOLE
FOR
STOP-
THREAD
CENTER LINE
SIDE SEAM OF CAN
CUT ALONG LINE
BOTTOM OF CAN (ABOVE LIP)

Before threading the thread through the four holes, tie a **small** toggle (see the preceding sketch) to the long end of the thread. (This toggle can easily be made of a very small sliver of wood cut about ⅜ in. long.) After the thread has been pulled through the four holes, attach a second toggle to the thread, about ½ inch from the part of the thread that comes out of the fourth hole. Then the thread can be pulled tightly down the side of the can and the second small toggle can be taped securely in place to the side of the can. (If the thread is taped down without a toggle, it is likely to move under the tape.)

The first toggle and all of the four holes also should be covered with tape, to prevent air from leaking into the can after it has been covered and is being used as an ionization chamber.

X. Make Two Separate 8-Ply Leaves of Standard [Not Heavy Duty*] Aluminum Foil

Proceed as follows to make each leaf:

1. Cut out a piece of standard aluminum foil approximately 4 inches by 8 inches.

2. Fold the aluminum foil to make a 2-ply (=2 thicknesses) sheet approximately 4 inches by 4 inches.

---

*If only heavy duty aluminum foil (sometimes called "extra heavy duty") is available, make 5-ply leaves of the same size, and use the table for the 8-ply KFM to determine radiation dose rates. To make a 5-ply leaf, start by cutting out a piece of foil approximately 4 inches by 4 inches. Fold it to make a 4-ply sheet approximately 2 inches by 2 inches, with one corner exactly square. Next from a single thickness of foil cut a square approximately 2 inches by 2 inches. Slip this square into a 4-ply sheet, thus making a 5-ply sheet. Then make the 5-ply leaf, using the FINISHED-LEAF PATTERN, etc. as described for making an 8-ply leaf.

3. Fold this 2-ply sheet to make a 4-ply sheet approximately 2 inches by 4 inches.

4. Fold this 4-ply sheet to make an 8-ply sheet (8 sheets thick) approximately 2 inches by 2 inches, being **sure** that the two halves of the second-fold edge are exactly together. This third folding makes an 8-ply aluminum foil sheet with **one corner exactly square.**

5. **Cut out** the FINISHED-LEAF PATTERN, found on the following Pattern Page B. Note that this pattern is **NOT** a square and that it is **smaller** than the 8-ply sheet. Flatten the 8 thicknesses of aluminum foil with the fingers until they appear to be a single thin, flat sheet.

6. Hold the FINISHED-LEAF PATTERN **on top of** the 8-ply aluminum foil sheet, with the pattern's THIRD-FOLD EDGE on top of the third-fold edge of the 8-ply aluminum sheet. Be sure that one lower **corner** of the FINISHED-LEAF PATTERN is on top of the **exactly square corner** of the 8-ply aluminum sheet.

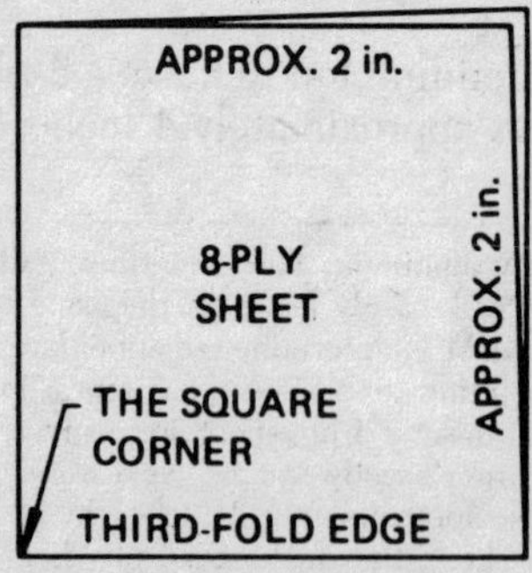

7. While holding a straight edge along the THREAD LINE of the pattern, press with a sharp pencil so as to make a shallow groove for the THREAD LINE on the 8-ply aluminum sheet. Also using a sharp pencil, trace around the top and side of the pattern, so as to indent (groove) the 8-ply foil.

8. Remove the pattern and cut out the 8-ply aluminum foil leaf. Then, in order to prevent possible excessive electrical discharge from overly sharp points on the lower corners of the leaf, cut about 1/16-inch (▲) off each of its two lower corners.

9. While holding a straight edge along the indented THREAD LINE, lift up the OPEN EDGE of the 8-ply sheet (keeping all 8 plies together) until this edge is vertical, as illustrated. Remove the straight edge, and fold the 8-ply aluminum along the THREAD LINE so as to make a **flat-folded** hem.

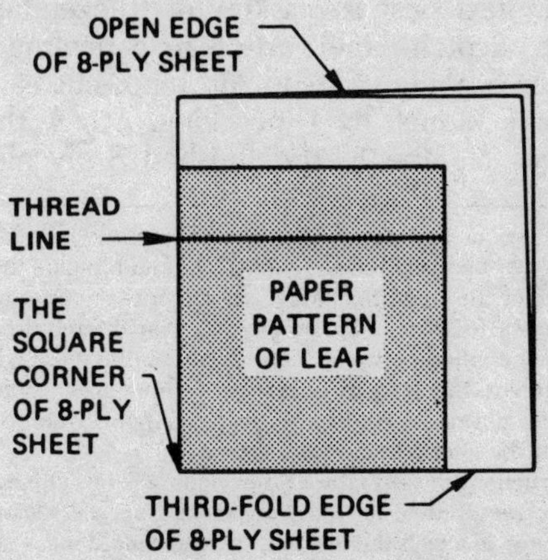

10. Open the flat-folded hem of the finished leaf until the 8-ply leaf is almost flat again, as shown by the pattern, from which the FINISHED-LEAF PATTERN has already been cut.

11. Prepare to attach the aluminum-foil leaf to the thread that will suspend it inside the KFM.

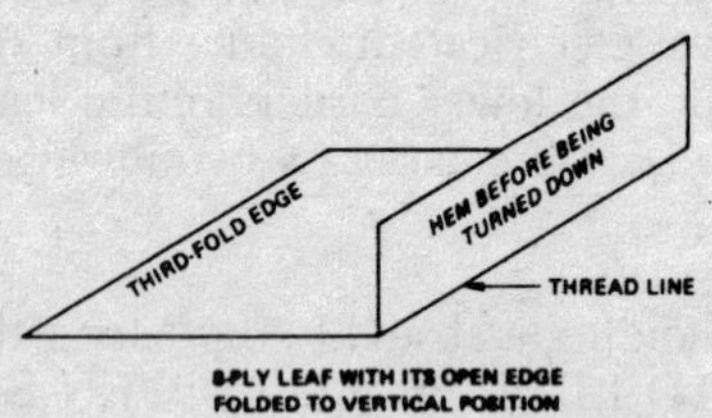

8-PLY LEAF WITH ITS OPEN EDGE FOLDED TO VERTICAL POSITION

If no epoxy glue* is available to hold down the hem and prevent the thread from slipping in the hem, cut two pieces of tape (Band-Aid tape is best; next best is masking or freezer tape; next best, Scotch tape). After first peeling off the paper backing of Band-Aid tape, cut each piece of tape ⅛ inch by 1 inch long. Attach these two pieces of tape to the finished 8-ply aluminum

---

*If using epoxy or other glue, use only a **very** little to hold down the hem, to attach the thread securely to the leaf and to glue together any open edges of the plied foil. Most convenient is "one hour" epoxy, applied with a toothpick. Model airplane cement requires hours to harden when applied between sheets of aluminum foil. To make sure no glue stiffens the free thread beyond the upper corners of the finished leaf, put no glue within ¼ inch of a point where thread will go out from the folded hem of the leaf.

The instructions in step 11 are for persons lacking "one hour" epoxy or the time required to dry other types of glue. Persons using glue instead of tape to attach the leaf to its thread should make appropriate use of the pattern on the following page and of some of the procedures detailed in steps 12 through 18.

leaf with the sticky sides up, except for their ends. As shown by the pattern on the following pattern page, secure ⅛ inch of one end of a tape strip near one corner of the 8-ply aluminum foil leaf by first turning under this ⅛-inch end; that is, with this end's sticky side down. Then turn under the other ⅛-inch-long end, and attach this end below the THREAD LINE. **Slant** each tape strip as illustrated on Pattern (C).

Be sure you have read through step 18 before you do anything else.

12. Cut an 8-½ inch piece of fine, unwaxed, **very clean** thread that has not been anti-static treated. See INSTRUCTIONS, Pages 149 and 152 for excellent insulating threads and substitutes. In 1986 most sewing threads are anti-static treated and are too poor insulators for use in a KFM.

    Cut out Pattern (C), the guide sheet used when attaching a leaf to its suspending thread. Then tape Pattern (C) to the top of a work table. Cover the two "TAPE HERE" rectangles on Pattern (C) with pieces of tape, each piece the size of the rectangle. Then cut two other pieces of tape each the same size and use them to **tape the thread ONTO the guide sheet,** on top of the "TAPE HERE" rectangles.

    Be very careful **not to touch** the two 1-inch parts of the thread next to the outline of the finished leaf, since oil and dirt even on clean fingers will reduce the electrical insulating value of the thread between the leaf and the top rim of the can.

PATTERN (B)

PATTERN FOR CLEAR-PLASTIC COVER FOR KFM CAN

The paper patterns on the next two pages are the exact size for the clear plastic cover for a KFM can. Cut out these patterns and glue them together so that the center line between the two leaves aligns exactly. Overlap areas on both pages should make this easier.

Caution: Xerox copies may be slightly too large.

PATTERN (B)

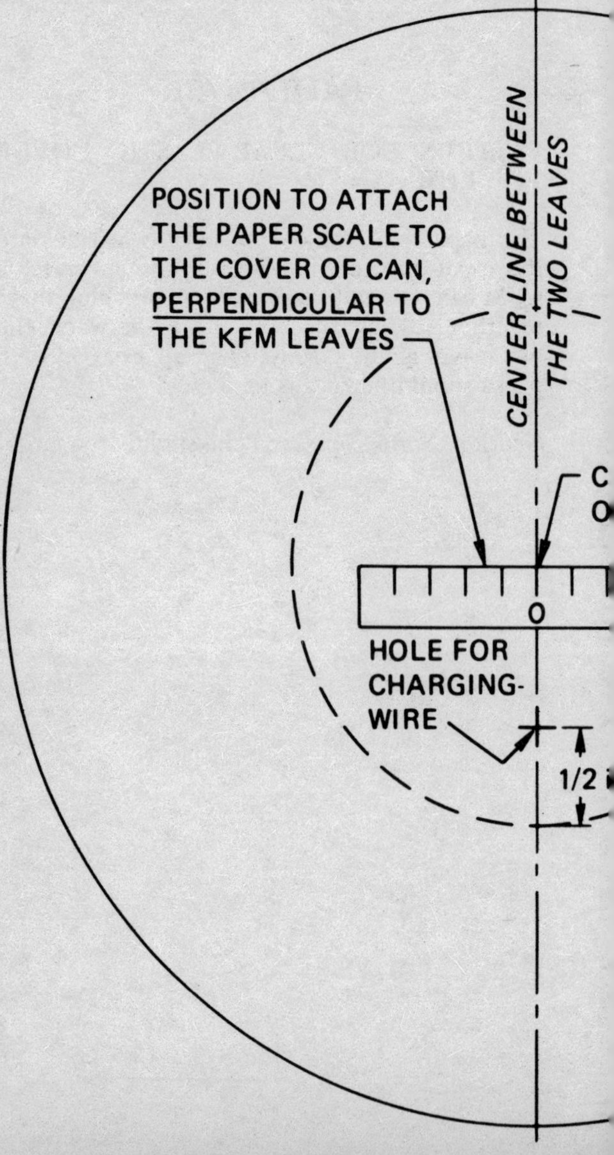

CENTER LINE BETWEEN THE TWO LEAVES

POSITION TO ATTACH THE PAPER SCALE TO THE COVER OF CAN, PERPENDICULAR TO THE KFM LEAVES

C
O

0

HOLE FOR CHARGING-WIRE

1/2

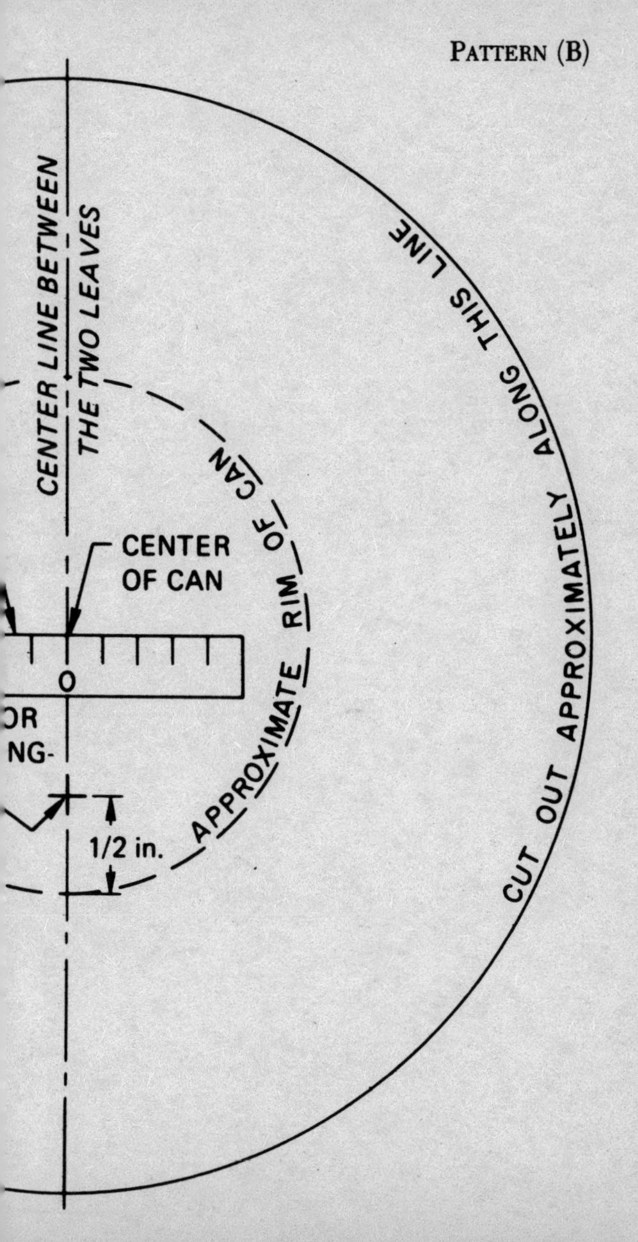
CENTER LINE BETWEEN
THE TWO LEAVES
CENTER
OF CAN
O
OR
NG-
1/2 in.
APPROXIMATE RIM OF CAN
CUT OUT APPROXIMATELY ALONG THIS LINE

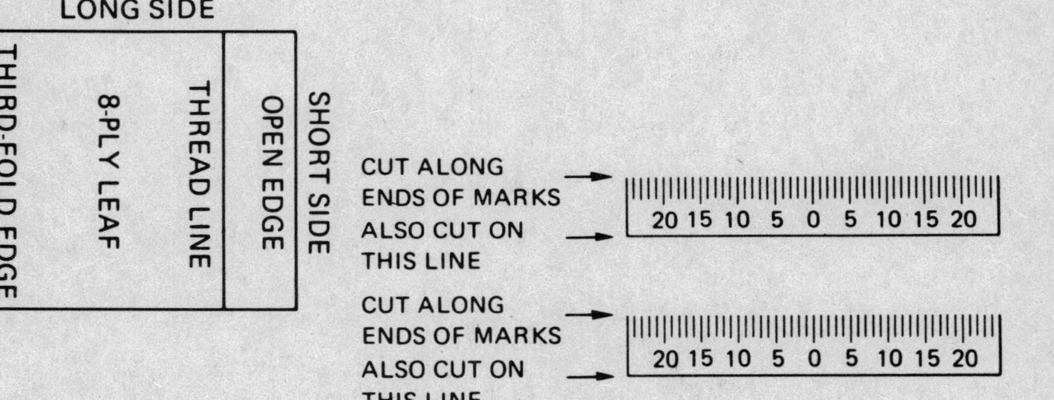

FINISHED-LEAF PATTERN
(CUT OUT EXACTLY ON SIDE LINES)

PAPER SCALE (TO BE CUT OUT)

CAUTION: XEROX COPIES OF THE FINISHED-LEAF AND THE SCALE PATTERNS MAY BE SLIGHTLY TOO LARGE.

13. With the thread still taped to the paper pattern and while slightly lifting the thread with a knife tip held under the center of the thread, slip the finished leaf **under** the thread and into position exactly on the top of the leaf outlined on the pattern page. Hold the leaf in this position with two fingers.

14. While keeping the thread straight between its two taped-down ends, lower the thread so that it sticks to the two plastic strips. Then press the thread against the plastic strips.

15. With the point of the knife, hold down the center of the thread against the center of the THREAD LINE of the leaf. Then, with two fingers, carefully fold over the hem and press it almost flat. Be sure that the thread comes out of the corners of the hem. Remove the knife, and press the hem down completely flat against the rest of the leaf.

16. Make **small** marks on the thread at the two points shown on the pattern page. Use a ballpoint pen if available.

17. Loosen the second two small pieces of tape from the pattern paper, but leave these tapes stuck to the thread.

18. Cut 5 pieces of Band-Aid tape, each approximately ⅛-inch by ¼ inch, this small.

Use 2 of these pieces of tape to secure the centers of the side edges of the leaf. Place the 5

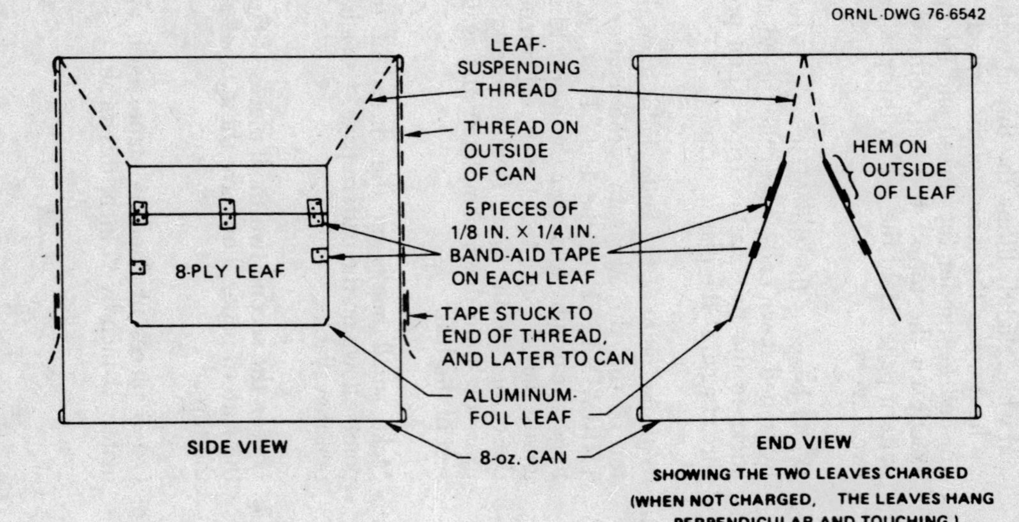
ORNL-DWG 76-6542
LEAF-
SUSPENDING
THREAD
THREAD ON
OUTSIDE
OF CAN
5 PIECES OF
1/8 IN. × 1/4 IN.
BAND-AID TAPE
ON EACH LEAF
8-PLY LEAF
TAPE STUCK TO
END OF THREAD,
AND LATER TO CAN
ALUMINUM-
FOIL LEAF
8-oz. CAN
HEM ON
OUTSIDE
OF LEAF
SIDE VIEW
END VIEW
SHOWING THE TWO LEAVES CHARGED
(WHEN NOT CHARGED, THE LEAVES HANG
PERPENDICULAR AND TOUCHING.)

PATTERN (C)

The paper patterns on the next two pages must be cut out and glued together so that they align exactly. Then tape the entire pattern to the top of a work table. Cover the two "TAPE HERE" rectangles with same-sized pieces of tape, in order to keep from tearing this pattern when removing two additional pieces of tape. Then, by putting two other pieces of tape this same size on top of the first two pieces, tape the thread ONTO this pattern, and later attach a leaf to the taped-down thread.

Warning: The parts of the thread that will be inside the can and on which the leaf will be suspended must serve to insulate the high-voltage electrical charges to be placed on the leaf. Therefore, the suspended parts of the thread *must be kept clean.*

Pattern (C)

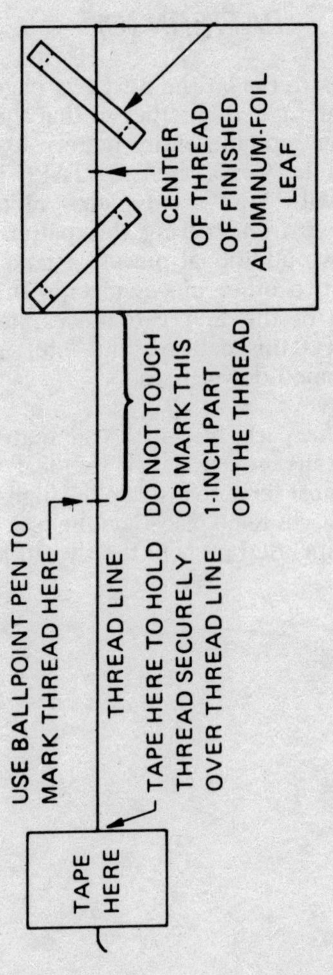
USE BALLPOINT PEN TO
MARK THREAD HERE
THREAD LINE
TAPE HERE TO HOLD
THREAD SECURELY
OVER THREAD LINE
DO NOT TOUCH
OR MARK THIS
1-INCH PART
OF THE THREAD
CENTER
OF THREAD
OF FINISHED
ALUMINUM-FOIL
LEAF
TAPE
HERE

PATTERN (C)

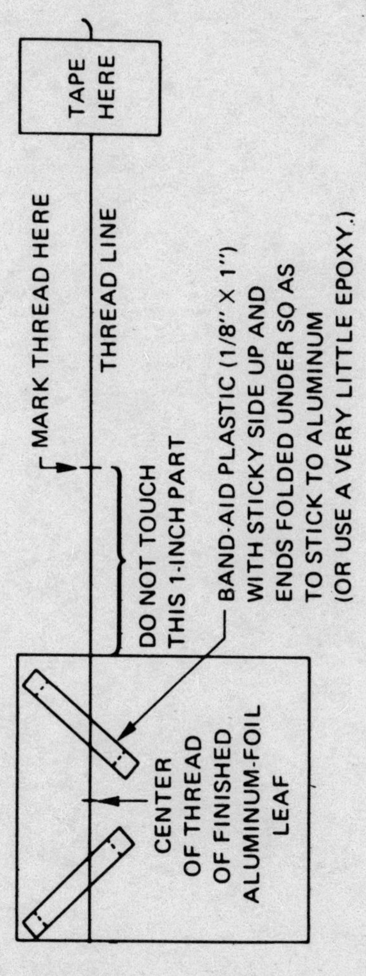

TAPE HERE
MARK THREAD HERE
THREAD LINE
DO NOT TOUCH THIS 1-INCH PART
BAND-AID PLASTIC (1/8" X 1")
WITH STICKY SIDE UP AND
ENDS FOLDED UNDER SO AS
TO STICK TO ALUMINUM
(OR USE A VERY LITTLE EPOXY.)
CENTER OF THREAD OF FINISHED ALUMINUM-FOIL LEAF

pieces as illustrated in the SIDE VIEW sketch. Or use tiny droplets of epoxy, applied with a needle, to secure the side edges and to hold down the hem.

19. To prevent possible partial discharge from overly sharp lower corners of the leaves, use scissors to cut about 1⁄16-inch (▲) off each lower corner of the two leaves. (Partial discharge from an overly sharp corner may prevent a KFM's leaves from being adequately charged and adequately separated.)

20. To make it easier to take accurate readings:

    a. Make a black stripe 1⁄8-inch wide on the hem side of the lower edge of each leaf, if the drying agent to be used is white anhydrite made from gypsum, or light blue Drierite. It is best to use a waterproof marker, such as black Marko by Flair.
    b. Make a white stripe, if the drying agent to be used is dark blue silica gel. Liquid Paper correction fluid, or white ink, serves well.

XI. Install the Aluminum-Foil Leaves

1. In preparation for suspending the leaves inside the can, make two shallow notches in the top of the rim of the can. Make one notch above each of the two lines ("FASTEN THREADS HOLDING ALUMINUM LEAVES HERE") on the paper Pattern attached to the outside of the can. Make flat-bottomed notches by first filing a V-shaped notch, and then using a fine-toothed hacksaw blade to make the notch rectangular. (If a file and/or a hacksaw blade are not available, the leaf-suspending threads can be taped to the top of the rim of the can.)

2. Use the two small pieces of tape stuck to the ends of a leaf-suspending thread to attach the thread to the outside of the can. Attach the tapes on opposite sides of the can, so as to suspend the leaf inside the can. See END VIEW sketch. Each of the two **marks** on the attached thread MUST **rest exactly in a notch** (or on the top of the rim of the can, if you are unable to make notches). Be sure that the hem-side of each of the two leaves will face outward. See END VIEW sketch.

3. Position and secure the second leaf, being sure that:

    a. The smooth sides of the two leaves are not wrinkled or bent and face each other, and are flush (="right together") when not charged. See END VIEW sketch and study the first photo illustration, "An Uncharged KFM."

    b. The upper edges of the two leaves are suspended side by side and at the same distance below the top of the can.

    c. The leaf-suspending threads are in their notches in the top of the rim of the can (or are taped with Band-Aid to the top of the rim of the can) so that putting the cover on will not move the threads.

    d. No parts of the leaf-suspending threads inside the can are taped down to the can or otherwise restricted.

    e. The leaf-suspending parts of the threads inside the can do not cross over, entangle or restrict each other.

f. The threads come together where they go over the rim of the can, and the leaves are flat and hang together as shown in the first photo illustration, "An Uncharged KFM."

g. The leaves look like these photographed leaves. If not, make new, better leaves and install them.

4. Cover with tape the parts of the threads that extend down the **outside** of the can, and also cover with more tape the small pieces of tape near the ends of the threads on the outside of the can. Or use epoxy or other waterproof glue to attach the parts of the threads on the *outside* of the can securely to the can.

5. To make the SEAT, cut a piece of a wooden pencil, or a stick, about one inch long and tape it securely to the side of the can along the center line marked SEAT on the pattern. Be sure the upper end of this piece of pencil is at the same position as the top of the location for the SEAT outlined on the pattern. The top of the SEAT is ¾ inch below the top of the can. Be sure not to cover or make illegible any part of the table printed on the paper pattern.

6. Cut out one of the "Reminders for Operators" and glue and/or tape it to the unused side of the KFM. Then it is best to cover all the sides of the finished KFM with clear plastic tape or varnish. This will keep sticky-tape on the end of an adjustment thread or moisture from damaging the "Reminders" or the table.

XII. Make the Plastic Cover

1. Cut out the paper pattern for the cover from the Pattern Page (B).

2. From a piece of clear, strong plastic, cut a circle approximately the same size as the paper pattern. (Storm-window vinyl film, 4 mils thick, is best.)

3. Stretch the center of this circular piece of clear plastic over the open end of the can, and pull it down close to the sides of the can, making small tucks in the "skirt," so that there are no wrinkles in the top cover. Hold the lower part of the "skirt" in place with a strong rubber band or piece of string. (If another can having the same diameter as the KFM can is available, use it to make the cover—to avoid the possibility of disturbing the leaf-suspending threads.)

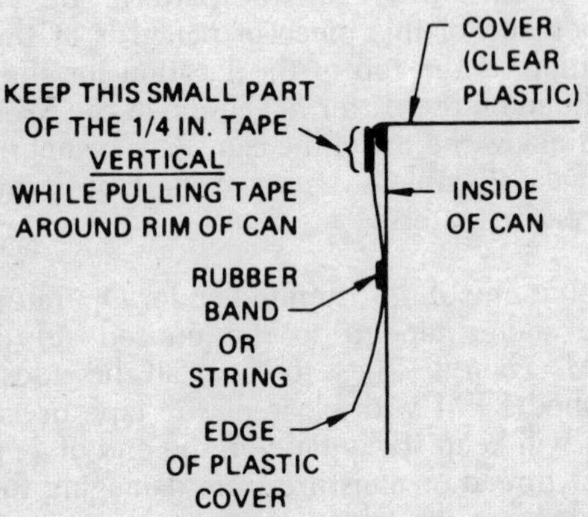

4. Make the cover so it fits snugly, but can be taken off and replaced readily.

REMINDERS FOR OPERATORS

The **drying agent** inside a KFM is O.K. if, when the charged KFM is **not** exposed to radiation, its readings decrease by 1 mm or less in 3 hours.

Reading: With the reading eye 12 inches vertically above the seat, note on the mm scale the separation of the **lower** edges of the leaves. If the right leaf is at 10 mm and the left leaf is at 7 mm, the KFM reads 17 mm. Never take a reading while a leaf is touching a stop-thread. Never use a KFM reading that is less than 5 mm.

Finding a dose rate: If before exposure a KFM reads 17 mm and if after a 1-minute exposure it reads 5 mm, the difference in readings is 12 mm. The attached table shows the dose rate was 9.6 R/hr during the exposure.

Finding a dose: If a person works outside for 3 hours where the dose rate is 2 R/hr, what is his radiation dose? Answer: 3 hr x 2 R/hr = 6 R.

Finding how long it takes to get a certain R dose: If the dose rate is 1.6 R/hr outside and a person is willing to take a 6 R dose, how long can he remain outside? Answer:
6 R ÷ 1.6 R/hr = 3.75 hr =
3 hours and 45 minutes.

Fallout radiation guides for a healthy person not previously exposed to a total radiation dose of more than 100 R during a 2-week period:

6 R per day can be tolerated for up to two months without losing the ability to work.

100 R in a week or less is not likely to seriously sicken.

350 R in a few days results in a 50-50 chance of dying, under post-attack conditions.

600 R in a week or less is almost certain to cause death within a few weeks.

REMINDERS FOR OPERATORS

The **drying agent** inside a KFM is O.K. if, when the charged KFM is **not** exposed to radiation, its readings decrease by 1 mm or less in 3 hours.

Reading: With the reading eye 12 inches vertically above the seat, note on the mm scale the separation of the **lower** edges of the leaves. If the right leaf is at 10 mm and the left leaf is at 7 mm, the KFM reads 17 mm. Never take a reading while a leaf is touching a stop-thread. Never use a KFM reading that is less than 5 mm.

Finding a dose rate: If before exposure a KFM reads 17 mm and if after a 1-minute exposure it reads 5 mm, the difference in readings is 12 mm. The attached table shows the dose rate was 9.6 R/hr during the exposure.

Finding a dose: If a person works outside for 3 hours where the dose rate is 2 R/hr, what is his radiation dose? Answer: 3 hr x 2 R/hr = 6 R.

Finding how long it takes to get a certain R dose: If the dose rate is 1.6 R/hr outside and a person is willing to take a 6 R dose, how long can he remain outside? Answer:
6 R ÷ 1.6 R/hr = 3.75 hr =
3 hours and 45 minutes.

Fallout radiation guides for a healthy person not previously exposed to a total radiation dose of more than 100 R during a 2-week period:

6 R per day can be tolerated for up to two months without losing the ability to work.

100 R in a week or less is not likely to seriously sicken.

350 R in a few days results in a 50-50 chance of dying, under post-attack conditions.

600 R in a week or less is almost certain to cause death within a few weeks.

Just below the top of the rim of the can, bind the covering plastic in place with a ¼-inch-wide piece of strong tape. (Cloth duct tape is best. Use two thicknesses. If only freezer or masking tape is available, use three or four thicknesses.)

Keep vertical the small part of the tape that presses against the rim of the can while pulling the length of the tape horizontally around the can so as to bind the top of the plastic cover snugly to the rim. If this small part of the tape is kept vertical, the lower edge of the tape will not squeeze the plastic below the rim of the can to such a small circumference as to prevent the cover from being removed quite easily.

5. With scissors, cut off the "skirt" of the plastic cover until it extends only about one inch below the top of the rim of the can.

6. Make a notch in the "skirt," about one inch wide, where it fits over the pencil SEAT attached to the can. The "skirt" in this notched area should be only about ⅝ of an inch long, measured down from the top of the rim of the can.

7. Remove the plastic cover, and then tape the lower edges of the "skirt," inside and out, using short lengths of ¼-inch-wide tape. Before securing each short piece of tape, slightly open the tucks that are being taped shut on their edges, so that the "skirt" flares slightly outward and the cover can be readily removed.

8. Make the charging-wire by using the full-size, exact-size pattern.

Doorbell wire with an outside diameter of about 1/16 inch is best, but any lightweight insulated wire, such as part of a lightweight two-wire extension cord split in half, will serve. The illustrated wire is much thicker than bell wire. To stop tape from possibly slipping up or down the wire, use a very little glue.

If a very thin plastic has been used for the cover, a sticky piece of tape may need to be attached to the end of the bare-ended adjustment thread, so both threads can be used to hold the charging wire in a desired position.

The best tape to attach to an end of one of the adjustment-threads is cloth duct tape. A square piece ¾ inch by ¾ inch is the sticky base. To keep this tape sticky (free of paper fibers), the paper on the can should be covered with transparent tape or varnish. A piece about ⅛ inch by ¾ inch serves to stick under one end of the sticky base, to hold the adjustment-thread. A ¾ inch by 1-¼ inch rectangular piece of tape is used to make the finger hold—important for making adjustments inside a dry-bucket.

With a needle or pin, make a hole in the plastic cover ½ inch from the rim of the can and directly above the upper end of the CENTER LINE between the two leaves. The CENTER LINE is marked on the pattern wrapped around the can. Carefully push the CHARGING-WIRE through this hole (thus stretching the hole) until all of the CHARGING-WIRE below its Band-Aid-tape stop is inside the can.

9. From the Pattern Page (B) cut out the SCALE. Then tape the SCALE to the underside of the plastic cover, in the position shown on the pattern for the cover, and also by the drawings.

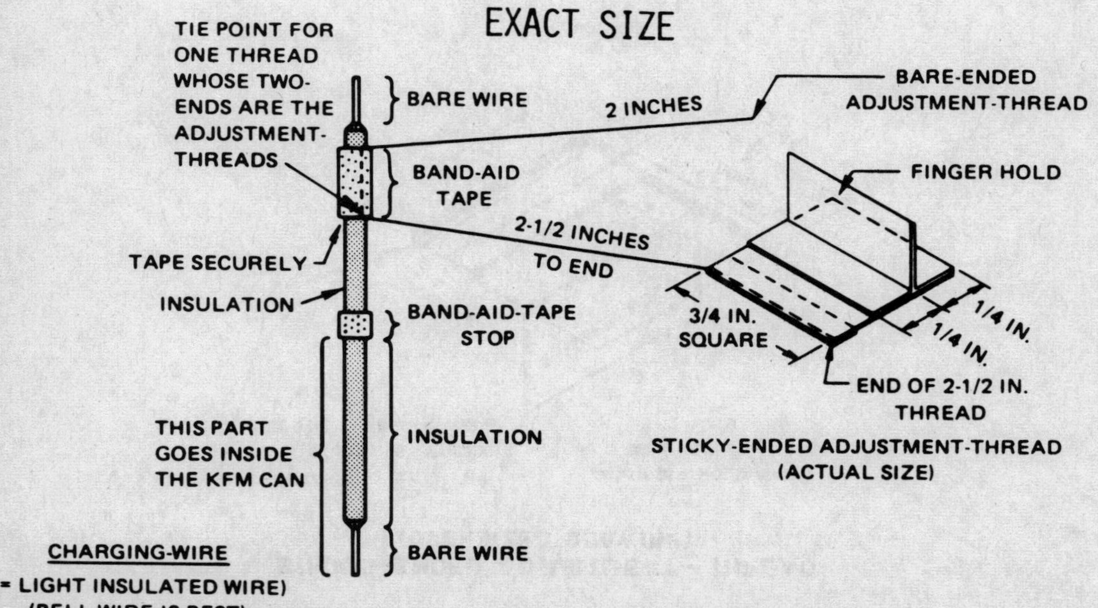
EXACT SIZE
TIE POINT FOR ONE THREAD WHOSE TWO-ENDS ARE THE ADJUSTMENT-THREADS
BARE WIRE
BAND-AID TAPE
TAPE SECURELY
INSULATION
BAND-AID-TAPE STOP
THIS PART GOES INSIDE THE KFM CAN
INSULATION
BARE WIRE
CHARGING-WIRE
(= LIGHT INSULATED WIRE)
(BELL-WIRE IS BEST)
2 INCHES
BARE-ENDED ADJUSTMENT-THREAD
FINGER HOLD
2-1/2 INCHES TO END
3/4 IN. SQUARE
1/4 IN.
1/4 IN.
END OF 2-1/2 IN. THREAD
STICKY-ENDED ADJUSTMENT-THREAD (ACTUAL SIZE)

STICKY—ENDED ADJUSTMENT—THREAD
(OVERSIZED DRAWING)

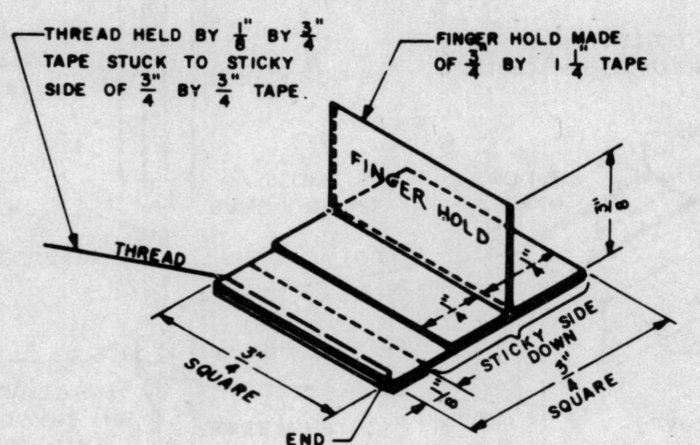

Preferably use transparent tape. Be careful not to cover with tape any of the division lines on the SCALE between 20 on the right and 20 on the left of 0.

10. Put the plastic cover on the KFM can.

XIII. Two Ways to Charge a KFM

When preparing to charge a KFM, be sure its anhydrite is fresh. (Under humid conditions, sometimes in only 2 days enough water vapor will go through the plastic cover to make the drying agent ineffective.) Be sure no piece of anhydrite is on top of another piece. Re-read VIII 7 and VIII 8.

1. Charging a KFM with Hard Plastic Rubbed on **Dry** Paper.

   a. Adjust the charging-wire so that its lower end is about 1⁄16 inch above the upper edges of the aluminum-foil leaves. Use the sticky-tape at the end of one adjustment-thread to hold the charging-wire in this position. Stick this tape approximately in line with the threads suspending the leaves, either on the side of the can or on top of the plastic cover. (If the charging-wire is held loosely by the cover, it may be necessary to put a piece of sticky-tape on the end of each adjustment-thread in order to adjust the charging-wire securely. If a charging-wire is not secure, its lower end may be forced up by the like charge on the leaves before the leaves can be fully charged.)

   b. Select a piece of Plexiglas, a draftsman's plastic triangle, a smooth plastic ruler, or other piece

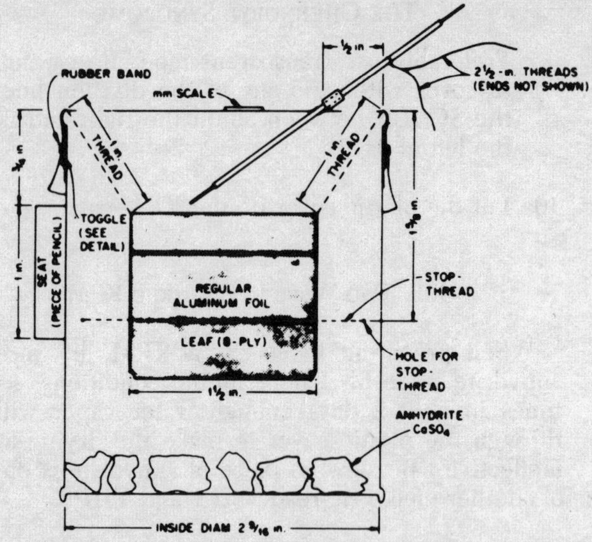

of hard, smooth plastic. (Unfortunately, not all types of hard plastic can be used to generate a sufficient electrostatic charge.) Be sure the plastic is dry.

For charging a KFM (especially inside a dry-bucket), cut a rectangular piece of hard plastic such as Plexiglas about 1-½ by 6 inches. Sharp corners and edges should be smoothed. To avoid contaminating the charging end with sweaty, oily fingers, it is best to mark the other end with a piece of tape, and to hold it only by its taped end.

c. Fold **DRY** paper (a piece of clean paper bag, or other smooth, clean paper) to make an approximate square about 5 inches on a side and 15 to 20 sheets thick. (This many sheets of paper lessens leakage to the fingers of the electrostatic high-voltage charges to be generated on the hard plastic and on the rubbed paper.)

d. Fold the square of paper in the middle, and move the hard plastic rapidly back and forth so that it is rubbed **vigorously** on the paper in the middle of this folded square—while the outside of this folded square of paper is squeezed firmly between thumb and little finger on one side, and the ends of three fingers on the other. To avoid discharging the charge on the plastic to the fingers, keep them away from the edges of the paper. See sketch.

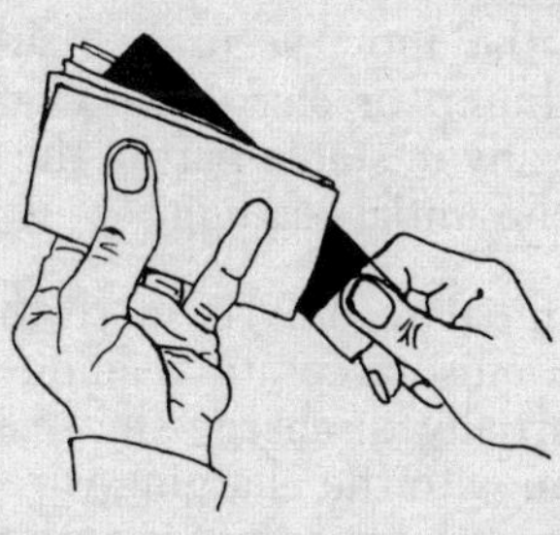

e. Move the electrostatically charged part of the rubbed plastic rather slowly past the upper end of the charging-wire, while looking straight down on the KFM. Keep the hard plastic approximately perpendicular to the charging-wire and about ¼ to ½ inch away from its upper end. The charge jumps the spark gaps and charges the leaves of the KFM. Charge the leaves sufficiently to give a reading of at least 15 mm.

f. Pull down on an insulating adjustment-thread to raise the lower end of the charging-wire. (If the charging-wire has been held in its charging position by its sticky-ended adjustment-thread being stuck to the top of the clear plastic cover, to avoid possibly damaging the threads: (1) pull down a little on the bare-ended adjustment-thread; and (2) detach, pull down on, and secure the sticky-ended adjustment-thread to the side of the can, so as to raise and keep the lower end of the charging-wire close to the underside of the clear plastic cover.) **Do not touch the charging-wire,** because its insulation usually is not good enough to prevent the charge from bleeding off into the fingers.

g. To get the most accurate readings possible, lightly bump or shake the charged KFM (to remove any unstable part of the charge) before taking the initial reading.

h. If the initial reading is more than 20 mm, to get the most accurate reading possible carefully partially discharge the leaves (by touching them with the charging-wire while guiding the wire with your fingers on its insulation), to reduce to 20 mm or slightly less the initial reading that you will use. Or completely discharge, and recharge to 20 mm or slightly less.

i. To keep a KFM in excellent condition and to enable its drying agent to last much longer before becoming ineffective, put the whole KFM in an airtight container, such as a large peanut butter jar, with drying agent about an inch deep on its bottom. Or at least keep the charging paper and the hard plastic charging strip dry in a sealable container, such as a Mason jar, with some drying agent.

2. Charging a KFM from a Quickly Unwound Roll of Tape. (Quick unwinding produces a harmless charge of several thousand volts on the tape.)

a. Adjust the charging-wire so that its lower end is about 1/16 inch above the upper edges of the aluminum-foil leaves. Use the sticky-tape at the end of one adjustment-thread to hold the charging-wire in this position. Stick this tape approximately in line with the leaves, either on the side of the can or on the plastic cover. (If the plastic cover is weak, it may be necessary to put a piece of sticky-tape on the end of each adjustment-thread, in order to hold the charging-wire securely. If a charging-wire is not secure, its lower end may be forced up by the like charge on the leaves before the leaves can be fully charged.)

b. The sketch shows the "GET SET" position, preparatory to unrolling the Scotch Magic Transparent Tape, P.V.C. electrical tape, or other tape. Be sure to first remove the roll from its dispenser. Some of the other kinds of tape will not produce a high enough voltage.

c. **QUICKLY** unroll 10 to 12 inches of tape by pulling its end with the left hand, while the

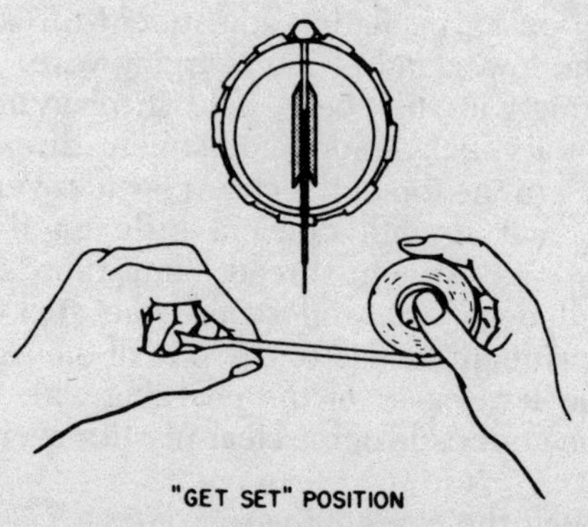

"GET SET" POSITION

right hand allows the roll to unwind while remaining in about the same "GET SET" position only an inch or two away from the KFM.

d. While holding the unwound tape tight, about perpendicular to the charging-wire, and about ¼ inch away from the end of the charging-wire, **promptly** move both hands and the tape to the right **rather slowly**—taking about 2 seconds to move about 8 inches. The electrostatic charge on the unwound tape "jumps" the spark gaps from the tape to the upper end of the charging-wire and from the lower end of the charging-wire to the aluminum leaves, and charges the aluminum leaves.

Be sure neither leaf is touching a stop-thread.

Try to charge the leaves enough to spread them far enough apart to give a reading of at least 15 mm, but no more than 20 mm after the KFM has been gently bumped or shaken to remove any unstable part of the charge.

e. Pull down on an insulating adjustment-thread to raise the lower end of the charging-wire. If the charging-wire has been held in charging position by its sticky-ended adjustment-thread being stuck to the top of the clear plastic cover, it is best first to pull down a little on the bare-ended adjustment-thread, and then to move, pull down on, and secure the sticky-ended adjustment-thread to the side of the can so that the lower part of the charging-wire is close to the underside of the clear plastic cover.

Do not touch the charging-wire.

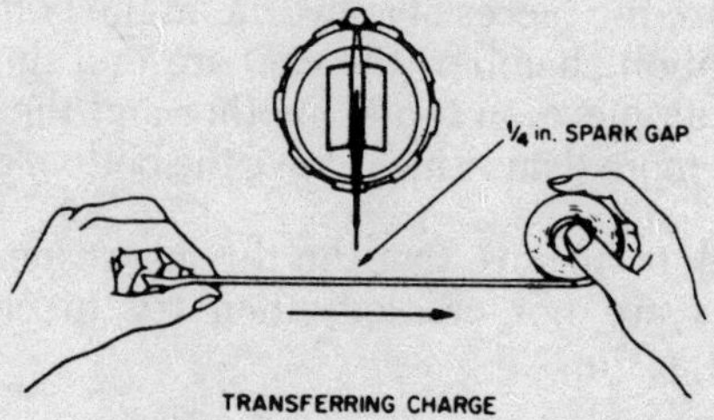

TRANSFERRING CHARGE

f. Rewind the tape **tight** on its roll, for future use when other tape may not be available.

Testing Your KFM to Learn if it Can Accurately Measure Low Dose Rates

Put fresh drying agent in your KFM and then charge and test the KFM in a location where it is **not** exposed to abnormal radiation. Take an initial reading. If after 3 hours its reading has decreased by 1 mm, or less, this means that its leaf-suspending threads are good insulators and that your KFM can reliably measure dose rates as low as 0.03 roentgens per hour (30 milliroentgens per hour). By post-attack standards, 30 mR/hr is a low dose rate. In a whole month of continuous exposure (an impossibility, because fallout decays), 30 mR/hr would result in a dose of 21.9 roentgens—not enough to incapacitate. **Warning:** In heavy fallout areas, for the first few days after fallout deposition the dose rates inside even most good shelters will be higher than 0.03 R/hr.

Trouble Shooting

If charging does not separate the two leaves sufficiently, take these corrective actions:

1. Be sure the pieces of anhydrite in the bottom of the ionization chamber (the can) are in a single layer, with no piece on top of another and the top of no piece more than ½ inch above the bottom of the can.

2. Check to be sure that the threads suspending the leaves are not crossed; then try to charge the KFM again.

3. If the KFM still cannot be charged, replace the used anhydrite with fresh anhydrite.

4. If you cannot charge a KFM when the air is very humid, charge it inside its dry-bucket.

5. If you cannot charge the KFM while in an area of heavy fallout, take it to the place affording the best protection against radiation, and try to charge it there. (A dose rate of several hundred R/hr will neutralize the charges on both the charging device and the instrument so rapidly that a KFM cannot be charged).

If a KFM or other radiation measuring instrument gives unexpectedly high readings inside a good shelter, wipe all dust off the outside of the instrument and repeat the radiation-measurements. Especially when exposing a fallout meter outdoors where there is fresh fallout, keep the instrument in a lidded pot, plastic bag, or other covering to avoid the possibility of having it contaminated with fallout particles and afterwards getting erroneously high radiation measurements.

XIV. Make and Use a Dry-Bucket

By charging a KFM while it is inside a dry-bucket with a transparent plastic cover (see illustration), this fallout meter can be charged and used even if the relative humidity is 100% outside the dry-bucket. The air inside the dry-bucket is kept very dry by a drying agent placed on its bottom. About a cupful of anhydrite serves very well. The pieces of this dehydrated gypsum need not be as uniform in size as is best for use inside a KFM, but do not use powdered anhydrite.

A dry-bucket can be readily made in about an hour by proceeding as follows:

1. Remove the handle of a large bucket, pot, or can preferably with a top diameter of at least 11 inches. A 4-gallon bucket having a top diameter of about 14 inches and a depth of about 9 inches is ideal. A plastic tub approximately this size is satisfactory. If the handle-supports interfere with stretching a piece of clear plastic film across the top of the bucket, remove them, being sure no sharp points remain.

2. Cut out a circular piece of clear plastic with a diameter about 5 inches larger than the diameter of the top of the bucket. Clear vinyl 4 mils thick, used for storm windows, etc., is best. Stretch the

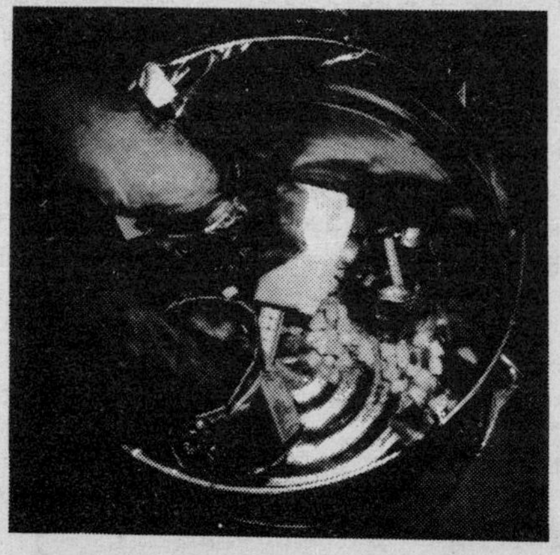

plastic smooth across the top of the bucket, and tie it in place, preferably with strong rubber bands looped together to form a circle.

3. Make a plastic top that fits snugly but is easily removable, by taping over and around the plastic just below the top of the bucket. One-inch-wide cloth duct tape, or one-inch-wide glass-reinforced strapping tape, serves well. When taping, do not permit the lower edge of the tape to be pulled inward below the rim of the bucket.

4. Cut two small holes (about 1 inch by 2 inches) in the plastic cover, as illustrated. Then make the radial cuts (shown by dotted lines) outward from the small holes, out to the solid-line outlines of the 3 inch by 4 inch hand-holes, so as to form small flaps.

5. Fold the small flaps upward, so they are vertical. Then tape them on their outer sides, so they form a vertical "wall" about ¾ inch high around each hand-hole.

6. Reduce the length of two ordinary plastic bread bags (or similar plastic bags) to a length that is 5 inches greater than the height of the bucket. (Do not use rubber gloves in place of bags; gloves so used result in much more humid outside air being unintentionally pumped into a dry-bucket when it is being used while charging a KFM inside it.)

7. Insert a plastic bag into each hand-hole, and fold the edge of the plastic bag about ½ inch over the taped vertical "wall" around each hand-hole.

8. Strengthen the upper parts of the plastic bags by folding 2-inch pieces of tape over the top of the "wall" around each hand-hole.

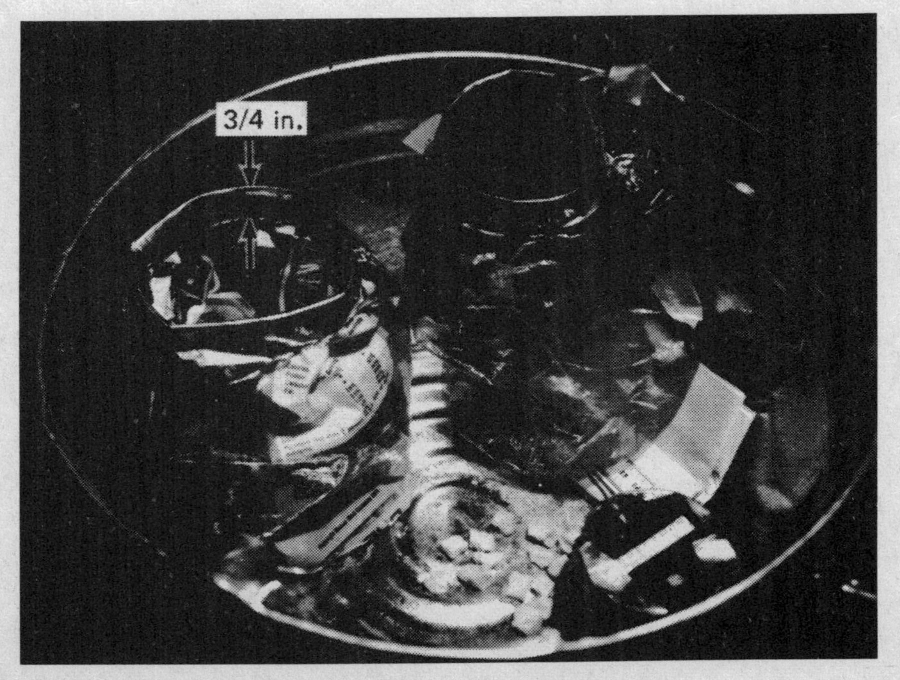
3/4 in.

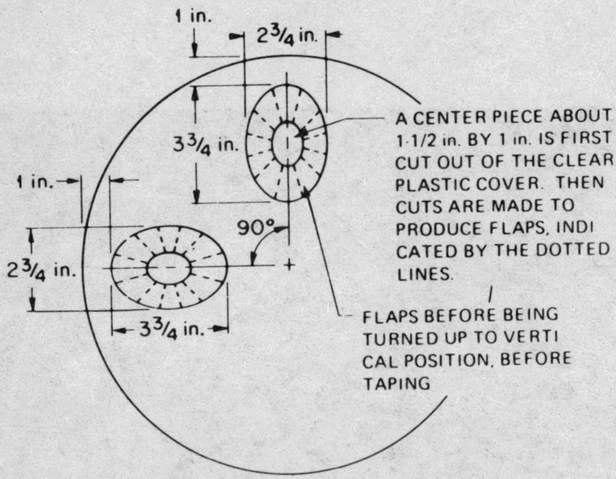

9. Make about a quart of anhydrite by heating small pieces of wall-board gypsum, and keep this anhydrite dry in a Mason jar or other airtight container with a rubber or plastic sealer.

10. Make a circular aluminum-foil cover to place over the plastic cover when the dry-bucket is not being used for minutes to hours. Make this cover with a diameter about 4 inches greater than the diameter of the top of the bucket, and make it fit more snugly with an encircling loop of rubber bands, or with string. Although not essential, an aluminum-foil cover reduces the amount of water vapor that can reach and pass through the plastic cover, thus extending the life of the drying agent.

11. Charge a KFM inside a dry-bucket by:

    a. Taking off wrist watch and sharp-pointed rings that might tear the plastic bags.

    b. Placing inside the dry-bucket:

(1) About a cup of anhydrite or silica gel;

(2) the KFM, with its charging-wire adjusted in its charging position; and

(3) dry, folded paper and the electrostatic charging device, best a 5-inch-long piece of Plexiglas with smoothed edges, to be rubbed between dry paper folded about 4 inches square and about 20 sheets thick. (Unrolling a roll of tape inside a dry-bucket is an impractical charging method.)

c. Replacing the plastic cover, that is best held in place with a loop of rubber bands.

d. Charging the KFM with your hands inside the plastic bags, operating the charging device. Have another person illuminate the KFM with a flashlight. When adjusting the charging-wire, move your hands very slowly. See the dry-bucket photos.

12. Expose the KFM to fallout radiation **either** by:

a. Leaving the KFM inside the dry-bucket while exposing it to fallout radiation for one of the listed time intervals, and reading the KFM before and after the exposure while it remains inside the dry-bucket. (The reading eye should be a measured 12 inches above the SEAT of the KFM, and a flashlight or other light should be used.)

b. Taking the charged KFM out of the dry-bucket to read it, expose it, and read it after the exposure. (If this is done repeatedly, especially in a humid shelter, the drying agent will not be effective for many KFM chargings, and will have to be replaced.)

XV. How to Use a KFM after a Nuclear Attack

A. Background Information

If during a rapidly worsening crisis threatening nuclear war you are in the place where you plan to take shelter, postpone studying the instructions following this sentence until after you have:

(1) built or improved a high-protection-factor shelter (if possible, a shelter covered with 2 or 3 ft of earth and separate from flammable buildings), and

(2) made a KAP (homemade shelter-ventilating pump) if you have the instructions and materials, and

(3) stored at least 15 gallons of water for each shelter occupant if you can obtain containers.

Having a KFM or any other dependable fallout meter and knowing how to operate it will enable you to minimize radiation injuries and possible fatalities, especially by skillfully using a high-protection-factor fallout shelter to control and limit exposures to radiation. By studying this section you first will learn how to measure radiation **dose rates** (roentgens per hour = R/hr), how to calculate **doses [R]** received in different time intervals, and how to determine **time intervals** (hours and/or minutes) in which specified doses would be received. Then this section lists the sizes of doses (number of R) that the average person can tolerate without being sickened, that he is likely to survive, and that he is likely to be killed by.

Most fortunately for the future of all living things, the decay of radioactivity causes the sandlike fallout particles to become less and less dangerous with the passage of time. Each fallout particle acts much like a tiny X ray machine would if it were made so that its rays, shooting out from it like invisible light, became weaker and weaker with time.

Contrary to exaggerated accounts of fallout dangers, the radiation **dose rate** from fallout particles when they reach the ground in the areas of the heaviest fallout **will decrease quite rapidly.** For example, consider the decay of fallout from a relatively nearby, large surface burst, at a place where the fallout particles are deposited on the ground one hour after the explosion. At this time one hour after the explosion, assume that the radiation dose rate (the best measure of radiation danger at a particular time) measures 2,000 roentgens per hour (2,000 R/hr) outdoors. Seven hours later the dose rate is reduced to 200 R/hr by normal radioactive decay. Two days after the explosion, the dose rate outdoors is reduced by radioactive decay to 20 R/hr. After two weeks, the dose rate is less than 2 R/hr. When the dose rate is 2 R/hr, people can go out of a good shelter and work outdoors for 3 hours a day, receiving a daily dose of 6 roentgens, without being sickened.

In places where fallout arrives several hours after the explosion, the radioactivity of the fallout will have gone through its time period of most rapid decay while the fallout particles were still airborne. If you are in a location so distant from the explosion that fallout arrives 8 hours after the explosion, two days must pass before the initial dose rate measured at your location will decay to 1/10 its initial intensity.

B. Finding The **Dose Rate**

1. Reread Section IV, "What a KFM Is and How it Works." Also reread Section XIII, "Two Ways to Charge a KFM," and actually do each step immediately after reading it.

2. Charge the KFM so that it reads at least 15 mm. Next raise the lower end of the charging wire. Then gently bump or shake the KFM to remove any unstable part of the charge. Read the apparent separation of the lower edges of the leaves while the KFM rests on an approximately horizontal surface. If the reading is larger than 20 mm, bleed off enough charge to reduce the initial reading to 20 mm or slightly less, for maximum accuracy. Never take a reading while a leaf is touching a stop-thread.

3. To prevent possible contamination of a KFM (or of any other fallout meter) with fallout particles, keep it inside a plastic bag or other covering when there is risk of fallout particles being deposited or blown onto it. An instrument contaminated with fallout particles can give too high readings, especially of the low dose-rate measurements made inside a good shelter.

4. Expose the KFM to fallout radiation for one of the time intervals shown in the vertical columns of the table attached to the KFM. (Study the following table.) If the dose rate is not known even approximately, first expose the fully charged KFM for one minute. For dependable measurements outdoors, expose the charged KFM about **3 feet above the ground.** The longer outdoor exposures usually are best made by attaching the KFM with 2 strong rubber bands to a stick or pole, being careful never to tilt the KFM too much.

5. Read the KFM after the exposure, while the KFM rests on an approximately horizontal surface.

6. Find the time interval that gives a dependable reading—by exposing the fully charged KFM for

one or more of the listed time intervals until the **reading after the exposure is;**

(a) Not less than **5 mm.**

(b) At least **2 mm** less than the reading before the exposure.

7. Calculate by simple subtraction the **difference** in the apparent separation of the **lower** edges of the leaves before the exposure and after the exposure. An example: If the reading before the exposure is 18 mm and the reading after the exposure is 6 mm, the **difference** in readings is 18 mm – 6 mm = 12 mm.

8. If an exposure results in a difference in readings of **less** than **2 mm**, recharge the KFM and expose it again for one of the **longer** time intervals listed. (If there appears to be **no** difference in the readings taken before and after an exposure for one minute, this does not prove there is absolutely no fallout danger. Take a longer reading.)

9. If an exposure results in the **reading** after the exposure being **less than 5 mm,** recharge the KFM and expose it again for one of the **shorter** time intervals listed.

10. Use the table attached to the KFM to find the **dose rate** (R/hr) during the time of exposure. The dose rate (R/hr) is found at the intersection of the vertical column of numbers under the time interval used and of the horizontal line of numbers that lists the calculated difference in readings at its left end.

    An example: If the time interval of the exposure was **1 MIN.** and the difference in the readings was **12 mm,** the table shows that the **dose rate** during

TABLE USED TO FIND DOSE RATES (R/HR FROM KFM READINGS

DIFFERENCE BETWEEN THE READING BEFORE EXPOSURE AND THE READING AFTER EXPOSURE (8 PLY STANDARD FOIL LEAVES)

DIFF.* IN READ-INGS	TIME INTERVAL OF AN EXPOSURE 15 SEC. R/HR	1 MIN. R/HR	4 MIN. R/HR	16 MIN. R/HR	1 HR. R/HR
2 mm	6.2	1.6	0.4	0.1	0.03
4 mm	12.	3.1	0.8	0.2	0.06
6 mm	19.	4.6	1.2	0.3	0.08
8 mm	25.	6.2	1.6	0.4	0.10
10 mm	31.	7.7	2.0	0.5	0.13
12 mm	37.	9.2	2.3	0.6	0.15
14 mm	43.	11.	2.7	0.7	0.18

the time interval of the exposure was **9.2 R/HR** (9.2 roentgens per hour).

Another example: If the time interval of the exposure was **15 SEC.** and the difference in readings was **11 mm,** the table shows that the dose rate during the exposure was halfway between **31 R/HR** and **37 R/HR;** that is, the **dose rate** was 34 R/hr.

11. Note in the table that if an exposure for one of the listed time intervals causes the **difference** in readings to be 2 mm or 3 mm, then an exposure 4 times as long reveals the same dose rate. An example: If a 1-min exposure results in a difference in readings of 2 mm, the table shows the dose rate was 1.6 R/hr; then if the KFM is exposed for 4 minutes at this same dose rate of 1.6 R/hr, the table shows that the resultant difference in readings is 8 mm.

    The longer exposure results in a more accurate determination of the dose rate.

12. If the dose rate is found to be greater than 0.2 R/hr and time is available, recharge the KFM and repeat the dose-rate measurement—to avoid possible mistakes.

C. Calculating the **Dose Received**

The **dose** of fallout radiation—that is, the **amount** of fallout radiation received—determines the harmful effects on men and animals. Being exposed to a high **dose rate** is not always dangerous—provided the exposure is short enough to result in only a small **dose** being received. For example, if the **dose rate** outside an excellent fallout shelter is 1200 R/hr and a shelter occupant goes outside for 30 seconds, he would be exposed for ½ of 1 minute, or ½ of 1/60 of an hour, which equals 1/120 hour. Therefore, since the dose he would receive if he stayed outside for 1 hour would be 1200 R, in 30 seconds he would receive 1/120 of 1200, which equals 10 R (1200 R divided by 120 = 10 R). A total daily **dose** of 10 R (10 roentgens) will not cause any symptoms if it is not repeated day after day for a week or more.

In contrast, if the average dose rate of an area were found to be 12 R/hr and if a person remained exposed in that particular area for 24 hours, he would receive a **dose** of 288 R (12 R/hr × 24 hr = 288 R). Even assuming that this person had been exposed previously to very little radiation, there would still be a serious risk that this 288 R **dose** would be fatal under the difficult conditions that would follow a heavy nuclear attack.

Another example: Assume that three days after an attack the occupants of a dry, hot cave giving almost complete protection against fallout are in desperate need of water. The dose rate outside is found to be 20 R/hr. To backpack water from a source 3 miles away is estimated to take 2-½ hours. The cave occupants estimate that the water backpackers will receive a dose in 2-½ hours of 50 R (2.5 hr × 20 R/hr = 50 R). A dose of 50 R will cause only mild symptoms (nausea in about 10% of persons receiving a 50 R dose) for persons who previously have received only very small doses. Therefore, one of the cave occupants makes a rapid radiation survey for about 1-½ miles along the proposed route, stopping to charge and read a KFM about every quarter of a mile. He finds no dose rates much higher than 20 R/hr.

So, the cave occupants decide the risk is small enough to justify some of them leaving shelter for about 2-½ hours to get water.

D. Estimating the **Dangers** from Different Radiation Doses

Fortunately, the human body—if given enough time—can repair most of the damage caused by radiation. An historic example: A healthy man accidently received a daily **dose** of 9.3 R (or somewhat more) of fallout-type radiation each day for a period of 106 days. His total accumulated **dose** was at least 1000 R. A dose of one thousand roentgens, if received in a few days, is almost three times the dose likely to kill the average man if he receives the whole dose in a few days and after a nuclear attack cannot get medical treatment, adequate rest, etc. However, the only symptom this man noted was serious fatigue.

The occupants of a high-protection-factor shelter (such as a trench shelter covered with 2 or 3 feet of earth and having crawlway entrances) would receive less than 1/200 of the radiation dose they would receive outside. Even in most areas of very heavy fallout, persons who remain continuously in such a shelter would receive a total accumulated **dose** of less than 25 R in the first day after the attack, and less than 100 R in the first two weeks. At the end of the first two weeks, such shelter occupants could start working outside for an increasing length of time each day, receiving a **daily dose** of no more than **6 R** for up to two months without being sickened.

To control radiation exposure in this way, each shelter must have a fallout meter, and a daily record must be kept of the approximate total dose received each day by every shelter occupant, both while inside and outside the shelter. The long-term penalty which would result from a dose of 100 R received within a few weeks is much less than many Americans fear. If 100 average persons received an external dose of 100 R during and shortly after a nuclear attack, the studies of the Japanese A-bomb survivors indicate that no more than one of them is likely to die during the following 30 years as a result of this 100 R radiation dose. These delayed radiation deaths would be due to leukemia and other cancers. In the desperate crisis period following a major nuclear attack, such a relatively small shortening of life expectancy during the following 30 years should not keep people from starting recovery work to save themselves and their fellow citizens from death due to lack of food and other essentials.

A healthy person who previously has received a total accumulated dose of no more than 100 R distributed over a 2-week period should realize that:

> 100 R, even if all received in a day or less, is unlikely to require medical care—provided during the next 2 weeks a total additional dose of no more than a few R is received.
>
> 350 R received in a few days or less results in a 50-50 chance of being fatal after a large nuclear attack when few survivors could get medical care, sanitary surroundings, a well-balanced diet, or adequate rest.
>
> 600 R received in a few days or less is almost certain to cause death within a few days.

E. Finding the **Protection Factor** of a Shelter

To avoid the necessity of repeatedly going outside a shelter to determine the changing dose rates outside, find the shelter's protection factor (PF) by measuring the dose rate inside the shelter as soon as it becomes high enough to be reliably measured. Then promptly measure the dose rate outside. The uncontaminated shelter's

$$PF = \frac{\text{Dose Rate Outside}}{\text{Dose Rate Inside}}$$

An example: If the dose rate inside is found to be 0.2 R/hr and the dose rate outside is 31 R/hr, the shelter's

$$PF = \frac{31 \text{ R/hr}}{0.2 \text{ R/hr}} = 155$$

Then at future times the **approximate** dose rate outside can be found by measuring the dose rate inside and multiplying it by 155. Approximate Dose Rate Outside = Dose Rate Inside × PF.

F. **Using a KFM to Reduce Radiation Doses Received**

If a charged KFM is discharged and reads zero within a second or two after being taken outside a good shelter, this means that the dose rate outside is hundreds of roentgens per hour. Get back inside! Also remember that a 15-second reading is not as accurate as are readings made in longer specified exposure times.

Inside most shelters, the dose received by an occupant varies considerably, depending on the occupant's location. For example, inside an expedient covered-trench shelter the dose rate is higher near the entrance than in the middle of the trench. In a typical basement shelter the best protection is found in one corner. Especially during the first several hours after the arrival of fallout, when the dose rates and doses received are highest, shelter occupants should use their fallout meters to determine where to place themselves to minimize the doses they receive.

They should use available tools and materials to reduce the doses they receive, especially during the first day, by digging deeper (if practical) and reducing the size of openings by partially blocking them with earth, water containers, etc.—while maintaining adequate ventilation. To greatly reduce the slight risk of fallout particles entering the body through nose or mouth, shelter occupants should cover nose and mouth with a towel or other cloth while the fallout is being deposited outside their shelter, if at the same time ventilating air is being blown or pumped through their shelter.

The air inside an occupied shelter often becomes very humid. If a good flow of outdoor air is flowing into a shelter—especially if pumped by briefly operating a KAP or other ventilating pump—a KFM usually can be charged at the air intake of the shelter room without putting it inside a dry-bucket. However, if the air to which a KFM is exposed has a relative humidity of 90% or higher, the instrument cannot be charged, even by quickly unrolling a roll of tape.

In extensive areas of heavy fallout, the occupants of most home basements, that provide inadequate shielding against heavy fallout radiation, would be in deadly danger. By using a dependable fallout meter, occupants would find that persons lying on the floor in certain locations would receive the smallest doses, and that, if they improvise additional shielding in these locations, the doses received could be greatly reduced. Additional shielding can be provided by making a very small shelter inside the basement where the dose rate is found to be lowest. Furniture, boxes, etc. can be used for walls, doors for the roof, and water containers, books, and other heavy objects for shielding—especially on the roof. Or, if tools are available, breaking through the basement floor and digging a shelter trench will greatly increase available protection against radiation. If a second expedient ventilating pump, a KAP, (or a small Directional Fan), is made and used as a fan, such an extremely cramped shelter inside a shelter usually can be occupied by several times as many persons as can occupy it without forced ventilation.

END OF INSTRUCTIONS

Finding Truly Responsible Physicians

We all know about the group of physicians who claim that nuclear survival training is A Bad Thing; they call themselves the Physicians for Social Responsibility (PSR). I've debated these folks in public forums in two countries, and have spoken to them privately on many occasions. It's time, I believe, to air some observations. More about those in a moment; but how many of us are familiar with a group of physicians who actively *support* Civil Defense?

I learned of the Doctors for Disaster Preparedness (DDP), a national organization, through one of its most active members: Jane M. Orient, M.D., of Tucson. My first impressions of Dr. Orient after a panel discussion some time ago were of a calm, competent, rather attractive physician who thinks much and talks relatively little. I soon learned that she and the DDP have much to say, and they say it very well—notably in a newsletter which they have managed to make available at no charge. As a friendly outsider I'd say the DDP takes the position that physicians, and indeed all of us, should take steps to be prepared against disasters of all kinds. Nuclear disaster is among the worst; chemical and biological warfare are other front-runners. The DDP addresses them all, as well as the fact that Soviet citizens seem better prepared for such disasters than American citizens are. This, I assert, is true social responsibility.

You can obtain the DDP Arizona Newsletter by writing your request to Dr. Jane M. Orient, 1601 N. Tucson Blvd., Suite #9, Tucson, AZ 85716. Need I add that the price is right? It's the price of your postcard, though I feel that Dr. Orient would not refuse donations to defray costs. You can also join the national DDP and get its *Journal of Civil Defense*. National membership is $40 for doctoral members, $30 for the rest of us, and only $15 for students. Send your check and national membership request to DDP, P.O. Box 1057, Starke, FL 32091.

Why, if the DDP is a national organization dedicated to our survival, don't we hear as much about it as we hear from the anti-Civil Defense PSR? Maybe because it goes about its business quietly, without a lot of hoopla. Frankly, I wish the DDP had the money to hire more public relations experts. In contrast, the PSR has about *five dozen* public relations people in Cambridge, and a whopping budget to carry its anti-Civil Defense message to us. The PSR sponsors a lot of media events, and from personal acquaintance I believe its members have their hearts in the right place. They truly believe that Civil Defense measures tend to make us more warlike, so they consider it unethical to promote CD.

On the other hand, some PSR members say publicly that nuclear disarmament must be verifiable and mutual—a stand most of us would applaud. The PSR members I know personally are not Soviet sympathizers, and I have no evidence suggesting that the PSR's strings are being pulled by America's opponents.

Where the PSR fails—and where some of its own members admit that it fails—is where it leaps headlong into illogical positions. For example: in its own hour long propaganda movie, one of the PSR's doctors says that a 40-rad dose of radiation is an "intolerable" dose. This is one tenth of the dose generally accepted as 50% lethal; ask any radiologist yourself! Did the speaker mean he wouldn't like to tolerate it? Did he really not know his own business? What the devil *did* he mean? Remember, the PSR itself prepared that movie; if this blunder was a slip of the tongue, why was it not edited out? God knows, thousands of physicians have heard that statement. How much wild exaggeration does the film contain? We can only harbor suspicions . . .

Another absurd position: that in the interest of preventing nuclear war, it is unethical for any physician to promote emergency nuclear survival measures beforehand. When faced with this position in debate, I always explain that it's a way of saying "preventive measures are the only ethical ones." And if that's true, every hospital emergency room is unethical.

In other words, the PSR seems to feel that promoting post-accident emergency procedures tends to make us more willing to tempt that accident. You only need ask yourself whether you, personally, are more willing to risk catastrophe whenever you think of a hospital emergency room nearby. Thinking about emergency rooms tends to make me more cautious, not more foolhardy.

Some of the PSR's media events work for them, especially when they control the whole event ahead of time; but they are sometimes betrayed haphazardly by their own members. On a Canadian network TV panel show, one PSR member said that if he knew a nuke was scheduled for Toronto, he would rush to a fine rooftop restaurant there and order a wonderful meal. If he timed it right, he wouldn't have to pay the check. It earned him the laugh he seemed to expect. The rest of us on the panel disagreed with his serious position: he hoped to ride a fireball to Heaven rather than try to save his medical knowledge to help survivors. My personal feeling was that he might find that fireball carrying him somewhere else than Heaven. This same gentleman waited until the end of the program before tossing out a fast slur to the effect that we Civil Defense people were warmongers. I had little time to make my objection—but I used what little time I had.

During another public debate, a PSR psychiatrist whispered to me that she was about to charge me with immorality for my Civil Defense stand—but that I mustn't think it meant I was a bad person. Or something to that effect; I was too busy trying not to guffaw at this outrageous attempt at manipulating me. She seemed too young to have several children, but during the debate she admitted that she and her kids lived in a prime target area. I pointed out that our own children were growing up in a small town as far as we could get from prime targets and from age 6 they have known self-reliance tactics anyhow, and that the audience could draw its own conclusions as to which parent was the more moral, she or I.

Sometimes the PSR pays for an event that wasn't billed as a debate, but turns out to be a *very* lively debate when the sponsored expert lacks expertise. One such touring speaker told a public gathering several interesting tidbits which I felt compelled to set right, roughly as follows:

Speaker: Military policy is no longer debated even among the military.

Ing: I have recently served on three defense-related groups including military men in which policy and strategy were debated.

Speaker: What good is point defense? Soviet warheads can be salvage-fused so that, even if we hit them, they will go off anyway.

Ing: If a U.S. point defense hits them ten miles in

the air, we get high air-bursts and relatively little fallout. If they are allowed to hit their targets, we get ground-bursts and tremendous amounts of fallout. The choice is obvious.

Speaker: Soviet ICBMs can defend against our beam defenses during launch merely by adding insulation to the "bird."

Ing: If they did, the added insulation weight would cut the missile's range by thousands of miles.

Speaker: What good is our European-based Pershing missile if it is targeted against "empty holes" after Soviet missiles have already been fired from those holes?

Ing: Soviet missiles are now designed so that their silos—their "holes"—can be reloaded quickly. We would hit holes while they were being reloaded, before they could launch a second salvo.

The discussion was civil, even friendly, and perhaps useful. In off-the-cuff talks with PSR members I find most of them genuinely interested in getting the facts separated from unsupported opinion. Perhaps the worst that can be said of the PSR is that, as famed physicist Freeman Dyson wrote of the PSR's Helen Caldicott (whose humanity he admires), they are sometimes careless about technical details and they do not think naturally in quantitative terms. In other words, they sometimes get the numbers all wrong, and their expertise is often shallow. These are serious charges against physicians; would you want to be treated for a hangnail by such a person? Well, yes; because the wrong numbers, and the shallowness, are often outside the field of medicine. And this is exactly my point: all too often, we give a physician credit for expertise in some field where his knowledge may not be as broad, or as deep, as your own.

Maybe the best that can be said of the PSR is that their bottom line is the survival of the human race, and they rightly think that *prevention* of catastrophe is better than cleaning up after one. In this, of course, we can all agree. The PSR becomes socially irresponsible, in my view, chiefly when it gets the facts all wrong, or proclaims that educating our civilian population in Civil Defense is an immoral act.

And what's the worst we can say of the staunchly determined Doctors for Disaster Preparedness? I'm not sure; maybe that it isn't famous enough to get the media coverage it deserves. We can all fix that by becoming members, and by letting reporters know they can get both sides of these issues by contacting DDP. I had intended to cite the *best* we can say of the DDP, but there are too many "bests" to choose from. Of one thing, you can be sure: the DDP is one group of physicians that wants to help you survive come-what-may. Here, at last, we find physicians whose ideas about social responsibility are geared to our survival, tomorrow.

Is Nuclear Winter Exaggerated?

You have a right to know when your news is biased, especially when that news sends a freezing wind of futility howling up your spine. The nuclear winter scenario was made public in *Science* in December 1983. Briefly, the idea was that numerous nuclear blasts would produce enough smoke to obscure the sun for months or years, with global freezing as a result. Ever since that publication, headlines screamed that any sizeable nuclear exchange would almost certainly cause a long, murderous global nuclear winter. No crops, no people, no hope, no place—or so we're invited to believe.

Those headlines have triggered a lot of second thoughts during the past year. Why bother with surviving a war, if we're all going to flunk the following life-support exam anyway: right? But that 'IF' should be printed heavily in our minds, because responsible scientists are now admitting that nuclear winter appears to be a *very* iffy scenario. Actually, some of the very people who helped with the original 'TTAPS' study (for authors Turco, Toon, Ackerman, Pollack, and Sagan) disagreed with the pessimism of those five authors.

I was first brought up against this disagreement about a year ago, while in Canada for a media event on nuclear survival. Another of the guest panelists, one of the unlisted scientists who helped with the 'TTAPS' study, complained to me that he felt the perils of nuclear winter had been much exaggerated. He was none too happy about the way his honest work had been slanted in what appeared to be a scare tactic. Apparently he wasn't the only one.

As a one-time professor who took a lot of flak for speculating on the future, I can even dredge up a little sympathy for the likes of Carl Sagan. A *very* little, of course, when he's snowing on my parade. I agree that the possibility of any sudden climate change is reason enough for Sagan to grab his speculative whistle and blow it until his ears pop. *But not to offer that speculation as virtual certainty.*

Maybe there would have been no good, solid follow-up studies without those gloom-and-doom warnings—in the *Scientific American* of August 1984, for example, by the same 'TTAPS' authors. But the tone of the TTAPS speculation was very, very pessimistic. Rather than admit that their findings might be considerably in error in either direction, they kept hinting that they'd been so conservative in their estimates that the reality was likely to be far worse than their findings. There was little evidence that they thought reality might be the tiniest bit milder than their scenario. You must bear in mind that Carl Sagan is not only a man of science; he's also a media man. Science and the media are strange bedfellows but Sagan crowds them both into the same hammock. Don't expect truth to be the first thing that spills over the side.

Well, if the TTAPS team was whistling for attention, they certainly got it. But if Sagan was expecting close agreement, he was in for serious disappointment. In December of 1984, a panel of experts in the

National Research Council reported on their follow-up studies. While saying that severe climate effects seemed a possibility and should be taken seriously, they admitted that extensive uncertainties kept them from making any firm statements about a nuclear winter.

TTAPS's Richard Turco manfully admits that the NRC *did not* confirm the TTAPS work, but labels the panel's report a 'weak endorsement' because both reports agree that the problem is worthy of more research. (Which is a little like saying the neutral Swiss were a weak endorsement of Mussolini.)

But how did the popular little weekly magazine, *Science News*, report on the lack of agreement? Its headline read: "MORE SUPPORT FOR NUCLEAR WINTER THEORY." The fine print was a different story, but that headline was worthy of any tabloid. A lot of science teachers are going to recall that headline. Too bad.

And what can the reader glean from all these reports? Quite a bit, actually. First, now we know that Sagan is far out on his own speculative limb. His worst fear *could* still, possibly, be correct—but few other scientists are willing to say it's very likely. Second, since most nuclear exchanges would be expected in the Northern Hemisphere, the effects in the Southern Hemisphere would be delayed and probably much reduced. Anyone for New Zealand?

The bad news comes third: if half the nuclear arsenals were expended in a 6500 megaton war, much of the northern temperate zone might *possibly* suffer darkness and temperatures 20 to 45 degrees Fahrenheit below normal for weeks, with subnormal temperatures gradually rising in the weeks following. Further, our air would be laced with nitrogen oxides and other dangerous chemicals from the firestorms. Nobody would be dumb enough to deny that these effects would be hazardous to our health.

The not-so-bad news comes fourth: a lot of this smoke pall might be localized, with very large areas comparatively free from suspended particles in the air. In some regions near the West Coast, winds off the sea might keep temperatures from dropping much.

We can't make any predictions from all this, so we just have to run with the best estimates we have. If you live far from firestorm areas, you might live through a month of depressed temperature and diminished sunlight. Crops might not mature unless they were planted near the end of that period. Certainly your food stocks would be crucial; and with independent electricity and artificial lighting in a small greenhouse, your chances would be immeasurably improved. Gas masks, preferably with charcoal filters, would help when you're outside for the first few weeks. Inside air should be drawn through filters too.

But virtually all of these things can be handled by the serious planner. They make the job of survival tougher, but they don't call for abject surrender. Yes, a medium-to-severe nuclear winter seems possible; and no, most of the pundits don't seem to think it's very probable—indeed, some of them never did. It's altogether possible that a nuclear winter could come and go in a week or so, passing almost as soon as fallout danger. Those of us who are interested in such things will welcome further upcoming studies—and we will know better than to rely on those outrageous headlines.

NON-
NUCLEAR
CALAMITY

Snowshoe Summer
Confessions of a High-Country Hiker

Let me begin with a confession: I've always been a summer soldier. From age ten, I loved the high country and took vacations there whenever possible. But that was summertime, as the song goes, when the livin' is easy. I never thought the day would come when I'd be navigating Fernandez Pass alone in 20 feet of snow, on jury-rigged snowshoes. If you're a summer soldier, perhaps this memoir will help you survive the kind of dumb decisions *I* made.

In 1955, California Fish and Game wanted a masonry dam at a place called Rutherford Lake. That's in Minarets, a wild area east of Yosemite. The pay was laughable but you couldn't fault the view from 10,000 feet. That was a normal year; around the first of July the high-country snow faded fast. Most years, you can get a string of mules up the Sierra trails as far as Rutherford by then.

I spent that summer with a Barco gasoline-powered jackhammer, a dreadful device with one virtue: It peeled off every ounce of me that wasn't absolutely essential. But during the long evenings in the Sierra I hiked, fished and learned every square foot of the place within miles of our new spillway.

In later years I packed in to Rutherford several times, always in July or August. The trails seemed to get worse each time—but by 1975 I didn't use them much anyway, figuring I knew the shapes of the peaks and passes from memory. Mine was the unconscious arrogance of the summer soldier, that sense of knowing where you are and how you're doing, whether you do or not. All that changed in 1980.

From all reports of the Minarets area, 1980 featured the latest thaw in human memory. The high-country snow load was simply stupendous, they said; the bears would be hungry and the lakes would still be frozen above 8,000 feet in July. Any middle-aged flatlander trying a solo higher than that, they said, was either very good at winter camping, or three pints low on brains. None of this fazed me. Maybe two quarts low was more like it; I thought of Rutherford like a toddler thinks of his playpen.

The first day was a foretaste. I parked the VW for a downhill start at the trailhead, in case the battery fell asleep during its week of idleness. (It turned out to be two weeks.) Two sets of vibram soles had punched holes in the rotting snow before me, and ancient trail blazes on the trees greeted me like old friends. I decided to stick to the trail awhile; this familiar turf was beginning to look stranger by the moment.

Of course, "turf" isn't the right word. The only real dirt I saw was at the base of a few granite boulders, warmed by a bright mid-July sun. Most of what I saw was white, below a hard blue sky, and within an hour I had to modify my sunglasses. It took only a few moments to run strips of tape across the lenses, after which I peered through the narrow slits with much less discomfort.

The real discomfort was from the snow, which deepened with every hundred feet of altitude. My feet were protected by mink-oiled boots and two pairs of socks, but my thigh muscles soon complained at having to lift each foot high to make any headway. Sometimes I could barely drag my feet through the snow—and sometimes a hard crust tripped me. It took me a while to learn that you maintain a better pace imitating a show horse than by pushing your way through. I stopped frequently in sunny areas; not only because it was bitter-cold in shadow, but because all that high stepping tired me fast.

My first stupid error came only a mile from the little chain of lakes I had set as my day's goal. The thaw had begun, and the chuckling stream I normally crossed in a steep ravine was now a thundering torrent. I could even hear the sound of big rocks grinding in it before I saw the cataract. Well, there went those tracks, skirting up the ravine; I'd find where that first pair crossed, or tried to.

Sure enough, 100 yards up the ravine, a dead fir spanned the creek where someone had recently crossed. I studied the fir and judged it stable. What I didn't judge was my own stability; I was tired, and this was my first day carrying 50 pounds of gear. I should've rested, then gone across without the pack to test my footing and handholds before harnessing up again. Instead, I started across immediately. White water boiled four feet or so beneath the fir, and the slope of the tree was downward. Naturally, when I leaned forward to grab a handhold halfway across, the unfamiliar weight of my pack overbalanced me.

To anybody watching it might've looked comical; I moved forward fast to regain balance, missed a branch with one gloved hand, and tripped headlong, grabbing thin air and then falling with one knee on the trunk. The pack swung me around and suddenly I was hugging the trunk, one leg hooked around a branch, the other dangling in spray. I managed to find purchase to push upward from that branch and hauled my sodden freight the rest of the way, literally crawling between branches to safety.

Only one leg was wet a little above the knee. I climbed the nearest dry boulder, shucked my pack and wrung out the bottoms of my elkhide trousers without removing them. Elkhides let you stay relatively warm even when they're wet, so I'd done one thing right. My boots were hightops with accordion tongues—not the sexy overlap-closure kind—so my feet weren't wet. The tops of my socks were, though. I changed socks, wrung out the wet ones and placed them inside my shirt to dry. Then I sat back and reviewed the event that could've dumped me into a cold mixmaster.

It was a simple matter of balance, one I knew perfectly well but had somehow managed to forget; with the bellyband carrying half the weight of the pack over my hips, I didn't feel the full weight of the pack until I bent over. Then 25 apparent pounds became 50. During the first day, before you're accustomed to the weight, any quick bending or twisting can result in sudden weight shifts that could literally kill you.

From there to the lower lakes I pondered my vulnerability. My predecessors, a pair of young stalwarts, had stopped at the first lake; I coveted their two-man tent. I pressed on to the uppermost lake in the chain. It's astonishing how much difference a few hundred feet can make; the lowest lake was virtually free of ice, while the others were progressively more frozen. The uppermost lake was clear at the spillway and for a few yards around most of the shore, but wind-driven snowdrifts still undulated on blue ice across the lake. A few trout lazed near the shore. I located a granite slab and made a bough bed under my mummybag with an hour of light left, set up my little one-kilo woodstove and tried for a trout supper. No dice; I ate gorp and swilled it down with a peach-brandy slurpee, feeling like a pathfinder again. Mine were the first human tracks of the year to Upper Chain Lake.

My only shelter was a poly tarp rigged over parachute cord. With more cord, I hung my pack from a nearby fir branch to keep it high above prowling varmints, then crawled into the sack and pulled my mosquito net into place. This net, by the way, works even when repellents don't.

I woke to the noise of someone whetting a rusty saber. It was a big whiskeyjack, warning another jaybird away from his treasure. I'd never known a jay to wriggle inside a packflap—even a loose one—but this one did, joyously gouging into my gorp mixture. I worked one hand up to the zipper and gave it a tug, with a startlingly lovely result: Ice crystals flew up from the zipper, creating an instant rainbow in the direct sunlight. Not 'til I'd heaved a stick of firewood

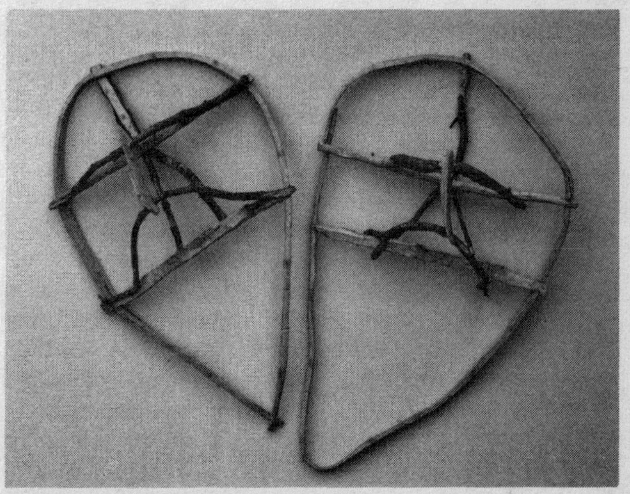

"Bearpaw" snowshoes

at the thieving jay did I crawl completely out, donning jacket and gloves quickly. Soon I was hobbling around with aching thighs, stoking up the stove and taking care not to mash the sparrows.

I think they were white-crowned sparrows; in any event, they were so intent on a handout they had no fear whatever. One of the idiots perched on my knee to share a biscuit. Never before or since have I seen wild critters so eager to infest a campsite, and before grabbing my packrod I snugged the flap tight on my backpack. I had lost only a handful of gorp to the whiskeyjack.

Fishing was pointless; during the night, the shallows had refrozen and I got no action at the spillway. By midafternoon, though, the shoreline ice had melted, and I pulled in a few pan-sized rainbow trout. They might've been asleep for all the fight they showed but, broiled with almonds from my gorp, they redeemed themselves.

The next day was much the same. I figured the steep peaks kept the sun off the lake, and that I might have better luck farther up. On the following morning I let sparrows eat from my hand before starting my climb, then puffed my way over the towering ridge toward Breeze Lake.

The lake was higher, so solidly frozen that I heard the gunshot reports of pack ice shifting at noon. It was fairly easy coming down, despite the herringbone pattern on snowfields with the "grooves" a pace apart. I had no crampons and didn't collect a hefty walking staff until tobogganing on a slick patch. After that, the staff saved me every time I started to slip.

Something akin to good sense kept me from exploring the snowfields around Breeze. No other human tracks were in evidence, and the unearthly stillness—shattered by those echoing reports of shifting ice—gave the place a sinister appeal. I spent the night there, judging from the looming ridges of Gale Peak that the sun wouldn't melt that ice for weeks.

The next morning I started for Rutherford, taking my bearings from Merced Peak. Only it must've been another peak, disguised by snow. Instead of using my map and compass, I assumed I knew what I was doing and wound up in a moraine meadow boasting another lake chain I recognized as Fernandez Lakes.

Heading down to the meadow, I heard a creek nearby. Of course I couldn't see it because it was directly beneath me—but I *could* fall through an innocent-looking depression of snow, and I did.

Again I had fool's luck. The drop was only six feet or so, and the staff across collapsing snow let me down easily. I banged a knee against a rock, and those spongy-wet elkhides absorbed half the blow. Still, there was the small matter of getting the hell out of ankle-deep water and out of the hole. I was in a waist-high tunnel made by the stream. Incredibly, my feet *still* weren't wet, but the socks were wicking cold water downward. I floundered to stand on protruding stones, removed my pack and pawed the snow away as far as a pair of rounded boulders.

The staff was handy; I stuck it under a packstrap and shoved my pack out onto the snow, then used it to get onto a boulder. I sat there for a few moments swearing I'd never again cross a shallow depression in rotten snow without probing the stuff—especially when I could hear water running below! As soon as I found a bare, sunwarmed boulder I changed socks again, squinting furiously in the brilliant reflection of the snowfield. It wasn't until then that I realized I'd lost my sunglasses in the stream.

I went back, shivering, and searched fruitlessly for a half-hour before giving up. I needed to make camp and dry my clothes and gloves. When your hands are going numb and you can't stop shivering, hypothermia is on the way.

Within a few minutes I struck Post Peak Trail, recognizable only by a campsite I knew from earlier hikes. This time I scuttled around and built a typical tenderfoot fire, one big enough to make a broad bed of coals. To warm myself I brewed soup and sat without my pants, wrapped to my sternum in the mummybag. If the weather had been bad I would've had a lot rougher time of it.

Bare hands thrust under my armpits, I planned each picayune detail of setting everything straight again. I had hours of daylight; maybe enough that my trousers and gloves would sun-dry if I stuck them up on poles for air circulation. The pins-and-needles of circulation were in my hands and, within an hour, I was warm enough to trim the poles for my clothes. Hanging well above the coals in the sun, the well-wrung trousers and gloves dried while I made Eskimo goggles from wire and a cardboard food carton. I had a lot of time to think—mostly about going back to lower elevations.

But Rutherford was hardly a mile away now, just over the next ridge. If I kept well above the meadows and studied the slopes ahead, surely I could avoid plummeting into any more holes. That sturdy hiking staff had served me well, but what I really needed was snowshoes. Well, I didn't have any. For that matter, I had never worn them. At that point, I was already committed to making a set, but didn't know it yet.

My leathers dried slowly because I'd suspended them high above the coals, turning everything over frequently. Since I hadn't worn longjohns, I thrust my legs through the armholes of my spare T-shirt and wore it like shorts to cut the breeze. That central hole in the shirt created a mighty breezy gap until I pinned it shut!

By sundown, I was once again in business. Fernandez Lakes were frozen and, though I tossed stones through the ice and tried ice fishing, I dined on hard salami and pan bread. This time I found no birds to share it with. The isolation and some ominous clouds made me cautious enough to rig my shelter on a raised granite slab between small firs, with snow banked around the edges of my poly sheet. I'd been in midsummer storms there that wouldn't let you see 20 feet in front of you at high noon.

The next morning I hied off for Rutherford early and found it without trouble, making my favorite site homey before hiking around the lake perimeter. Rutherford gets a lot of sun despite the thousand-foot ridge on one side and, though I had to clear away 18 inches of snow from my campsite, this was a familiar isolation. I spent most of a week there, even though the deep volcanic lake never did thaw. Ice fishing, again, proved fruitless. I read a lot and watched a hefty marmot scuttle around my stove for crumbs whenever I was more than five paces away from it.

There was a marten, too, a nut-brown tube of muscle two feet long who tried to flank the marmot. The marmot wasn't stupid; he always got to his hole in the rocks with time to spare. I expected the marten—not as broad-beamed as his prey—to go into the hole, but he never risked it. Perhaps he knew there were more marmots inside.

He also knew when I was napping. I hadn't seen him nearer than 20 yards but was rudely awakened one afternoon by paws scampering directly over my legs. I looked around to see the marten, bobbing on his hind legs, watching me closely. If I hadn't moved, would he have returned for a tentative taste of me? Maybe not, but I was the only thing at 10,000 feet that wasn't desperately hungry. I heaved a few snowballs in his direction as he made for the rocks.

Then one afternoon I had real, honest-to-God company, a man from Fish and Game who'd hiked in from the ranger station to open the spillway gate. It hadn't been touched in over 20 years, he said, and the wheel that opened the floodgate was chained, and they'd lost the key to that lock many years before.

I helped cut the chain and bellyflopped to turn that big iron wheel, feeling like something from the Jurassic period as the trickle at the base of the dam became a roar. I had taken that wheel from a mule's back a generation earlier, when the wheel was fresh with scarlet paint. Some of the paint still adhered, but for all I knew nobody had touched the wheel since I had mounted it on the long screw shaft in 1955. I tried to explain, but my companion just stared, perhaps in disbelief, and I quickly changed the subject.

Before he left, he mentioned a group of hikers some miles below who hadn't been as lucky as I. One of them made it to the ranger station, and a rescue chopper had found the others—one with an inguinal hernia and one with a broken ankle. It was that treacherous rotten snow, said my informant; he was crazy to be up this far without snowshoes. And so, by implication, was I.

I mentioned that I intended to go out through Fernandez Pass.

"Not this year, you won't," he grinned. "The chopper pilot says it's choked with 20 feet of snow."

"I think I'll give it a try," I said, realizing what I'd have to do.

"Maybe in September," he replied. "But it's impassable now—without snowshoes."

That settles it, I thought, watching him stride off. Snowshoes he wants, and snowshoes I'll get.

A small fir provided the wood. I botched a couple of long splits but finally trimmed a pair of good six-foot lengths of frame to a roughly rectangular cross-section using my sheath knife. In cross-section the lengths were seven-eighths by five-eighths of an inch, more or less. Even with gloves, my hands were tender as boils, because a sheath knife makes a lousy plane.

The green wood bent readily so that, with matching notches cut near the ends of a frame, I could make a frame shaped roughly like a teardrop. I needed roundish "bearpaw" snowshoes, not the long-tailed type they use in flat country. These didn't look much like the sketches made by Ernest Thompson Seton, but by God, they sure looked good to me. I toyed with the idea of trapping the marten for gut to bind the frames, but it seemed criminal somehow. Instead, I used 25-pound test monofilament line from the quarter-mile spool I always carry. By the time I had two frames bent, notched and tightly bound, it was dark and my hands were raw meat.

It took all of next day to finish the job. I made grooves for each wrapped joint and used small branches for crosspieces. I then set each boot in place and ran flexible branches over the toe and instep, binding the branches to the cross-frames, resulting in loose boot bindings. For cross-lacing, I ran monofilament line from side to side and at angles. I intended to weave strips of T-shirt through this network of line, but it wasn't necessary. Odd as it seems, a cross-hatch of nylon line with the framing was enough to support me and my lightened pack.

By then, there were about 10 pounds less of me, as well. I'd relied so much on soup the past few days that I had mild diarrhea. That last morning on Rutherford I breakfasted on pancakes and, for good measure, the last of my cheese. While stowing gear I kept stealing glances across the lake, wondering when it would thaw and if Fernandez Pass would seem as unfamiliar.

For an hour or so, I found easy going as long as I

kept my feet well apart and leaned back a bit on the downhill stretches. The tips of my snowshoes didn't bend upward enough, repeatedly digging into the snow when I wasn't careful. Again, I felt the ache of muscles unused to a particular activity, mostly along my shins.

I followed the trail to the pass for a mile, but eventually the blazes on trees were swallowed by five feet of snow. Finally I was shuffling across steep snowfields with rounded mounds revealing small trees, their tops curled under the snow load. The now-familiar herringbone pattern in the snow wasn't easy to cross. Without those snowshoes, it would have been tougher.

To make it worse, I had to admit finally that I did not know where the hell I was anymore. Peering through the slits of my sunshades I saw, far below, what might have been one of the Fernandez Lakes. But I couldn't be sure. Maybe I could puzzle it out from a nearby prominence. Eventually, standing on a ridge that *might* be Fernandez Pass, I shucked my pack and half-climbed crusty snow to the top of a ledge. It was smooth, windblown, innocent of herringbone ridges, and I crawled across its icy flat top to the overlook.

It was an overlook, all right; I had climbed onto a classic cornice. During the next five seconds, I learned several things. One, the saddleback behind me *was* Fernandez Pass. Two, my wind-sculptured cornice was soft below its crust. And three, the icy lip that crumbled away below my outstretched arm had been undercut by wind to a thin ledge. Far, far below me lay a snowfield, its herringbone pattern seemingly no bigger than corduroy from my dizzying height. I had crawled out on a projecting lip of snow, and only that overhang of cold cotton candy lay between me and a 400-foot fall. My heart jumped like a deer.

Face down, flat as I could get, I began to squirm

backward like a swimmer. Not until sliding back down to where I'd left the snowshoes did I lift my head again.

I leaned against a boulder in the throat of the pass, sucking hard candy and waiting out the five-minute fit of trembles that followed. I had seen cornices while skiing, years before, but all the warnings I'd ever heard didn't keep me off that lethal overhang. Why not? For one thing, those sunshades weren't very effective; all that white-on-white was deceptive. For another, I hadn't thought carefully about the odd, slick streamlining of the snow where I was climbing. The wind had done that streamlining because it was whipping unopposed over the mountaintop. And you can expect cornices there, if your wits are working. The only thing working for me had been dumb luck.

I eased down the pass and crossed to Breeze Lake again, curiously lighthearted, studying every cornice in sight. When one of the boot bindings came loose, I elected to proceed with the snowshoes on my pack. I can't remember ever feeling more of that high-country elation than I did back at Upper Chain Lake that night, feasting on fairly scrappy trout and peach brandy.

Next day, I packed out again. It wasn't merely that I was short on rations; I found myself fighting temptation to make some ice-climbing experiments for which I wasn't equipped. In particular, I tended to think how "easily" I'd come through the errors, to tell myself I was on a roll of luck and that nothing could hurt me. That's why I hauled my hardware down to the trailhead before something *did.*

My kids laughed when they saw the warped, heat-dried bearpaw snowshoes, the nylon lacings now slack. They talked a lot about what fun I'd had. Well, they were right, but they can't possibly understand the respect I've developed for the experienced high-country winter hiker. I know now just how much I needed a companion for safety's sake—but I enjoy the solo trips too much. That's why I'll always be just a summer soldier.

The Woodpacker: Backpackable Woodstove

It's hard to say exactly when the Woodpacker stove became a viable alternative for me. It may have been the first time I watched a friend troubleshoot his nifty little gasoline stove in fading light, two miles high in the sierra; or the time a friend found that his liquid fuel had leaked into his granola supply; or the time I saw the weighing-in of stove fuel for a three-week pack trip. You get the idea—at some point I decided that the Basque shepherds were just as well off with their little woodstoves.

The trouble with traditional shepherd stoves is that they are so infernally heavy. I needed a woodstove that would fit into the top of a medium-sized backpack and would weigh roughly two pounds. It couldn't be temperamental—it must work as high as trout streams run, clear up above the timberline—and I wanted to build it mostly from parts available at any hardware store.

As it turned out, the image in my mind's eye took some detours and required lots of development before it became a reality in my pack. I toyed with several versions of the "comet," a tin-can fire carrier used by Europeans during WWII, but soon abandoned the notion. A comet doesn't draw much of a draft, and I wanted something that could draw like Pablo Picasso. I studied the packable stainless-steel woodstoves developed by the U.S. Army, and wondered why the devil they made such poor use of the heat in the wood. Then I stoked some old-fashioned Swedish stoves, and wondered why I'd never seen one that could be carried in a backpack. Finally I roughed out some specifications and headed for the hardware store in search of ready-made parts.

Satisfaction came after three months of development in a series of little breakthroughs. Now I have a woodstove that:

- will cook a meal for two with one charge of wood
- weighs 40 oz. including the high-country stack extension
- is both cookstove and space heater, with an adjustable elbow to let its smokestack angle out through tent flaps
- has a telescoping stack that doubles as a protective metal sheath for my fiberglass pack rod
- can be built in a single evening
- has cooked hundreds of meals and shows little sign of deterioration
- isn't an *open* fire.

This stove (Fig. 1) is not the first model I built; I snipped a lot of sheet metal before getting all the dimensions right. But it's the first one that incorporates all the design innovations. I began using it seven years ago and haven't needed to build another; I just wash and repaint it now and then.

Figures 1 and 2 show the stove burning a charge of

Fig. 1. Woodpacker portable stove is a nifty addition to any campsite.

wood the size of the chunks resting on the flat stone to the right of the stove. Though the elbow and stack joints aren't truly airtight, the stack draws so well that virtually no smoke issues from anyplace but the top of it.

Fig. 2. With the damper in place, a fire will burn a half-hour or longer in the Woodpacker.

After starting the fire with kindling, you add a preliminary charge of twigs the size of your finger. When these are blazing, you stuff the stove full of much bigger chunks, pull the stoke-hole door down using its folding wire handle and adjust the damper. The damper handle, a wire loop, is visible in Fig. 2, protruding from the base of the stack elbow. Once the full charge of wood is burning well, you can slow its combustion with the damper and have a fire that will burn for a half-hour or more, depending on the kind of wood you use.

A word of caution about your choice of wood: don't burn pine cones or other pitchy wood unless you want to ream bubbles of carbonized creosote from the stack every day or so. However, if you *do* find your stack clogging with creosote, you can clean it

Fig. 3, prefabricated parts, and one evening's time, are all you need to construct the Woodpacker.

with small pine cones. Just keep stuffing them into the disassembled stack until full, then push them out the other end with a stick.

The Woodpacker illustrated here has a high-country stack extension fitted atop the basic lower stack. If you're not going higher than 6,000 feet, you can leave the extension at home. I generally carry it in the Cascades anyway because, at any elevation, it lets me cook more cleanly, and it projects fewer sparks.

The flat stones flanking the stove aren't merely work surfaces. They are also weights, resting atop wire pieces that protrude from the sides of the stove. The stove body is so light that the stack tends to tip it over. The wire stabilizer feet, like the stoke hole cover handle, fold flat for stowage.

Figure 3 shows how the elbow can be adjusted to let the stack extend at various angles. This is especially useful when you're using the stove in a tent or other shelter because you can direct the stack outside at any angle you choose. The stack can get hot enough to char tent fabric, so be sure to obtain plenty of clearance. I drilled small holes at the lip of the stack pieces so that the stack can be guyed in place with wire. Normally, though, I don't need guy wires, as the stones atop the stabilizer feet help anchor the Woodpacker.

Fig. 4, "Model" baffle is held beneath completed Woodpacker.

The Baffling Secret: The secret of the Woodpacker's efficiency lies in the shape of its internal baffle. While experimenting, I gauged the stove's efficiency by the time it took to boil a cup of water. (On an electric stove this takes a bit over six minutes). In my first disheartening trials with my little rig, it needed nearly 15 minutes! But that was before I added baffling to it.

I cut boiling time down to 12 minutes when I first added baffles. Then I built a sloping addition to the baffle that forced the hot gasses to sweep up and forward, then past a baffle lip that guided the gasses beneath the cooking surface before letting them exit up the stack. By changing the dimensions of that sloping baffle and curving it slightly, I eventually got the boiling time down to eight minutes. No amount of tinkering and torture of sheet metal made it any better, though I did get a five-minute boil by using an aluminum cup with a cover. Every little nuance of heat transfer is important.

Could the Woodpacker be improved? Sure. For a start, you could rig a metal-foil wind guard to keep breezes away from the cooking surface. You could also make a wire grid (or use pebbles as I do) to keep a biscuit pan elevated off the cooking surface and prevent the biscuits from browning too fast on the bottom. You could build a tent-flap guard to fit around your stack. Or, even though the Woodpacker doesn't shed much light, you could further lower your night profile by installing a metal-mesh trap over the top of the stack and prevent that occasional spark from escaping.

Figure 3 proves that you can build your Woodpacker with prefabricated parts. The smokestack is made from a pair of 22-inch lengths of two-inch-diameter rainspout. They're made of galvanized steel, but the zinc will soon disappear from the lower stack. Note that the upper-stack extension was slit down its entire length with a modeler's saw. Simply curl one

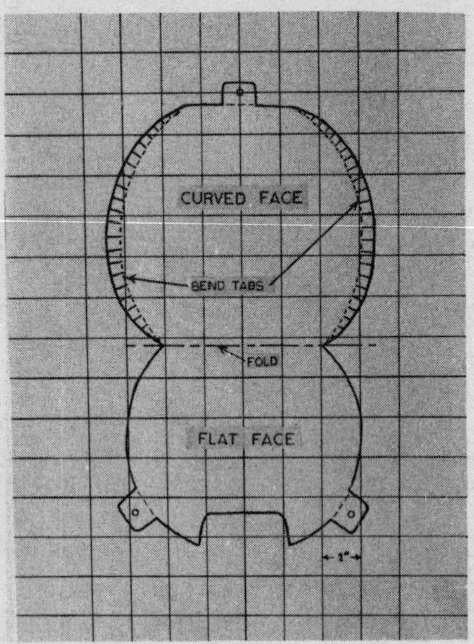

Fig. 5, lay out a full-size pattern on one-inch grid lines and make a cardboard mockup before starting with actual materials.

edge of this extension under the matching edge, forcing its diameter a bit smaller so that it slides down inside the basic stack for stowage. It projects a few inches from my pack and protects my five-piece fishing rod.

The elbow is another piece of rainspout hardware, articulated so that you can angle it up to 90 degrees. The damper is built into the elbow; it's merely a disc of steel pierced by a length of cast-hanger wire. The wire pivots in holes drilled in the elbow. Both ends of the wire should be looped: that way it can't fall out, and the loops make handles to adjust the damper.

The elbow's crimped end fits into a prefabricated collar (yes, more rainpsout hardware!) which I spot-welded into a hole cut into the stove body as shown in Fig. 3. If you can't spot-weld, you might get by with wire anchors threaded through drilled holes, but I don't recommend it. Soldered joints would melt immediately.

The stove body (Fig. 4) is nothing more exotic than a three-pound coffee can with some holes, a baffle system and a few spot-welds. Make sure the can's major seam is not joined by solder alone, but is a folded sheet-metal joint. Opposite the elbow collar is the stoke hole, roughly four inches wide and three-and-a-half-inches high. The stoke hole is cut near the bottom of the coffee can, leaving the rolled bottom lip of the can intact for strength. When cutting the stoke hole, fold the metal edges inward to avoid sharp edges.

The rolled top and bottom lips of the coffee can are very useful because they're sturdy enough to let you spot-weld a pair of strong steel wires (coat-hanger wire or even 1⁄16″ welding rod) from the top to the bottom lip. Weld the wires so that they flank the stoke hole (see Fig. 4). They will become the guides for your stoke-hole cover, permitting you to slide the cover up and down.

The stoke-hole cover is made from another coffee can, its bottom incorporating the can's rolled lip for added strength. Save the rest of the can; you'll need it to build the baffle. Notice the four tabs on the stoke-hole cover (Figs. 3 and 4). They slip between the stove body and the spot-welded wire guides. Curl the tabs enough to keep the cover from slipping loose, but not enough to prevent it from sliding up and down over the stoke hole. The wire handle for the stoke-hole cover fits into small drilled holes, with the ends of the wire sharply bent so that the wire handle will fold flat but cannot come loose.

At this point you could assemble the stove, but it wouldn't be efficient without the baffle system or rest securely without the stabilizer feet. The feet are a pair of sturdy U-shaped wires, the U about three inches wide and five inches long. Drill small holes in the stove body, just above the lower rolled-metal lip, and mount one stabilizer foot through the holes on each side of the stove body (Fig. 4). Curl the wire ends so that the stabilizer feet can fold against the stove body or lie flat on the ground. When the feet are weighted with big stones, the stove will be stable, even with its stack extended at an angle.

Now you're ready to build the baffle. Study the pattern in Fig. 5, lay out a full-size pattern on one-inch grid lines and make a mockup pattern from thin cardboard first. Bend all the tabs down and fold the cardboard into the hand-held shape shown in Fig. 4. Next try fitting your cardboard pattern into the stove body. It should fit snugly. It may take a bit of trimming, especially on all the small tabs that surround the edge of the lower part of the baffle.

When the cardboard pattern is in place, you'll see that the shallow U-shaped cutout in the flat (upper) face of the baffle is to provide clearance for the elbow collar, which protrudes into the stove body slightly. You'll also find that you can get your fingers inside the collar to locate the mounting holes of the two large tabs on the baffle. The third large mounting tab is at the bottom of the curved (lower) face of the baffle, clearly visible when you turn the stove body upside down. I'm not sure why the slight curvature of the sloping face of the baffle aids the stove's efficiency, but it works best that way.

Since it's possible to orient the baffle poorly, note that the main fold of the baffle should be at the front of the stove, with its flat upper face only about a half-inch below the cooking surface. It will be anchored with screws through the three large tabs. The lower face of the baffle curves down toward the back of the stove, and the bottom tab will be anchored about halfway down the stove body.

Now it's time to cut the steel baffle from the remains of the second coffee can. You may be tempted to use aluminum. Don't; it would melt the first time you used it. Be sure to bend all tabs, including the small ones, downward as shown in Fig. 4. These smaller tabs help keep hot gasses from short-cutting past the folded lip of the baffle.

When the steel baffle assembly is shaped, push it into the stove body and drill the screw holes for the mounting tabs. Instead of my fingers, I cobbled up pieces of wood for holding the two hidden tabs in place while drilling blind holes through the stove body and tabs. If you're not confident about blind drilling, take several careful measurements to make sure the drill bit won't miss the tab. The bottom tab is easier to hit accurately because you can eyeball it. I used very small, steel machine screws and nuts to hold the three baffle tabs, but you could probably use sheet-metal screws. Don't use aluminum screws or fiber nuts; they can't take the heat.

What's next? Assembly and stoking! I find that the Woodpacker operates best with the stoke-hole covered almost completely. Your first model may take a full day of snipping, pattern-making, cussing and spot-welding, but the result should last for years. You won't ever curse a needle valve or spill lethal, flammable stove fuel on your knickers while packing with this stove. If fishing above timberline, you'll find that a single sackful of dry wood can keep you cooking for nearly a week. My Woodpacker kept me cozy through a two-week solo in knee-deep Sierra snow during the frigid July of 1980.

Common sense tells you the Woodpacker won't cook for more than two or three people: its cooking surface is just right for a scout cook kit, but barely adequate for a 10-inch skillet. The same common sense will tell you to be careful about stoking up when fire danger is high. The stack *will* blurt out a few sparks. The stove body gets hot enough to ignite twigs or paper lying next to it. Never place a Woodpacker directly on humus or other flammable material, nor place stones such as quartz near enough that they might burst from the heat.

You could, of course, build a larger stove from a bucket. It might bulge in your pack, but it would serve more people, too. My feelings wouldn't be hurt if someone improved on the model I use but, just as it stands, the Woodpacker has a permanent place in my backpack. You may find it, at the very least, an interesting alternative—and you must admit that the price is right!

Safetynet: Pest-Proof Headgear

Confound those mosquitoes! Whether you're in a serious survival situation, day camping, fishing, watching an outdoor event or just snoozing, you have to be able to avoid the pests. But what if you're out of repellent, or if the bugs just seem to ignore it?

You really should have a bug-free backup system, unless you want to risk going nuts from clouds of mosquitoes or similar pests. Ever hear stories of people driven to suicide by insect-induced madness? I've seen hikers in full panic, swinging wildly and hopelessly at their tiny tormentors, running around blindly, staggering, colliding with trees. I've also seen hikers build smudge fires and deliberately stand in the smoke to escape mosquitoes, preferring instead the danger of inhaling all those particulates.

During the height of mosquito season, some campers won't budge from a tent within an hour of dawn or dusk—hours when mosquitoes are most ravenous—and some will lug enormous net-equipped tents on their backs rather than provide a meal for the bugs.

Others will seek the breeziest site for camp, regardless of what the wind may do to fires or general

The author models a Safetynet while wearing full backpack gear. The net can come clear down to the waist without impeding hand movement. To fit the net over yourself and backpack, gather the netting into a roll and place it atop your pack before you shrug into your straps.

comfort, because mosquitoes can't hack a spanking breeze.

We wear dark clothing, select second-rate campsites, chew smoke, lurk indoors, haul big tents and sometimes flatly refuse to engage in outdoor activities, all because of mosquitoes. It's truly a maddening, saddening problem. But, if you avoid wearing shorts or trousers that the bugs can penetrate, and

The author's first stab at an effective Safetynet (right) lacked the requisite stiffness to keep mosquitoes away from the body. The current design (left), made of two yards of stiff netting, solved the problem. It's roomy enough to do the job, and folds into a sandwich-size packet. Photos by Dana Ing.

get yourself two yards of stiff mosquito netting, a solution is at hand.

Locate good, sturdy nylon netting that will hold its shape fairly well. Buy the stuff a yard wide, two yards long and in a dark hue, if possible. Then fold it double and sew it closed along the two opposing selvages (the non-ravel self-edging on any bolt of cloth), leaving the long, bottom edge open. You now have a yard-square upper-body hood, resembling a big net pillowslip, that will fold into a packet smaller than a ham sandwich and is a whole lot more useful. I've dubbed it the Safetynet.

I've kept a half-dozen Safetynets around for years, ever since I camped on a swampy lake boasting a mind-boggling mosquito hatch, and tried covering my exposed surfaces with mud to escape the consequences. I figured there had to be a more elegant solution!

Affluent campers always had a partial solution: a tent with mosquito netting. But this was 1960, and I was a penniless backpacker who enjoyed solos. It took me an entire week to deduce the obvious: If your lower body is covered with jeans, leathers or sleeping bag, you need only enough net to cover your upper body. On my next trip into high country, I had a Safetynet.

Only, it wasn't a very good one. I still have it, chiefly as a bad example. It's a lot better than nothing, but its weave is gossamer. It lacks stiffness, so it lies close to your skin and mosquitoes can lance you right through it. The solution is stiffer netting which stands away from your body a lot better.

You can wear your Safetynet while hiking, working or even biking near beehives. In Figure 1, I'm wearing full pack and Safetynet. The capacious net comes clear down to the waist, but your hands are free and your vision is almost unimpeded (the netting does deepen shadows a bit). You may find it easier to get the net over you and a backpack if you gather the netting into a roll and place it atop your pack before you shrug into your straps. You can leave the netting raised, resting above and behind your head, when on a long trek—ready to be tugged down whenever you run into a swarm of trouble.

I sometimes smoke a pipe, and it's no trick to do it while wearing a Safetynet. Squadrons of your insect enemies can whine and fizzle in frustration around you, but rarely does one find its way up inside the net. And that's one that won't get away!

Have you ever felt that mosquitoes gang up on you when fly fishing is at its best? Well, just don your Safetynet and go to it. Yes, the net does impede you a little but, on balance, I don't mind. It sure beats getting bitten until my eyes swell shut.

While sleeping, you'll want to fluff your Safetynet out, or perhaps rig it tentlike with rubber bands, barbless hooks and monofilament line. And try not to toss and turn; there's a definite knack to it. If you move around so that the netting is against your unprotected skin, you're candy for the bugs.

So, if mosquitoes are keeping you or your loved ones from camping experience, give Safetynets a try. Wear 'em in good health.

The Backpacker's Saw Quandary

They say geese come in gaggles and eggs in clutches, and after years of testing, I'm convinced that saws for survivalists and backpackers come only in quandaries. Which should you carry? You can't tote them all, and no single choice is best for every job you're likely to need a packsaw for, so: a quandary it is.

Having growled the bad news first, I'll admit that the other news is good. After evaluating a dozen small portable saws over the past several years in rough country, I can report on a few that might save your bacon in different tight spots. What's more, you may decide to avoid some models as flimsy, ill-chosen, or just plain dangerous.

Let's start with the smallest of the lot, the ringsaw—often called a wiresaw, and sometimes adapted as a bowsaw. Boy scout suppliers sell them for pocket change. Figure 1 shows three of 'em. Each saw is a tempered and twisted steel wire with toothed edges, both ends swaged (squeezed) into terminals that connect to hefty steel rings. In theory, and often in practice, the ringsaw is a great bargain in compact survival tools. But it's no bargain if it breaks. The thinnest of my ringsaws (also the longest, 19½ inches

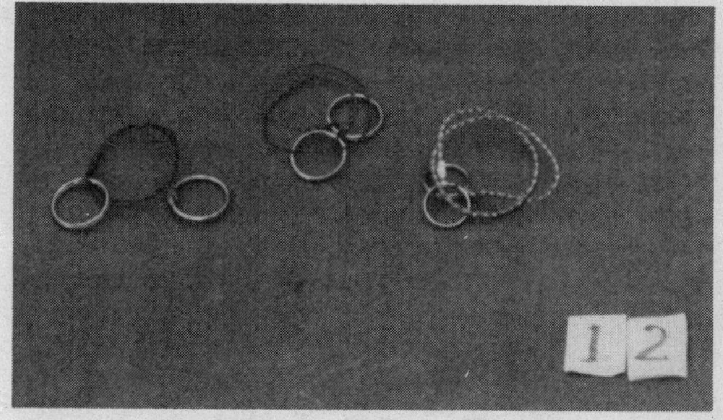

Figure 1

between rings) broke at the swaged terminal before I'd sawn through a dozen four-inch poles of green fir. I tied it to the loose ring and kept at it, the tied end nicking the thumb of one glove several times, while cutting more poles. The *other* terminal broke after a few more poles. Enough said.

In this test I used the ringsaw in its most primitive way, with gloved thumbs through the rings, pulling back and forth to keep tension on the wire as its teeth bit into the poles. Later I bought another and tried it as a bowsaw, bending a flexible, finger-thick green hardwood stick as the bow (you can anchor the rings by simply cutting slots into the ends of the bow and pressing the saw wire into the slots like a bowstring). Well, maybe I just expected too much; this one broke too, on similar saplings. The wire was very thin and made excellent cuts, and for light exact cuts like a coping saw, it might serve. Don't count on its stamina.

Thicker ringsaws are a bit shorter. Mine survived fairly heavy use, both as bowsaws and with my thumbs through the rings. The swaged terminals for this thicker wire were heavy enough to last. The thicker the wire, the more energy you use,—generally true for saw blades—and I now keep a medium-thick ringsaw tightly coiled in my fishing vest with a thicker one in my pack. The things weigh almost nothing and once, fishing a bramble-choked ravine, I used one to fell an alder ten inches thick so I could climb out. Recommendation: get one of the sturdy type and keep it on you when you're in rough country.

Under the heading of "sportsaws" are the three shown in Figure 2. Let's get the cheapest of the lot out of the way immediately. I call it the Chinese Switchblade because it comes from Taiwan for $2, opens and locks like some pocket knives, and might have some use in pruning twigs or brandishing at a small unarmed intruder. Both the blade and the lock mechanism are too flimsy. That toothed nine-inch blade will snick out easily and might scare off a mugger. It sure didn't scare two-inch hardwood limbs.

Next comes a rugged little brushnipper by Knapp with a hollow cast-aluminum handle (ideal for stashing waxed matches), weighing 9 oz. with its leather scabbard. Elk hunters sometimes use saws like this to quarter a carcass because they'll cut through bone. It could serve as a nasty weapon, close at hand in its belt scabbard, because in addition to its teeth the ten-inch blade has a wicked, daggerlike point which can bore reasonably well through wood. One edge of the blade has small, unbeveled "ripsaw" teeth for fine cuts, and it tends to bind in green wood. The other edge means business; its teeth are coarser, with alternate top bevels. That means even-numbered teeth lean slightly to one side while odd-numbered teeth lean slightly to the other side. It clears out a wider cut, keeping the blade free of binding in deep cuts.

Footnote: a saw intended merely to cut with the grain often has simple, undifferentiated "chisel" teeth for ripping through wood. A saw for cutting cross-

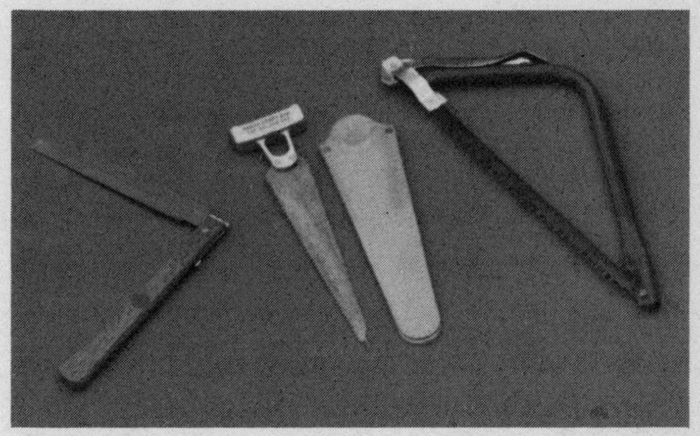

Figure 2

grain needs each tooth set so that both its top bevel and the bevel of the cutting edge alternate with every other tooth. The little Knapp saw would be perfect for more jobs, in my opinion, if its teeth also had alternating face shear—that is, if the bevel of each tooth's cutting face alternated as well. Maybe that's an extra we shouldn't expect for fifteen dollars, and a saw sharpener will do the job for you for a couple of dollars. E.M. Barr, author of *The 'How To' Book For Woodcutters* (reviewed in this book) reminds us that saw sharpening is an art and that you really should learn it, if your local expert will teach you about raker and cutter teeth, bending ("setting") teeth for alternate bevel, and so on. An hour's meticulous work with pliers and a slender dressing file can quadruple your productivity with a saw.

The Stansport bowsaw is made in Taiwan, but don't despair; its foot-long blade is locked into the tubular steel bow under high tension and will fell a six-inch fir in seconds. It has both cutter and raker teeth to keep the sawdust flying, though I could ask for better bevels on the teeth. Yes, the blade is replaceable. Consider buying a length of blade stock and making your own spares. Or maybe you'd rather carry several different types of blades: hacksaw, ripsaw, cross-cut, and so on. That's always an option when bandsaw blade stock can be ground and bored to fit your saw. Stansport's little lopper is a wonderful bargain at $4, is fairly sturdy, and weighs 12 oz. It has only two drawbacks: its bow is not collapsible; and as furnished, its blade (12″ of teeth) is not long enough to cut logs of the thickness suggested by its coarse teeth. If you're cutting poles four inches thick, it might be the tool of choice.

For felling real trees, you need one of the saws in Figure 3. The Pennsylvania bowsaw is a whopper, really too big for any but the most cavernous packs because its blade is 27″ and the tubular bow isn't collapsible. It's marginally big enough to be used as a two-person bucksaw on 18″ logs, the blade is replaceable, and its teeth are too coarse for fine work. Building a cabin? Keep the teeth set and sharpened, and bring a friend to haul on the opposite end during the heavy work.

The Sven-saw is my all-around favorite, a triangular collapsible bowsaw that stows as a slender elegant package. Its high-quality blade has 19″ of medium-coarse teeth with alternate top bevels and alternate face shear, so it cuts like a scatback both coming and going. The blade scissors to hide in an extruded aluminum arm, and the whole assembly slides into the anodized aluminum handle, locked by a wingnut both in use and for stowage. It costs about $18, takes up very little packspace, and weighs only 13 oz. I've seen them hung from belts by thongs. Don't; its pendulum swing will drive you batty. It will do fairly fine work and has cleared a trail of snags a foot thick though it's a bit of a hassle for anything larger. The first one I ever bought is still useable after cords of firewood, years of heavy use, and several resharpenings.

This isn't to suggest that it's still like new. That aluminum arm will take a permanent kink, and the slender socket hole in the aluminum handle does get sloppy in time. I narrowed the socket again by boring a small hole and looping several turns of wire through the socket mouth. I straightened the arm so that it once again held the blade in tension. The point is that it's such a great saw, you really won't want to toss it when it begins to fail. Nor do you have to; with careful repair it will last a decade.

Finally we come to a Taiwanese copy of the Sven-saw, a few dollars cheaper with what looks like an improvement in the steel handle: a socket hole that won't deform as easily. It weighs an ounce more and its arm is two inches longer, with excellent teeth like the Sven-saw. The thing could have been an improvement, but its handle is an inch *shorter*. It is shorter at the handgrip, exactly where you want it longer. Further, its blade was obviously cut from bandsaw stock by somebody who didn't care whether the last few teeth engaged a tree, or the user's fore-

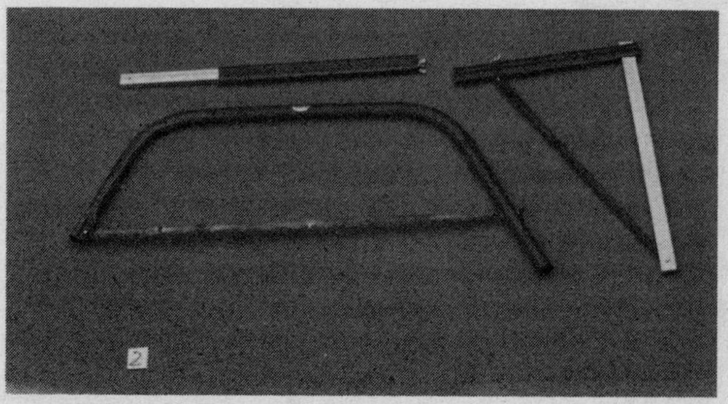

Figure 3

finger. I always use thin leather gloves, but I did not greatly appreciate having to sew mine up after ten seconds of using this abortive copy. Too bad; I could grind off those last teeth, but that handle simply won't accept the full grip of an adult's hand. Never buy a saw until you've handled it—unless you only intend to take pictures!

You can find several other saws, sold for tree-trimming or campsaws, but to date I've found nothing better than some of these. You *could* choose one (the Sven-saw, maybe), but I'd recommend that you pack three: a ringsaw coiled and taped in a patch pocket; the Knapp saw on your belt instead of a heavy Bowie; and of course, the matchless Sven-saw in your pack. All three come to 22 oz. and $35; a modest outlay. Together they'll cut through your quandary of saws.

Biker's "Second-Stage" Kit

Evacuation from urban disaster is generally conceded to be limited by traffic bottlenecks. We've come to think of urban evacuation (which the government terms 'crisis relocation') in terms of staged vehicles. Your family car is the big booster vehicle which you keep as long as it seems likely to convey you. Your bicycle(s), mounted atop the car where minor accidents can't wreck the bikes, qualify as second-stage vehicles.

Foot power is, by implication, your third stage. But you can carry a bike over obstacles or through water and if you part with that bike you'll probably regret it. One English officer, adventurous to the point of cheerful lunacy, was famous for his solo bike rides through Persia and India prior to World War I. Intent on a wild-boar hunt with fellow sahibs, he needed to cross the Ganges to join the fun. His minor problem: the Ganges was in flood—and the Ganges is no placid brook. Our ingenious madman removed his inner tubes, pumped them up much fatter than their usual diameter, and bound them to him as waterwings!

In a less daunting current, you could probably

bind those fattened inner tubes to your bike and float it across very considerable bodies of water. Just don't forget your bike pump. Oh, yes: did the barmy biker succeed? Well, the first time he tried it, *at night*, a passing tree trunk floated by and knocked him sensible. Next morning he had another go at it, and triumphantly swam the flooded Ganges wearing his rubber bandoliers.

We won't dwell here on the details of bikes and their elegant simplicity, but we'd like to show you a modestly-sized 8-lb. survival kit to be strapped to a second-stage vehicle. No doubt we've forgotten a few important items, and some of you will probably write to tell us so. Thanks in advance; try using this kit as a departure point for cobbling up your own. If you must finally abandon your bike, remember that you can strap this little kit inconspicuously onto your belt at the small of your back. By the way, we didn't forget the bike pump; it fits on the bike frame, not in the kit.

LEFT SIDE
(Top to Bottom)

Bike bag with:
- spare inner tube inside

Sealed baggie with:
- raisins
- salt container
- bouillon cubes

Sealed baggie with:
- caffeine tabs
- aspirin tabs
- needles
- fish hooks with leader
- safety pins
- heavy mending thread
- compass
- waxed matches
- razor blades

Wool yarn for sock repair.

Aluminum food grinder with:
- special tee-handle

Coil of wire with:
- stub candle inside

RIGHT SIDE
(Top to Bottom)

Baggie under its normal contents:
- bike repair tools
- spare chain links
- cold-patch kit

Baggie under its normal contents:
- spare eyeglasses
- waxed linen cord
- roll of dimes
- water purification tabs
- spare bootlaces
- flashlight
- ¼-mile spool, 25-lb. test nylon

Awl for leather and canvas repair.

2 large polyethylene garment bags.

Mechanic's kit in heaviest foil. Foil is heavy enough to be used to boil water or as reflector for a cooking fire. Note shape of kit, bound with huge slingshot rubber; kit can be swung as a truncheon. Thin mink-oiled leather gloves.

CONTENTS OF MECHANIC'S KIT

Small vise-grips
Hand drill (protruding) and bits
Adjustable-jaw wrench
Screw extractors
Screw taps
Small files, round and triangular
Razor blades in wax
Short hacksaw blades
Small nails
Screw and nut assortment
Machinist's pocket data book
6″ plastic slide rule

Keeping Those Wheels Unstuck

One fall day some years ago, I followed an old Oregon back-country road toward the coast in my VW bus. I was accompanied by two grade-school daughters and a teen-aged cousin. It was raining Persians and Poodles, but our map said the road went all the way.

The map lied. The road ended on a steep uphill slope and, trying to back down on a slippery high-crowned trail, I let the bus slip into the eroded ditch. That ditch was literally a mud-filled stream now, and I had no tow cable or winch.

I had snow treads on the bus, a trenching tool, a Sven saw, and tire chains stowed. (Why hadn't I put the chains on before starting up that slope? No fore-sight, that's why.) I cut two poles five feet long and, standing in the ditch with mud actually above one knee behind the bus, managed to insert the poles behind that buried rear tire. The girls laid tire chains down behind the other rear tire and laid brush along the chains. Then, while I pushed from the front, a teen-aged girl got the bus into reverse.

She learned quickly (with me yelling at her over the drumbeat of rain on the bus) to avoid turning the front wheels too sharply. The bus galumphed down that slope past the poles and then stopped again. I fished the poles out from under the bus and started all over again. It took us three hours to get that bus to a level place in the ditch which we filled with brush and poles, digging a trail for the half-buried rear wheel to follow out of that ditch. We also dug a cross-trench upstream to divert most of that ditchwater. It helped.

Surprisingly, the kids took it as a challenge and, finally, as a triumph. I took it as a warning because I do not relish being referred to as "the mudman" by young twits.

Now, our vehicles always carry LONG tow straps and one-ton, hand-operated ratchet winches with their own short cables. I also bought junkyard spare wheels with mounted snow-treads ($15 apiece). Now, switching over for slippery going is as quick as changing tires. If needed, chains can be installed *before* you mount the snow tires.

A limited-slip differential is useful because, even if one drive wheel is whirling without traction, the other wheel can exert traction. With ordinary differentials, including that of my old VW bus, if one rear wheel is spinning, the other delivers no traction. Four-wheel drive is a wonderful option; with aggressive treads and chains, it can get you through deep mud, snow, or ice.

But deep sand is another matter; heavy ribbed treads can bite in and dig a hole for your tires, and you can wind up buried to your frame. If you're heading across deep, loose sand, switch to "nonaggressive" smooth treads if possible. In any case, lower your tire pressures to roughly half the usual pressure; that means down to fifteen pounds or so for most of us. If you do it before you drive into the sand you may not get stuck at all. The low pressures let the tread squash out for a balloon effect, giving the tire a broad "footprint" to ride over the sand.

When you're past the sand traps and onto firmer footing, do not delay in reinflating your tires because under-inflation ruins a tire quickly. Yes, you can keep a small foot pump for this, but—have you ever reinflated four tires that way? Shinsplint pain will have you hobbling. Invest in a 12-volt motorized inflator instead. I've seen a van with a permanently-installed surplus air tank carrying high-pressure air and a long inflator hose. That's even faster, but in an accident that tank could rupture explosively. It's my guess that one day, special fiber-wrapped high-pressure air tanks will be a common option to run jacks, starters, and other systems on cars.

You only have to get stuck once to realize an instant payoff from your modest investment in a ratchet winch and long tow strap. A wire rope, or cable, is often cheaper per foot but it has its hazards, including frayed wire that can penetrate gloves (you do have leather gloves stowed?) and the possibility of snapping. Any logger can tell you what even a small chain or cable, under enough tension to snap it, can do as it whipcracks after parting. No ifs, ands, buts or exaggerations: it can cut you in two or, at the least, sever an arm or leg, before you can react.

A nylon strap, on the other hand, stretches a lot before parting, and tends to part with less violence. Avoid lightweight straps the size of seat belts and choose a strap that's rated at twice the weight of your vehicle. Why? Because when you're winching the vehicle in, it can lurch and apply extra loads. Besides, synthetics do tend to deteriorate in time, especially in sunlight, so keep the tow strap covered and clean in stowage. You don't want that strap to part. When researching full safety harnessing for racing cars, I watched tension tests on nylon straps. Dirt particles crushed in the webbing will literally pop, flying away with tiny dust trails, as the tension reaches extreme levels. Those particles are sharp and, as they pop out, can damage the fibers. No matter what kind of tow strap you use, imagine that it *will* part under tension and keep well clear. You can't tell which direction the frayed ends will take. The truth is, when operating that ratchet winch, you take a slight chance that it could snap. Don't risk exceeding its rated load. The little winch uses a few feet of steel cable, which can be extended to a distant anchor with the heavy nylon strap.

Most electric frame-mounted winches use steel cable. They can haul your hardware out of a hole in a hurry, but again, you'll be safer if you use a short cable and a long nylon strap. You may have to stop, pay out the cable again, and take up the slack on the strap. Take your choice, and your chances.

So what kind of anchor do we use to winch ourselves out of our mess? If it's a tree, wrap your strap around it as near the ground as possible. If there is no sturdy anchor handy, tie the end of the tow strap around something very sturdy, like a big tire tool, or a heavy hunk of firewood. Bury the sonofagun knee-deep in a hole ten yards or so from the vehicle and fill the hole, and watch carefully as you apply tension. A huge load may unearth that anchor, but it often works. If you can't find any single sturdy item to bury, try collecting a bundle of smaller items to strap and bury: small branches, for example. In a real pinch you might bury your auto jack or even your spare tire as an anchor.

Army manuals used to show how you can winch a truck up an open slope using a clever multiple anchor. In line with the direction of pull, you drive several long steel pegs, perhaps ten feet apart, deeply into the ground (sturdy wooden poles will do in a pinch). Each peg is driven so that it leans away from the truck, and each peg must stick up at least knee-high. Now tie the winch strap at the *base* of the nearest peg. Take a rope,—a tire chain might serve as well—and tie it without slack from the *top* of that same peg to the *bottom* of the next peg. Link the top of that next peg to the bottom of the third one, in the same way.

It may sound weird, but it affords tremendous leverage. As your winch tugs against the base of the nearest peg, it is trying to pull the leaning peg vertical. But the top of that peg is restrained by the rope (or tire chain) linking it to the base of the next peg, and so on. You may never have to use the Army way, but it's a good trick to know.

I knew that some desert roads were first made of planks, but I learned a very special trick from an elderly couple who won a loving cup three feet high for being the first tourists of the year to arrive at snowbound Lake Tahoe in the early 1920s. They made it, I believe, in February, by lashing a bunch of one-by-ten planks atop their touring car. When they got to heavy snow, they simply laid down a "road" of planks and drove over them for miles, removing and replacing planks to refresh the road ahead! It ought to work across loose sand, too.

Of course there are a million ways to get unstuck, some requiring shovels. Some branches, even low underbrush, can provide a lot of traction through mud, sand, or ice if you lay enough of it in the path of your wheels. Usually you'll improve matters by offloading the vehicle. The lighter your vehicle, the easier it is to get it unstuck (three of us once picked up a race car bodily and carried it a short distance). And the more assorted heavy cordage and tools you have, the broader your options for getting unstuck. Without flashlights or long extension cords, for plug-in lights, you would have a devil of a time employing any of the winch scenarios in the dark. And without that Sven saw and trenching tool, my old VW bus might still be mouldering away on a mountainside in Oregon.

The 12-Volt Solution

It doesn't take a global disaster for you to have a serious 110-volt problem. Virtually all of us have had it, and will again. Examples? About 20 years ago, my Texas kin huddled in a cyclone cellar while the infamous Lubbock tornado juggernauted overhead, dismantling most of their house in the process. In the center of a modern city, they and many others went without electricity for days—*unnecessarily*. That's what I mean by the 110-volt problem; it wouldn't be so much of one if we didn't unthinkingly depend so much on public utilities. Twice, in Oregon, winds and ice storms have left us bereft of house current for a day or so—yet we scarcely missed it.

There are ways to lessen that panicky feeling when your lights all wink out at once, your stereo groans to a halt and your coffee maker cools. First, you could get used to doing without; lots of folks do. Or you could assemble camping gear where you can find it in the dark, for use when house current fails. Or pile in the car and drive to a friend's—weather permitting—if your friend hasn't lost all his volts, too. We don't rely on this option because our place is reachable only by roller-coaster roads, and tire chains

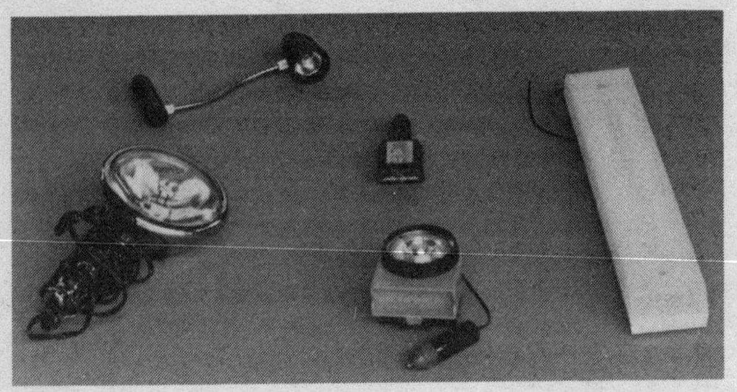

Clockwise from top: High-intensity map light, two-tube fluorescent lamp, magnet-backed trouble light with reel of cord, powerful spotlight, and (center) battery tester.

don't always keep us headed in the right direction during the worst weather.

Many people recommend home-generated electricity and, oddly enough, a few of us even have it! If you invest in a turbine or wind-generator system, you're talking about a lot of time and money. It's an excellent idea, but most of us probably won't do it. Then there's the emergency engine-driven alternator; they start at about $400 surplus, but usually cost several thousand. I can testify that they take up a lot of space, require maintenance, make noise, burp carbon monoxide and heat, and don't always work properly. The last time our power lines petered out, we didn't even start our two-kilowatt unit because we had a handier solution to an evening's inconvenience. We've dubbed it the 12-volt solution.

If you've ever converted a van into a camper, you may have guessed what I'm suggesting. The solution involves the family car. Naturally, you can't run a washer and dryer, or a microwave oven, off your standard auto battery—but it's astonishing how many amenities you *can* have if you don't overdo it. We've all seen 12-volt gadgets that plug into a car's cigarette-lighter socket. But have you noticed the extension cords for them? If you can't buy 12-volt auto extension cords locally, you can order them. Or you can sometimes buy male and female receptacles and attach them to standard 16-gauge insulated wiring of the sort normally used for household extension cords. It's best to avoid wiring thinner (with a *higher* number) than 16-gauge, because the thinner the wire, the greater your line losses—especially using direct

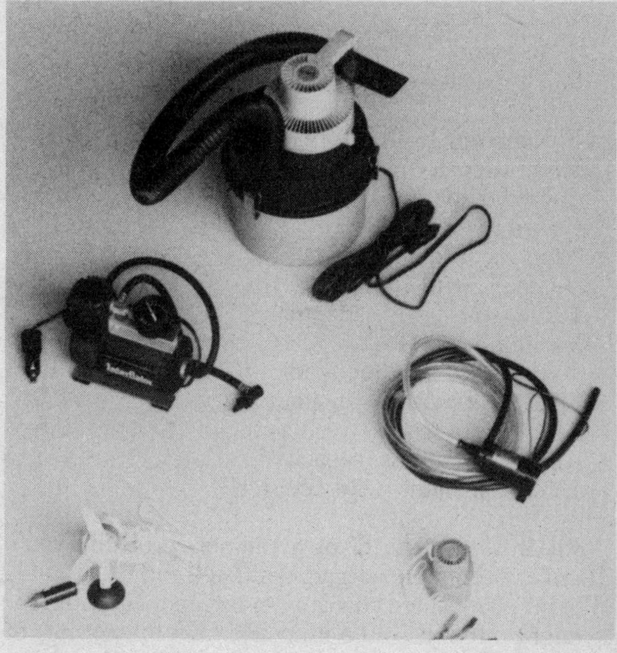

Clockwise from top: Canister vacuum cleaner, water pump with tubing, spark-plug sandblaster, fan, and 160-psi air pump.

current. Ten-gauge would be ideal, though costly, if you're cobbling up your own.

Those line losses needn't be great if you're using your car battery for things like low-amperage lights and radios with 12-volt adapters. Even here you can get cute with energy savings. A fluorescent lamp provides more light than most incandescents of the same power. You should buy your accessories with amperage ratings in mind.

But just how varied are those accessories? Very! A partial list of our 12-volt plug-ins includes:

Accessory	**Approximate Amps**
Small magnet-backed trouble light	less than 0.5
Fluorescent two-tube reading lamp	0.4
High-intensity map light	0.2
Powerful spotlight	2.1
Coffee maker	7 to 10
Tape recorder (small, with adaptor)	less than 0.5
Radio (small, with adaptor)	less than 0.4
Vacuum cleaner (powerful canister type)	about 10
Sparkplug sandblaster (motor-driven)	1.5
Electric fan (small)	0.5
Air pump (160-psi capacity)	3.5
Hand calculator (with adaptor)	0.1

Ask a friend who owns a camper; probably you'll discover even more accessories that'll run on 12 volts. What if you wanted to rig an emergency fluid pump? It might pump gasoline from one tank to another, or water from a brook up to your radiator. The pump shown in Figure 2 delivers about two gallons per minute, a pretty respectable volume—but it must be primed and won't push water uphill very far. For higher pressure, but a somewhat lower volume, you could use an electric fuel pump. After all, an electric automotive fuel pump was *designed* to run on 12 volts.

Your camper-owning friend might also introduce you to the inverter or voltage converter, which converts battery voltage to a level compatible with your household voltage, though it's likely to be fairly expensive. But his eyes are likely to gleam when he tells you about the auxiliary-battery idea. Many recreational vehicles have a second hefty battery which doubles the electrical-storage capacity in your car. Your alternator recharges them both, which works the alternator a bit harder. The auxiliary battery should be installed with a "battery isolator," a solid-state device that'll withstand a 500-amp surge and is available for under $20. The battery-isolator wiring is very simple; just don't install it in a high-temperature location. The gadget directs the alternator's output to whichever battery has the lowest charge and, better still, prevents the discharge of the main battery while you're draining power from the auxiliary. The cost of this whole auxiliary-battery system runs about $60 to $70, which is very near the total cost of all the accessories we've accumulated.

Do you own a word processor? Whether it's portable or not, check for an adaptor that converts it to 12 volts DC. If it's portable, chances are it can be converted easily.

With this array of gadgets, you could find your power lines down some evening before having friends over, and barely break stride. You can vacuum the living room, update the family records on your computer, make coffee, listen to weather reports, warm the baby's bottle, clean the sparkplug on your lawnmover for the heck of it and then entertain your friends with tape cassettes and mood lights—all using the 12-volt solution. You'd be smart to minimize use

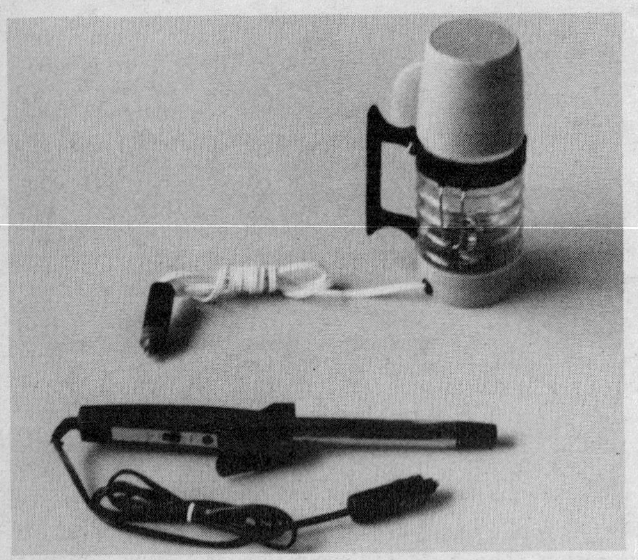

Top: Two-cup coffee maker. Bottom: Hair curler.

of heating elements, but the point is that you have a lot of options available.

So let's pretend your house current has gone belly-up temporarily, and your cars are near the house. The first thing to do is route your 12-volt extension cord(s) from the car through the nearest window. If your cars aren't near enough, see if you can push one of them within a dozen feet of a window. Don't start your car up with its battery to bring it nearer unless you have to, because starting the engine is a tremendous drain on the battery. (Car batteries could be a mere one-third the size they are, if it weren't for the huge jolt it takes to start a cold engine!)

On the other hand, you could start the car up and keep it idling for an hour or so, letting its alternator resupply the battery. Many cars will overheat if left idling very long, so monitor your engine's temperature if you're running it as an emergency-power plant. Since you might forget, perhaps you'd do better by just keeping tabs on the amount of amperage your 12-volt accessories are all using together.

Often the amperage rating is printed on the accessory—but all too often it isn't. The table in this article was compiled with the aid of a multitester, and can be used as a very rough estimate of the amperage drains you can expect. You'll find that any accessory which works primarily by generating heat, such as a curling iron, bottle warmer, coffee maker, etc., will use up lots more amperage than a gadget that produces a modest light, or runs a small motor. Big motors and spotlights make medium to heavy demands on your battery. If you intend to run

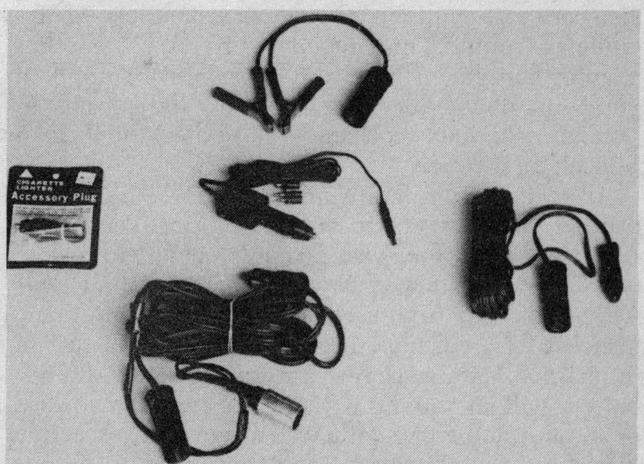

Clockwise from top: Direct-to-battery adaptor, 20-foot extension cord, extension cord with two outlets, male accessory plug, and (center) multiple-probe 6- and 9-volt adaptor. Photos by Dana Ing.

several accessories off the same lighter socket, you'd better know where its fuse is and have a spare. Ask a mechanic if your lighter-socket wiring can handle a somewhat higher fuse rating. Most fuses are literally two-bit items—unless you're one shy! I've been known to bridge a blown fuse with a piece of wire—but not to *recommend* it to anybody.

You'll surely want to run more than one device at a time, which can be done any of several ways. You could run extension cords from more than one car; run several extensions from the same car; or jury-rig a multiple-outlet from a single extension. Since few cars are factory-equipped with more than one lighter socket, you might have an extra socket or two installed. Or you can buy an extra socket with its own beefy little clips, and clip those leads directly onto the battery terminals.

I'm still searching for a commercial 12-volt extension cord with multiple "female" socket outlets. Meanwhile, I cobbled one together. It, and the other adaptor hardware I have, can be seen in Figure 4. If you're in doubt about how to wire the sockets in parallel, ask your mechanic—or perhaps he'll do it himself for a fiver.

After discussing how you do it, maybe I'd better caution you how not to *overdo* it. Most recent car batteries carry a four-year guarantee and, when new, will survive a drain of 25 amps for around an hour without damage from excessive discharge. (But many a socket fuse will blow before you reach that rate of discharge!) With a six-year guarantee, a new, heftier battery will let you draw that many amps for upward of an hour and a half without damage from excessive discharge. But whatever accessories you run off your car battery—without the engine and its alternator running—if they draw 20 amps for an hour, or 10 amps for 2 hours, you're in danger of overdoing it. You mustn't wait until your electric fan stops, or your reading lamp dims to a glow, because when low-amp accessories perform poorly you're running out of juice.

Soon after you detect a significant drop in performance of your accessories, unplug everything. Let the battery rest; it will regain some of its charge by itself. Or, if you're sure the car will start with very little cranking, make one attempt to start the engine and let its alternator revive the battery. You could even re-attach a low-amperage accessory or two once the engine's running. For that matter, there's a plug-in gadget that reads your battery's charge within broad limits and could let you monitor the drain you've laid on it. I use one, but I'm not sure it's a better monitor than the brightness of an incandescent bulb.

Finally, there's good news about the prices and the bulk of these accessories. Most accessories are priced right for a modest (even chintzy!) birthday or holiday gift. And they're compact enough that you can store them all in an apple crate. That means you can store them in your car, in case you develop a problem on the road. For years, I've chosen such gadgets and bought a half-dozen of them every November—for each of my close kin with a car. One by one, usually in highway emergencies, most of 'em have experienced a problem which dissolved with the 12-volt solution.

Making an Alternative Engine Oil

Piston engines have improved enormously since 1916, when Fokkers and Sopwiths tangled in dogfights over the trenches of Europe. Then, as now, military aircraft used the best lubricants money could buy for reliability. Petroleum-based oil was available, but many of those aircraft used castor oil instead!

Today we depend on cheaper engine oils. With detergents and other additives that keep the oils from thinning too much at high temperatures, these modern oils are better in some respects than castor oil. But in a pinch, we could use castor oil again.

Some years ago, I researched castor oil as an emergency alternative to petroleum-based lubricants. My own Porsche Special, and many of my competitors, used Castrol 'R,' the so-called bean oil, for racing. Castrol 'R' had its own additives, but basically it was still castor oil. Yes, it eventually causes a hard shellac to form on engine parts—but harmlessly; not on bearing surfaces. Yes, the durn stuff flows like glop when cold, and like water when it's hot—but as a thin-film lubricant it's great stuff. We wanted the best in engines turning 8500 rpm, and castor oil is slippery stuff. Yet, it is definitely a vegetable oil, since it comes from the bean of the castor bush—but this is one vegetable oil that could keep your VW going for a long time. If you're doubtful, check an engineering handbook on castor oil lubricant.

Some special engines still use castor oil though it is expensive. You may find model engine enthusiasts and go-karters using it for their expensive boytoys. Most of those engines are two-strokes with special fuels, and castor oil is added directly to the fuel, mixing well with alcohols too. But you may one day find it necessary to pour castor oil into the sump of your four-stroke engine. Be sure to drain your old oil completely before switching to castor oil, because castor oil doesn't mix with most other lubricants. It *does* mix with a few, notably a silicone-based racing lube called Steen 'C' which I can no longer find.

I've had a 50-50 mix of Castrol 'R' and Steen 'C' in the sump of my Corvair-powered Mayan Magnum (*see Road & Track*, May '68) for sixteen years now. I've never changed that oil. *Never*. Anyone who's willing to pay for an analysis of this much-used lubricant can put me to the test by draining a sample from the Magnum. All I ask is a copy of the analysis—I'm kinda curious about it myself! It may indeed be rotten junk by now, but the engine compression is still good. Oh, yes: I combined the two because the Steen oil didn't change its viscosity (thickness) much over a very wide range of temperature, and because castor oil is so lubricious (slippery). Will castor oil mix with some favorite multiviscosity lubricant of yours? I don't know; wish I had time to test every possible combination.

Okay, so castor oil is great; but it's exotic. How the devil can you get your hands on it during hard times? By processing it as I did. Correction: *almost* as I did. You'll see what I mean in a moment.

The castor plant, or Palma Christi, is a tall bush with large leaves often grown as an ornamental plant in warm climates, including much of California and sun-belt states. The plant and its seeds—beans to you and me—vary widely, so ask an expert to identify it for you. Many of the beans have a mottled shell, but the ones I collected from pods on the plant were a uniform grayish brown. I'm told some of the beans are quite large, but mine were smaller than common red beans. I was warned that the bean shells were hard, but found that I could crush one between thumb and forefinger. The oil-producing stuff inside was white and cheesy.

If I'd had a nut press, I could've expressed the oil by simply dumping my pound of beans into the press and squeezing until the oil came trickling out. Lacking a press, I decocted it. That is to say, I mashed the beans up, added water to make a soup, and boiled the whole mess for a half-hour, stirring as it simmered.

I drained the castor oil off the surface, then washed it—poured it into a mason jar with clean water and shook it—then poured it off the top and finally separated the oil from the water in a chemist's thistle tube. That wasn't difficult, since the clear light-yellow oil doesn't mix with water. The oil smelled right, looked right, felt right, and worked fine in my Ohlsson model engine.

Then I took a book and retired to the john. I did a lot of reading in the next twenty-four hours. I'm putting this as delicately as I can, but—you know the laxative properties of castor oil? Well, the confounded stuff works all too well when you're standing near while decocting it, too. An aircraft historian later told me, between fits of laughter at my sorry tale, that World War I fighter pilots made the same discovery. Sitting out there in God's open air behind an engine that wafted castor oil fumes back in his face, the pilot had good reason to make his flights brief. The historian swore that some flight suits, and pilot seats, were redesigned to provide fast, fast, fast relief for the suffering schnook in the cockpit. I don't know about the truth of that. I do know that if you decoct castor oil from beans, you'd be wise to use a fume hood or otherwise protect yourself from the fumes.

I extracted, if memory serves, only 50 ml. of oil from a pound of beans. Either I was klutzy or my beans were inferior; the *Britannica* says a hundred pounds of good beans will yield *five gallons* of oil. It might take a day to collect a hundred pounds of beans, and you'd have to grind them before decocting the oil. But it's a low-tech process.

Another text warns that the oil contains a violent alkaloid, ricin, which must be removed before the oil is taken medicinally. I don't know how that's done. Don't drink it; pour it into your VW. If your bug smokes a lot, lord help the fellow who chases you . . .

Teeth in Your Pocket

Food grinders are "must" items when it's time to grind cornmeal, leached acorns, tough meats, nuts (for oil, perhaps), or what-have-you. For a denture-wearer on a long trip afoot, a broken upper plate can be literally deadly unless you have a grinder. The short life-span of some Indians was partly due to health problems after their teeth deteriorated from grit in their stone-ground foods. We've seen skulls of people who died relatively young, with teeth completely worn down from grit.

The trouble is that hand grinders are so outlandishly shaped! The crank is big. So is the clamp, which isn't a "must" for your purpose. For our solution, study the photo.

We chose an aluminum-bodied unit for light weight, and we cut the unwieldy clamp off with a hacksaw because you can hold the throat of the grinder in one hand while you grind with the other. Then we made a tee-handle to replace the long one that came with the grinder. Notice that the tee-handle is short enough to fit down the throat of the grinder for easy carrying. A note about the tee-handle: any handyman can braze one for you. It should be sturdy, preferably of mild steel.

The grinder in the photo weighs a pound and will fit in a pocket, though this one usually rests in a bicycle kit. Once or twice a year it goes into a backpack.

Chimney Fires

One recent night, I was gazing across snowy rooftops when a column of fire and sparks began to rise in the near distance. It reminded me of a nose-down rocket test—but none of my neighbors have any old Shuttle boosters lying around! Someone burning Christmas wraps in his fireplace? Well, it started out that way. An awesome column of yellow flame, with tints of rose and deeper red, kept rising until it stood as high as a man above the chimney, tossing occasional bursts of sparks.

That pillar of fire stood on my horizon for a full minute before I got my buns in gear, slipping on the steep icy roadbed as I trotted toward my neighbor's place. I didn't know his name or I would have phoned.

He had no idea what was happening in his chimney flue, but one glance from his driveway told him the bad news. He did the two most important things fast: he levered the flue shut to choke off its air supply, and then he called the fire department.

Luckily, the fire truck was able to get up the icy patches to his place. The snow quenched all the sparks showering his roof, else we would've had to find an unfrozen garden hose to wet down the shingles. Closing the flue helped a lot, but the flame was still a foot high from his chimney when the firemen arrived ten minutes later.

We watched the professionals haul a second ladder to the roof and hook it over the roof peak before one man eased carefully near enough to the chimney to look down into that furnace. He had a hose with him, but did *not* squirt water down that hole! I asked him about that (and other things) later.

"The creosote was mostly burned out," said the fireman, "but the bricks in that flue liner were glowing red-hot. If I had shot water down that chimney, the thermal shock would have cracked those red-hot pieces of liner all the way through. And then somebody would either have to repair that whole chimney, or next time he started a fire he'd most likely burn the house down."

It was a judgment call, he said; sometimes a flue fire will crack the liner, and in such cases you must drown the flue fire to save the rest of the house. But it's an expensive option! In this instance, shutting off the damper kept the flue fire simmering along for quite awhile. Still, better that than having a pillar of fire two stories high that might well have ruined the upper part of the liner in its hellish combustion.

What could a homeowner do besides close the damper? This pro gave us a tip that could save lives: quickly get a ball of newspaper, half-soaked with water, and place it in the fireplace directly over the burning logs (or coals) *instead* of closing the damper. Great clouds of steam are generated fast; the ferocious draft created by the creosote burning in the flue will draw the steam up the chimney. That steam gets hot as you-know-what, but it chokes off the air supply as long as a good supply of steam is whirling up the chimney. You shut down the damper when the flue fire is out.

Doesn't a bit of the steam sometimes roil from the

fireplace into the room? Maybe, but this is no time for minor worries, guys: we've got a biggie up that flue! Of course it's a big help if your fireplace has a glass face so you can completely seal off the firebox from your living area.

When the flue fire is out, you're wise to wait an hour before building another fire. Without a seal over the mouth of your fireplace, you may have to drown the coals to avoid smoke damage in the meantime.

What else can a homeowner do? The obvious: keep the durn chimney clean of creosote deposits. The stuff is brittle and can be removed in an hour's sooty work.

ING'S

THINGS

Self-Reliance Scrapbooks

If you keep periodicals on self-reliance, you're probably serious about the notion. Chances are, you keep everything filed safely at home. That means you don't have them squirreled away in your car, or your backpack—but individual articles fairly beg to be collected, and stashed where you're most likely to need them.

Well, why don't you? Whichever vehicle you choose for survival wheels, you could profit from a scrapbook made up of articles on bugout kits, vehicles, and the right/wrong ways to operate them. Some of the best periodicals provide you with yearly indexes of articles. It shouldn't take you long to ferret out the pieces you want to reproduce. You can keep those as a scrapbook in your vehicle, just in case.

Several short articles can be cemented into a single sheet of heavy bond paper. Fixative spray can make each page highly resistant to water, oils, and smears. Reinforce each page for a loose-leaf binder. Number pages in boldface. You might type or print an index of those articles you've collected. Then consider doing the same thing for backpack or wilderness articles.

Meanwhile, there's an element of ethics (and of legality) to remember. It's illegal to reproduce entire issues of magazines, even though you've bought those issues. But there should be no problem if you reproduce individual articles for self-reliance scrapbooks.

* * *

Know Thy Neighbor

Many years ago, when everybody in a town knew all their neighbors, someone frantically called my grandmother on the phone one morning. A rabid dog, she learned, was on her property. She shot the poor creature dead as it was staggering toward two small children playing in the next yard. But all my Cherokee granny's cool determination would've been useless if a neighbor across the street had not known her name and phone number.

Recently I had to slither down icy slopes to inform a neighbor that he had a spectacular flue fire in his chimney—because, while I like the guy, I didn't know his name or number.

We can't know when we might need to make a fast call to give help, or to get it. It might be a good idea if we made simple maps of our locales, with names and phone numbers in boxes representing houses. I'm considering a block party soon, and I'll take that opportunity to pass the word. It might cost me $2 to xerox enough sheets for all my neighbors. It might also save me a bundle—or a life.

* * *

Getting Organized

How many clippings, books, and magazines do you have lying around with crucial data that you'd have to scratch hard to find again? It used to drive me nuts, knowing I had a crucial datum "somewhere," realizing I might spend two hours locating it. No more!

This may sound like a pain in the backside, but it becomes as easy as latching a seat belt and could be just as important, one day. Keep black and highlighter yellow flowpens and a pencil handy whenever you read any material you want to file; daily paper, pamphlet, whatever. When an extraordinarily useful item pops out at you, highlight it in yellow. If you have some comment you might forget, pencil it neatly in the margin. If the article is torn from magazine or newsprint, print your major topic boldly in black flowpen; a word or two will do.

File loose pages the same day you extract 'em. Your file might be a cardboard box and you'll find most items falling in perhaps twenty topics; food, transport, medicine, etc. Make topic separators and file your data by topic—but *chronologically*. New stuff always behind older stuff in that topic. Date everything you file. You may find conflicting reports and you'll want to know the more recent opinion when you look it up later.

When reading a book you own, index it as you go. Those blank leaves in front of the book are crying out to be used! Make a small dot in the margin next to an important passage, if you don't want to highlight it—but note the topic and page in the index you're compiling. You'll never be sorry; it's almost like having total recall.

* * *

Weatherproofing Your Papers

How many times have you found a map ruined by water or oil stains? It only has to happen once to get you lost, perhaps at a time when staying found is the difference between life and death. Think about your other crucial papers: a will, birth certificate, discharge papers, and so forth. If a flood or storm gets into your house, every scrap could be utterly, permanently ruined.

Well, it doesn't have to be that way. Years ago I began treating maps with Krylon-type clear spray coatings. One map of the high country got a cloth backing and plastic face, courtesy of the outfitter. Some of my paper chits have been encased in thin plastic: social security, professional society cards, and the like.

Several weatherproofing methods can be used. Check with print and copy shops, libraries, stationery and art supply stores, and camping outfitters. The combination of cloth back and flexible plastic facing has been wondrously useful; that map has survived a half-dozen Sierra trips. It's been doused with lamp oil, coffee, brandy (sorry 'bout that, but brandy and snow make a "slurpee" you wouldn't believe) and cooking oil. The darn thing is still in service.

If you use a spray, give your papers several light coatings. Encasing your papers in plastic can get modestly expensive, but how much would it cost to replace them? Don't trust your important papers to the elements.

* * *

Chimney Sweeping

If you burn wood, eventually you must clean your chimney or stovepipe, or risk a disastrous fire from accumulated creosote in the passages. You should have a chimney inspected annually, because loose bricks or rusted-out pipes can let your house burn down. Ideally you'll hire experts and watch to see how they do it, with sturdy bristled brushes and a rope that permits them to draw a brush up and down the chimney—among other things. If ever you must sweep your chimney alone and don't have the brushes to reach all the way down to your smoke shelf (just above the fireplace), you must do the best you can with a jury rig.

A bamboo pole or equivalent—a metal conduit tube may do the trick—gets you started. Get two grocery bags and stuff one inside the other (three bags, or a burlap sack, might be better). Fill the inner bag with small balls of newspaper. Stick one end of the pole inside the bag and firmly tape the bag's mouth around the pole, running tape both *around* the juncture of bag and pole, and *lengthwise* from bag to pole. Make it sturdy; if the bag rips inside the chimney, you may have to fish the balls of newsprint out with sticky tape or a handmade grappling hook.

Open the damper, then mask off the fireplace to prevent crud from cascading from your hearth. An old sheet, or plastic film, should serve.

Stand on a firm platform at the chimney top and insert the bag down the chimney. If it's a *very* tight fit, remove a few balls of paper and try again to get a medium-close fit. Use the pole and bag to brush all the way down to your smoke shelf, but do it in stages, three feet or so, scrubbing and twisting repeatedly. Haul the bag out and check for rips every few feet, then scrub down another three feet or so.

Soot and dried creosote will fall; some into the fireplace, some onto the smoke shelf. You must vacuum or brush the crud from the smoke shelf, unmasking the fireplace and reaching up from below. It's a nasty job, but you must clean the crud from that smoke shelf and check the job by flashing a light down the chimney, even if you have to do it with sunlight and a mirror. That creosote, if it burns, can generate more heat than most chimneys can take, cracking mortar or bricks from sudden heat.

If you have a stovepipe, be certain the sections are firmly attached at every joint. If you have a fireplace insert or some other complex woodburning rig, you may have special problems beyond the scope of this note. The main idea is to clean the soot, creosote, and other constrictions from your smoke passages while inspecting the system for damage.

Finally: if you're building a chimney, install a cleanout door just above the smoke shelf. That way, the nastiest part of the job becomes a cinch from outside the house.

* * *

Spring Outings

Sure, Spring is the time for bees and flowers—and also for sun, rain, wind or snow flurries. In other words, the weather's as capricious as a Spring lamb. A perfect time for a weekend outing!

Drag out your maps; there's sure to be someplace near where your family could hike or bike in a few hours, with medium packs and tents or "bivy sacks" for one night. Teenagers may seek excuses, but stand firm: if they knew half as much as they think, *they* could be feeding *you*. To sweeten the deal, promise to pack favorite junk foods. What the heck, it's only an overnighter. You could let them invite a friend if they're in the "joined at the elbow" phase.

These outings build confidence and muscle, and they remind us to repair or replace old equipment. When our kids were small, we played the "infiltrator spy" game. The idea was to leave the campsite so clean that one member, chosen as "spycatcher," could detect no sign we had ever been there. There were prizes for both sides, and it was great training.

Bring a camera and end the weekend at home with a dinner worth looking forward to. You can depend on its being a small adventure; and for many, a big boost in self-reliance skills.

* * *

Safe Bicycling

You've read about "two-stage" bugout kits: in a crisis, you use your car as the first stage "booster." The bike is your second stage if you must discard the car. But it's crucial that you stay in practice biking; and bike safety is always vital. To begin with, wear gloves and helmet.

Can your bike brakes skid both wheels? Good. Are your tires the fattest ones proper for your bike? Fine; thin racing tires require high pressures and sink down too far in soft turf. Do you have a big basket with tiedowns for your pack? Great. Can every member of your team patch a flat alone? Excellent!

Does your bike look snazzy and very stealable? Not so good. See if you can paint or otherwise crud-up its looks without hurting it. Would you be tempted to "hitch" onto a car or trailer while biking? It's a nonsurvival trick. Sure, maybe you can stop as fast as the vehicle towing you—but are you absolutely sure you want to? And if you hit one bump while hitching at over forty mph, you may have time to kiss your backside goodbye in midair.

A good headlight and tail reflector are essential. Reflective tape will make the bike still more visible—and if the time comes when invisibility is important, tape and reflectors can be stowed.

* * *

Shining Those Survival Wheels

Experts shrewdly advise you to paint your survival vehicle as a bird of drab plumage; a dull green, perhaps—or a sand-tan in arid country. But let's face it: until D +1, the day after "doomsday," we'll probably be driving our survival vehicles a lot as everyday transportation. Do we really want to blend in so well that average motorists might fail to notice us? I'd hate to get T-boned by some dude who wasn't paying attention, and who would argue in court that *of course* he couldn't see my bloody VW because it was camouflaged!

Well, we can have it both ways. Go ahead; get that inconspicuous paint job (including the bumpers). Then buy wide strips of highly reflective automotive striping favored by the "Hey, look at me" crowd. Apply the shiny tape in a pattern that outlines your vehicle (but not on your hood where reflection might dazzle your vision).

This way, you become just conspicuous enough to be safe in normal driving. And the day you need to become invisible, all you need to do is peel the shiny tape off; a five-minute conversion to pure camouflage!

* * *

Towing in Safety

Many folks keep trailers of various kinds, expecting to tow a trailerful of goods to safety in time of crisis. Towing is a learned skill—at best an art—and must be practiced under full-load conditions. Can you really turn and back up with it? Do you know how the entire rig handles fully loaded? Are the trailer's lights all working, rigged for instant plug-in to the tow car? Is the tow car heavy enough, with adequate brakes, to tow that load? Have you personally checked the towing regulations in the state(s) through which you'll drive? One "no" to any of the above, and you may have to abandon your trailer.

If the trailer has no brakes of its own, make certain your car's parking brake is in great shape. No inflated spare that fits your trailer? Put one where you can reach it quickly. Keep the trailer's side profile low, or side-winds may steer your rig where you least want it. This is especially important if the tow vehicle is small.

One item often ignored even by experienced drivers: a safety chain MUST be connected to the car without enough slack to let the tow bar hit the road if the hitch ever fails. A tow bar digging into macadam at fifty per, while still chained to your car, can have nightmarish results. Meanwhile, listen to people who tow often. And don't tow in a crisis unless you really must.

* * *

The Carton & The Candle

Soon after milk bottles became waxy cartons, my father began carrying a couple of half-gallon cartons in the trunk of his car. Whenever he squirreled something away in an unusual place it was usually worth my while to ask why; when he was a kid on the Texas plains, folks took self-reliance for granted.

Well, Dad kept fat candles and ashtrays inside the milk cartons. Highway flares are fine, he said, unless you need some to last several hours. Beacon batteries die after a year or two. But a thick candle sitting in an ashtray in the bottom of an empty milk carton will make the carton glow, and the carton stops the breeze. You can't see it as far away as you see a flare, but you can see it all night long!

Later he adapted the flare as a space heater. When he moved to Colorado Springs he had to park his VW bus outside, far from an electrical plug, in nights that were thirty below. He couldn't use an electric dipstick, but durn if a little cold weather would turn *his* oil to mud; no sirree. He got a gallon milk carton and a squat Christmas candle, lit up this rig like one of his highway flares, then shoved it under the casing of his VW engine every night. It burned all night and its heat was enough to keep the engine oil reasonably thin. He used up several candles that winter—but that engine started every time.

* * *

The Solar Trickle-Charge

Ever ignore your second car, or pickup or RV, for a couple of months only to find its battery dead when you *did* need it? Well, there's a fix for that; one that could also save your bacon in very hard times.

Both Radio Shack and auto aftermarkets (such as J.C. Whitney, P.O. Box 8410, Chicago, IL 60680) carry small solar panels which can be used to trickle-charge car batteries. If you're a gadgeteer with money to spare, you could buy a bunch of Radio Shack units; gang them together; and rig them to plug into the cigarette lighter of the pickup.

Or you could buy a 12-volt solar charger from Whitney, *et al*, for about $40. Just set it on the dash or wherever it gets plenty of sunlight, and plug it in.

And if the time ever comes when you need to power a shelter with a car battery, that solid-state solar charge can be worth a fortune!

* * *

Solder

There are several reasons why you should toss a bit of solder in your kit—even a bike kit. The most obvious use for solder is for electrical connections—for example, to repair a broken lamp wire or to rig a new one. But you can assemble light-duty structures from coat hanger wire with solder, too, or repair steel wire baskets.

When soldering steel wire structures, first scrape the structure's surface clean where the solder is to be added. Try to find enough fine soft wire (strands from an extension cord, or the equivalent, would be fine) to wrap a dozen turns around the connection before you solder it. The fine wire can bind the heavier wire joint, prevent molten solder from dripping so readily, and help form a soldered collar for the joint even if the heavier structure doesn't get hot enough to bond directly to the solder.

The first problem with solder, of course, is having a controlled source of heat to melt it. Unless you have a pocket torch—clearly the best solution but fairly expensive—you should ask your supply shop for solder **tape,** which often comes as a packet of small flat tabs of solder. In a pinch, you can actually solder wires together by wrapping the solder tab around the connection and applying a common match flame under the solder. You may need to do it twice to get the hang of it. In fact, try it on a paper clip or that loose lamp terminal as soon as you get home with the solder tape. One tip to save you from singed fingers and wasted matches: a candle flame is steadier and lasts longer. And you **do** have a candle in your kit—don't you?

* * *

High-Tech Pottery

It isn't likely that you'll ever be entirely without metals, but it could happen. That means no technology, right? Well, you already knew *that* was wrong. We've seen a functional water pump made of pottery with a wooden piston rod and pump handle and a leather valve flap. It has no metal parts, yet it's complete with a coarse pottery intake filter, and it will pump a half-inch stream of water from pottery pipe segments that are roughly two inches in diameter.

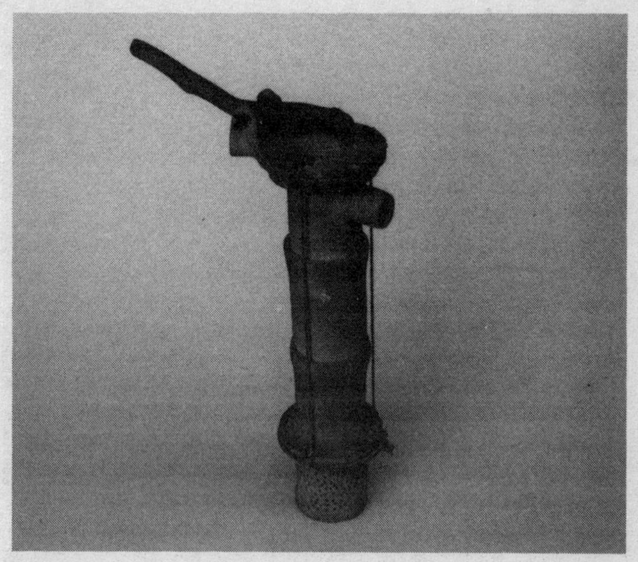

The potter who built this demonstration rig could've used glue to cement her fired clay segments together, but instead she used heavy twine and homemade putty. The twine, in tension, holds the segments snug. She could have made more segments and a bamboo piston rod to construct a much larger pump that would lift water ten feet or so.

So how about distilling water or alcohol with pottery? Distillation condensers and other hardware can be made entirely from fired clay. The potter must know how to make pottery glazes to seal the pores of the clay, and how to build a primitive kiln to maintain very high heat on the dried clay articles. It is of paramount importance that those glazes contain *NO* lead or lead salts if you ever intend to swallow anything that passes through that glazed pottery.

Yes, there's a whole technology behind pottery. You could build pumps, stills, and even bathroom

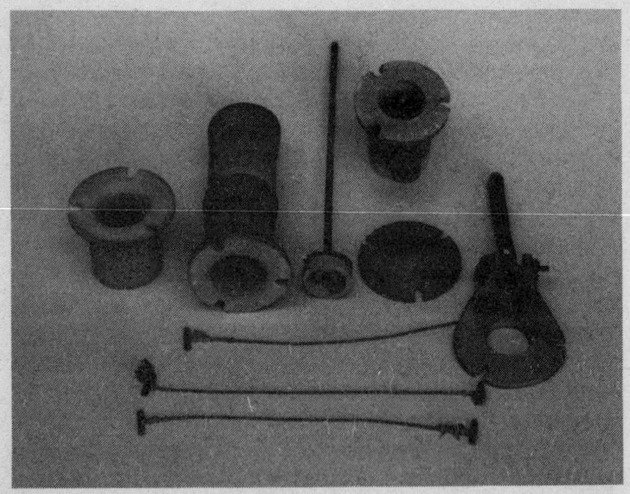

fixtures including spigots, without so much as a sliver of metal. The Romans stored and shipped such things as olive oil in large pottery vessels called amphorae. It's conceivable that you might want to store food this way. An amphora can protect its contents even when buried under damp soil.

*   *   *

Survival Shrubbery

During the fall and winter, most plants are relatively dormant. That's the time to plan our spring planting—well before we *do* it.

Too often we choose vines, shrubs, and dwarf trees without considering them as producers. Maybe you can't grow a dwarf lemon or lime, if it stays outdoors in bitter weather. But if it'll grow in a planter two feet across, why not wheel it indoors for the winter? We know folks in the Pacific Northwest who grow oranges and limes throughout the year this way, never risking them to frost.

For permanent planting of a shrub-sized tree with wondrous blossoms, how about a hardy quince, the kind that produces pear-sized fruit? Sure, its fruit is tough as old cheddar, and just about as sweet—but one day you may not have a Safeway handy to buy pectin for canning. Quince's middle name is "pectin"; diced quince is what our grandparents used to jell fruit jams and jellies. Quince jam, with nothing but honey and boiled quince, is rare today but still a delight. A wallop of lime juice makes it nicely tart.

And for natural borders, consider thickets of both wild rose and blackberry. Everyone knows how a berry thicket produces, but the thousands of orange-tinted rose hips on a thicket are wonderful producers of flavorful tea, and of Vitamin C. And in season, they carry masses of pink blossoms. After all, you devote lots of effort to your plants. Why shouldn't each one repay you with food and vitamins as well as beauty?

* * *

Rose Hip Tea

From the fall through winter, you can find rose bushes with healthy seed pod "hips." Dried briefly and ground up, rose hips can father a brew so wonderfully tasty that some users disparage tea leaves. It's also crammed with Vitamin C.

A bright red or orange shine on the pod says it's probably good. Use only shiny, bug-free pods; a child can gather a pint of them in a half-hour. This might even get kids interested. Wipe the pods clean, set them on a flat surface to dry for a day or so, then grind or chop them medium-fine, seeds and all.

Brew the stuff like tea, and try sweetening it with honey. This hot beverage is good for you, and could've sent Sir Thomas Lipton to the poorhouse.

* * *

Toolkit In A Tube

When collecting the contents of a survival pack, don't overlook the flexible adhesives. I've been testing one called "Shoe Goo" that has uses far beyond that of shoe repair. The stuff is amber in color and so thick, you can spread it to build up a partial sole on worn shoes or even repair holes in the uppers. But the stuff is so fiendishly sticky (and so tough and rubbery when cured), Shoe Goo turns out to be equally useful for many other repairs.

You could retread bike tires; seal punctures in metal or plastic containers; fix ripped upholstery; repair netting or clothing; make gaskets; seal glass panes; use to waterproof or insulate electrical connections—and cement many materials together where a waterproof flexible cement is needed.

Shoe Goo is flammable and it needs a few hours to become firm, but those are scant limitations. The same manufacturer offers a clear material called "Goop" which may be as good or better, but as yet I haven't tested it exhaustively.

* * *

An Emergency Sole for Shoes

If you lack the equipment to stitch new soles on shoes, you might learn an emergency alternative. Several thick rubbery adhesives are available which can be squeezed from tubes over shoe soles and will set firm in a few hours. "Goop" and "Shoe Goo" are two good backpacker examples.

You can provide thicker, long-lasting soles by cutting soles from a thin old tire casing and cementing the clean, roughened rubber to the bottom of your shoe, using clamps to hold the rubber firmly in place for hours. Tire treads make fairly decent lugged soles, as the Mexicans have shown us. Even old bike tires can be used in a pinch.

Finally, some craftsmen use tools to grind against the surfaces of old tire casings, catching the coarse "dust." The coarse rubber dust is then stirred into a (very!) thick paste with flexible goo, and spread over the shoe sole to a thickness of over a quarter-inch. It looks odd, but it's a true composition shoe sole that can last for months.

Why not try it on some comfortable old sneakers to gain experience? The goo also covers holes in the uppers. I never said it wasn't a gooey job, but I haven't bought new sneakers for years.

* * *

Weatherproofing Adhesives

Ever see layers of a sheet of plywood come unglued? Probably not, if it was originally put together with resorcinol resin, which is the stuff that makes exterior plywood work. Many of us employ adhesives—glues, cements, and varied stickums—that work perfectly when protected from the weather. But some otherwise tough adhesives can't hack the sun and rain, and even the bacteria.

High-tech adhesives were studied long ago for such applications as experimental aircraft and missile nosecones, both of which are made from wood sometimes. The areospace folks found that stuff such as the ancient hide-and-horn furniture glue, caseins, and some other white glues and mucilages, can be literally eaten from between layers of glued material by microorganisms. The bugs keep chomping until much of the glue is consumed and the layers, or laminations, then delaminated. Some solvent-evaporation cements (model cement is a common example) will deteriorate seriously with sunlight. When specimens of cemented plywood were pulled apart, we saw that the stuff has another drawback besides vulnerability to sun and heat. Much of the area we had smeared with cement had become air bubble, not cement, after the solvent evaporated. Only about half of the area actually had kept its adhesive. Surely there had to be some glue better than that.

Actually there are several. Resorcinols and epoxies avoid most of these problems and weather well, even for boats. If you build a kit aircraft and bond any of it with, say, caseins, chances are you will never get it certified. Epoxy and resorcinol? Okay. We've all seen the thick two-part epoxy liquids, some of which cure hard in minutes rather than hours. Resorcinol consists of a deep burgundy liquid and a powder. Properly mixed, with pressure on a wood joint, resorcinol resists just about any normal insult.

But no adhesive is much good if the joined area is contaminated with oils—and even a fingerprint can emperil a joint. You'll find that a very thin uniform coating, with clamp pressure, works better than a thick coating; and it uses less.

Some adhesives never harden; silicones and rubber cements, for example. Silicones won't furnish dessert for bugs, either, but they lack high tensile strength. Upshot: for permanent weatherproof joints I count on resorcinol, with wood screws as a backup. It's available under brand names at many a handyman counter. Don't forget to clamp the joint!

* * *

Toy Kits for Self-Reliance

There was a time when just about the only groans heard on Christmas day were the result of too much turkey. But the do-it-yourself craze spawned thousands of kits (presumably cheaper than a wholly-assembled gadget) and soon, all across the land, careful listeners could hear whole neighborhoods resounding on Christmas mornings with the groans of harried dads.

Today, many people agree that all this fumble-fingered home assembly was for our own good. I doubt if the manufacturers had that in mind; but the fact is, we can maintain our gadgets much better if we've assembled them to begin with!

I'm presuming for the moment that you, the reader, are the household assembler. So what happens if you're unable for any reason to do necessary trouble-shooting? In a survival situation, either a wife or son or daughter must puzzle out the solution, or there won't be any solution. What a godsend it will be if there's a "toy" kit of some sort on your shelf that lends immediate hands-on experience with the problem!

I've studied an array of these kits recently. Some of them have been around a long time—so long they're virtually antiques. Then there's the "science fair" kit; the kind that takes you through ten, or a hundred, such projects. It may be that your teenager will think you're barmy if you put such a present under the Christmas tree but there's hope that she may even get interested in it while you're fiddling with it later in the day. (Do your best to see that the parts don't get scattered.) It's all too true that many of our loved ones can't be bothered to understand even the basics of all the gadgetry they use. They probably won't bother until the day comes when their very survival depends on such understanding. Warnings seldom help; but if the "do-or-die" situation ever arises when there's no local community college course on appliance repair, our beloved boobs might just pull through because we bought a few of those 'toy' kits and kept them. The kits may be only part of there enforced training, but they can be a crucial part.

* * *

Trade Goods I: Cheap Today. Expensive Tomorrow?

We've seen these items dirt-cheap at flea markets, Goodwill and Salvation Army stores. Store them wisely, in quantity.

Slide Rules: When hand calculator batteries go south, slide rules will no longer be obsolete $.49 curiosities.

Thermometers: Oral, rectal, outdoor—worth their weight in penicillin.

12-Volt Auto Bulbs: Especially little ones from glove boxes, license lamps, directional signals of junked cars; for emergency lighting with a pirated car battery.

Meat Grinders: They grind corn, too. Anyone who breaks an upper plate *must* get one, or find an orthodontist.

Reading Glasses: Nonprescription Rexall-type specs are essential when we grow farsighted in middle years. Or would you rather grind your own lenses?

Wristwatches: The cheap wind-up Timex won't be so cheap when watch batteries become scarce. . . .

* * *

Trade Goods II: Cheap Today. Expensive Tomorrow?

Proper storage is essential; always store plastic and rubber materials in a cool, dark place.

Gloves: All sorts; throwaway plastic, heavy leather, thin leather, cotton, nylon, wool.

Baggies: All kinds and sizes, from flimsy produce bags to heavy-duty appliance and furniture covers.

Poly Sheeting: Rolls of polyethylene, four-mil or heavier.

Duct Tape:	This stuff has held our race-car panels together after foolish arguments with wet hay bales! Emergency upholstering, weatherproofing, bellows pumps, clothing repair, etc.
Cordage:	2-lb. to 30-lb. test nylon fishing line, wire, tow rope, waxed linen, parachute cord, cable.
Nails:	Include double-heads and broadhead roofing nails.
Salt:	For pickling, too . . .
Telescopes:	Crucial for cross-country jaunts, a small cheap model might bring a high barter-price.
12-V. Lights:	Never junk out any vehicle without saving every 12-volt bulb you can. Most are easily removed.

BOOK REVIEWS

The How To Book for Woodcutters, by E. M. Barr; Forest Grove, OR: EMBAR Endeavors Entre Nous, Inc., 1980. $5.95 softbound.

This little book has been around awhile without making the stir it deserves—perhaps because of the price. It isn't thick, and isn't hawked by a famous publisher, so how can it be worth six clamskins? Well, it can, and it is. The first time you really need to fell a tree in a certain precise direction, this text can be worth—well, the corner of your house, maybe. And so far as I know there is no, repeat **no**, place else you can get so much good clear information on all aspects of woodcutting in condensed form.

Barr's expert is elderly Herb Lange. No Paul Bunyan, Lange uses skill instead of sinew, which is perfect; his idea is to cut smarter, not harder. Many clear photos show how Lange eases his way through the big fir, from felling and bucking through splitting and ricking right down to kindling.

The text considers many odd things that can happen when you fell a tree, and explains the safest ways to approach the many variations using bucksaw, axe, or chain saw.

You'll enjoy learning some of the woodcutter's lingo. You'll learn why evergreens should be split immediately after felling, and why hardwoods should **not.**

Why hardwood actually splits more easily, and what kind of gloves to wear, and what legal strictures apply to chain saws, and why you shouldn't burn beach driftwood in your fireplace. There's even a canny two-page set of prescriptions for common problems in woodsplitting.

A critic always feels validated when he finds a nit to pick. I found only one, and then only because of an old back injury. Lange demonstrates the safe way to chop kindling, and he's right—only the photos show you must bend far over at the chopping block—which would have me in traction in ten minutes! I cut a fair amount of wood, but in splitting kindling I rig a block that, like a butcher's block, rises high enough to make bending unnecessary. (Lange would surely remind me to make sure it's stable.)

Upshot: author Barr reminds us, through Lange, of a great many things in the best interests of the woodcutter. Those reminders even include appendices with estimated load weights of wood and checklists for felling trees. If you cut wood, and if you haven't been taught by experts, you'll probably find this little text a steal at the price.

* * *

Urban Alert!, Mary Ellen Clayton with Bruce Clayton, Ph.D., Paladin Press, Boulder, CO, 1982. $12.95 clothbound.

The drawbacks of this little text can be quickly enumerated: it isn't indexed; it probably won't be distributed with suitable publicity where city-dwellers browse in urban bookstores; and most urbanites who do read it probably won't take its excellent advice. Obviously, the author can't be faulted for the last two complaints, and the first is a minor flaw since you should always, *always* index your own texts as you read them. (That way, you can always find the passage *you* thought so crucial—instead of seven hundred other passages some indexer thought you should consider crucial.)

Mary Ellen Clayton lives with her survivalist/author husband, Bruce, on the slope of the California sierra. *Urban Alert!* was written by an ex-urbanite *for* urbanites, on the premise that there are lots of urban emergencies (quake, cyclone, flood, blizzard,—finish the list yourself) which can overwhelm the city's ability to cope. When city officials can't help you, your continued survival in the anthill may depend upon your having made general preparations beforehand. In other words, what may be an urban disaster for the unprepared, may be only a minor disturbance for those who *did* prepare. Clayton addresses just about every facet of urban life-support, and hers is a frugal approach. Many of the supplies and gadgets she describes are also shown in photographs.

Clayton writes clearly and she doesn't bore you. When discussing emergency stoves, she gives names, prices, and model numbers; and she tells you exactly how long it takes to boil a quart of water, as well as levying criticisms on the gadgetry.

You may want to re-title some chapter headings, which get high marks for cleverness but may not immediately tell you where to look for a topic. "The Call of the Wild," for example, disguises a concise chapter on sanitation.

The virtues of Clayton's breezy, scholarly little text far outweigh its small vices. Even if you don't live in a city, buy several as Christmas presents for your loved ones who *do* live there. And be sure to read it through before gift-wrapping it; you're almost certain to expand your own survival lore.

* * *

High Frontier, by Lt. Gen. Daniel O. Graham, USA (ret.); New York: TOR Books, 1983. $6.95 softbound.

General Graham, with funding from the Heritage Foundation, compiled a $15 version of this book. The new updated version is substantially different and available at half the original price. It's only fair to tell you: this reviewer, who was the editorial consultant for this new edition, is biased in favor of the ideas in the book.

High Frontier was written by a score of experts in their chosen fields: defense technology, treaties, space systems, and civil defense, to name a few. They've worked out a national strategy that dumps Mutual Assured Destruction (which the Soviets never accepted anyway), and uses U.S. advantages in technology to outline a new strategy. It's a genuinely defensive strategy, which means that it would let us zap ICBMs without threatening a single Soviet citizen. Recently, President Reagan announced that he and the Joint Chiefs of Staff agree with the strategy.

Despite my best efforts the book isn't always breezy reading, but it gives fascinating details on ICBM-busters now under study, and it explains why we'll benefit so much from the peaceful side effects of a space-based missile defense. Wouldn't we welcome cheap electrical power beamed down from orbit? No more worries about nuclear power plants; and U.S. industry will gain a permanent beachhead in space with asteroid mining, solar power satellites, and special high-tech processing.

But what of the objections: domestic, foreign, and especially Soviet? They're handled here, along with details of a management system that can avoid the interminable, costly delays of recent years. We have no assurance that our final hardware along the High Frontier will be identical to the gadgetry described (and illustrated) in the book. The point is that we already have the technology to remove any aggressor's confidence in a first strike against us, by erecting a set of shielding systems. What we need is the will to employ this technology. To those who claim that a true defensive shield would be destabilizing, Graham's team replies that we should have no objection if the Soviets did the same.

This is a real departure from the hopeless old MAD strategy that holds our population hostage; and there's much in the book that the news analysts aren't discussing—yet. The price of the book isn't that daunting if you hanker to learn what it's all about. At the very least, it shows how your defense taxes can be spent on advanced systems that offer hope for our survival.

* * *

How To Make Nuclear Weapons Obsolete, by Robert Jastrow; Boston: Little, Brown and Company, 1985. $15.95 clothbound.

Your reviewer is envious of this book. It describes some steps world powers must take, and in fact *are* taking, to avoid nuclear Armageddon. Jastrow is a Dartmouth physicist with impeccable credentials, several readable books to his credit, and vast NASA experience. He has outlined, in simpler terms than I managed in two books, why the SDI "Star Wars" defense is crucial to our survival.

Jastrow makes it easy to understand why we originally boxed ourselves into treaties that outlawed a shield of antiballistic defenses. He also furnishes pictures and explanations to show that it's high time we all had those defenses. For one thing, he cites proofs that the Soviets have been building their own SDI systems for years, in violation of the treaties. For another, he demolishes most of the arguments by "scientists" who have tried to prove we can't, or mustn't, build our own SDI.

Will SDI be expensive? Jastrow admits that it will be; but far cheaper than developing ways to punch through a layered shield. This is true whether we're talking about a shield put up by Americans, Soviets, or anybody else. In short, a nation can afford to build a shield, but most could go broke trying to punch through one.

Will SDI mean the end of all nuclear weapons? Jastrow seems to imply that there may always be a few of them around. He adds some encouraging facts about the power of those weapons, though. As nations develop incredibly accurate guidance systems (putting a warhead down a particular smokestack, or impacting directly on the concrete lid of a missile silo), the warheads get very much smaller. And that means there will be little need for the huge H-bombs that could cause brief climate changers. Jastrow's figures show that in sheer "megatonnage," our nuclear stockpile has dropped by a factor of four during the past 25 years. That's because we don't need the big ones; our little ones make up the difference in accuracy. The same is true for Soviet weapons, allowing us to hope that most civilians everywhere would survive a war of small nukes—especially when our SDI shield can destroy most of them in space. Some of our existing SDI hardware is shown in excellent photographs Jastrow collected.

The book has a few small problems. It is, after all, a sixteen-buck book (though worth every cent). It fails to describe the economic advantage the U.S. enjoys, and our continued economic health while building our SDI (the Soviets will just have to cancel plans for a few thousand tanks; sorry 'bout that, Ivan). The book does not even mention the staggering wealth we can bring back from space manufacturing, which will almost certainly be a major result of placing SDI in orbit. And some of its most fascinating reading is stuck away in the notes and appendices where you might miss it.

So read it all. If you're an aerospace engineer, you already know many of the details Jastrow gives on defense against nuclear-tipped missiles—but he surprised me with a few unclassified details I didn't know. Most of those details add hope. If your local library does not have at least one copy of this important book, you have a right to ask why.

Enthusiastically recommended.

* * *

We Can Prevent WW III, by Sam Cohen; Ottawa, Illinois: Jameson Books, Inc., 1985. $13.95 clothbound.

Sam Cohen is an angry scientist, the father of the neutron bomb. Our NATO allies have rejected his weapon. Guess what Cohen wants to do with NATO?

This book was written at white heat by a man who, in middle age, remains furious at America for its stupidities. He believes that unless we make major policy shifts we will almost certainly fight *and lose* a nuclear war. A lambaster, not a politician, Cohen has much to say about naive Americans laying this nation on the line for lazy, subtle Europeans. He warns us never to risk nuclear war for any ally—but later says he does *not* suggest that we "precipitously abandon" our allies. He suggests, instead, that we abandon them by stages. Perhaps "weaning" them is a better way to put it. The heck of it is, many of his suggestions make enough sense to keep the high-tech liberals honest.

Cohen writes like a man who enjoys playing chess but who would jail a player, if he could, for a foolish move. H.L. Mencken tickled you into considering his curmudgeonly opinions with a feather, while Sam Cohen comes at you with a chain saw. Still, in all that fury he whittles out some sharp points.

Item: Our nation seems convinced that a nuclear war would be brief, yet the Soviets are planning for an *extended* nuclear war. Given their Civil Defense and our lack of it, who would bet on us?

Item: We should give crash priority to a full-fledged antimissile program of the "Star Wars" variety.

Item: More offensive weapons of the MX type cannot add to the security of the American people, but true *defenses* could.

Cohen has more items for our consideration in this book, and they make lively reading. We must listen to our gadflies (including Patrick Henry, Herman Kahn, and Sam Cohen) no matter how they sting our old opinions.

*　*　*

Down Home Ways, by Jerry Mack Johnson (Greenwich House, Distributed by Crown Publishers, New York, 1984 ed.).

This book is 240 pages of pure delight. Nope, it's not humorous, it's simply bursting with details on simple ways to do important things—a first-rate text in self-reliance.

How do you make paper, or adobe? Bread from zucchini? Sugar from beets, pectin from apples (reviewer's note: quince will serve as well)—even a batteryless *radio* from basic materials, for Pete's sake? Did you know most maples, not just sugar maples, will yield sugar sap? Could you sew a half-sole on so that the thread won't be quickly abraded away? How many kinds of sprouts can you produce? Could you make a quilt, or properly fire-temper clay pots, if you really needed to?

Johnson knows these things and hundreds more, and he tells you in words that are easy to understand. A former miner, oilfield worker and schoolteacher among other things, he's a rich man in the knowledge that counts. His table of contents and his index are thorough, and that's a huge "plus" in such a book.

Criticisms? Well, simple illustrations in a few cases would have clarified some details. Otherwise, this inexpensive hardback is just about perfect. For years, I've done a fair number of the projects he explains, and nowhere do I find a serious disagreement with his methods. You might find this book listed in a publisher's clearing house, as I did. It was a bonanza; get yours quick, before I buy 'em all up for Christmas presents.

* * *

Nuclear War Survival Skills, by Cresson H. Kearny; Oregon Institute of Science and Medicine, 2251 Dick George Road, Cave Junction, OR 97523. 1987. $9.50, large softbound; two for $16.

Kearny was a crucial figure at Oak Ridge during the development of low-tech fallout and blast shelters, and the incredible homemade Kearny Fallout Meter (KFM). He is still crucial, as this book proves. Updated, indexed, and 281 pages thick, the book is richly illustrated and includes such details as processing of grain and soybeans. Anyone contemplating a large shelter housing several people for weeks would be wise to study Kearny's plans for a whopping big plywood air pump. Worried about filtering fallout particles from water? Concerned about side-effects of taking potassium iodide after a nuclear accident? Interested in building your own fallout shelter, either above or below ground-level? Would you like to see pictures of average folks engaged in life-saving exercises according to Kearny's instructions? Well, all of it is in this big book, printed on slick paper for maximum quality illustrations.

Readers of *The Chernobyl Syndrome* who seek more robust gadgets for self-reliance will find Kearny's volume absolutely essential. Here is the measure of my admiration for it: if faced with a nuclear event, I would rather have Kearny's book than my own. Of course, they cover somewhat different topics, and nobody said you have to choose. I rank *Nuclear War Survival Skills* among the most important books for Americans during my lifetime—because it could extend millions of lives.

Put it this way: can you afford *not* to have one in your home?